HORIZON

ABOVE WORLD

BOOK THREE

HORIZON

JENN REESE

CANDLEWICK PRESS

Copyright © 2014 by Jenn Reese

First edition 2014

Library of Congress Catalog Card Number 2013951756
ISBN 978-0-7636-6417-6

14 15 16 17 18 19 BVG 10 9 8 7 6 5 4 3 2 1

Printed in Berryville, VA, U.S.A.

This book was typeset in Plantin.

Candlewick Press
99 Dover Street
Somerville, Massachusetts 02144

visit us at www.candlewick.com

For everyone
who's come on this adventure with me so far.

And for my first D&D friends —
Carolyn, Eddie, John, Michael, and Rick E. —
who were there when I fell in love with adventuring in the first place.

"IT'S TAKEN US A LONG TIME TO FIND ONE ANOTHER, BUT NOW WE HAVE. TOGETHER, WE'RE STRONG. STRONG ENOUGH TO FIGHT, AND STRONG ENOUGH TO WIN."

—The Dawn-bringer, born
Aluna of the Coral Kampii

CHAPTER 1

ALUNA UNHOOKED THE STRAP securing her tail to Vachir's saddle, shifted her weight, and slid to the ground. Over the last few months in the desert, her legs had fused together and sprouted a thick covering of greenish-gold scales. Delicate fins had formed along her thighs but stayed flat and lifeless under her skirt. Instead of feet, a large tail fin folded up and wrapped itself around her ankles and calves like a thin, glistening veil.

Her fins were sleeping, waiting to awaken with their first touch of water. Aluna longed to feel them unfurl in the ocean and show her what they were truly meant to do. *Swim swift as a seal, fast as a dolphin.*

But here, at the desert's edge, there were no waves to welcome her. Only dried earth, stubborn trees, and the crumbly beginnings of the distant mountains. When she stood, her whole body's weight rested painfully on what used to be the heel of her foot. Even with the sturdy leather tail sheath Hoku had designed for her, she could only hop a few meters. Or walk on her hands. She needed crutches to cross any significant distance. Kampii were not meant to live in the Above World.

She gripped Vachir's mane, grateful for her friend's four solid horse legs. *Vachir.* It had taken Aluna weeks to get used to calling her that instead of Tal, the horrible name the Equians had given her. *Tal* meant *half*, and Vachir was called that because she was born looking like a horse instead of a Human-horse mix like "real" Equians. After they'd defeated Scorch at the Thunder Trials, Khan Tayan had changed Tal's name to Vachir—*Thunderbolt*—a perfect match for her bravery and speed, and for her gray star-speckled coat. Now no other name seemed right.

Vachir nickered and stomped a hoof. Hoku, Calli, and Dash had dismounted their horses and disappeared into a tight cluster of shrubs and trees, leaving Aluna to follow behind at her own pace. She preferred it that way. The first few times the others had waited for her and watched her struggle. She'd found their patient stares unbearable. The new arrangement worked best for everyone.

Aluna unlatched her crutches from Vachir's saddlebag and slid her arms into the braces. Her fingers wrapped around the handgrips. She'd have preferred her talon weapons or a spear, but these were the tools she needed to master now.

The shrubs rustled and Hoku emerged. Aluna's special Kampii hearing devices carried his whispered words directly to her ears. "We found a group," he said. "It's the perfect size. Hurry, before they're out of sight!"

He disappeared again but she answered anyway, knowing his Kampii ears would pick up her voice. "I'll be there in two flashes of a tail." She turned to Vachir. "Keep an eye on the horses."

Vachir snorted and rolled her huge black eyes.

Distances seemed longer now that Aluna couldn't walk, and the terrain always seemed devious, as if it were trying to surprise her by being too soft or too hard or covered in twisty sticks and tumbling rocks. When she got to the shrubs, she hooked her crutches to her belt, dropped to the ground, and dragged herself forward on her hands. Her palms, callused from years of weapon training and her recent crutch use, were now tough as sharkskin.

She found Hoku and Calli crouched at the lip of a ridge, Calli's huge tawny wings pressed firmly against her back. Dash had scrambled up one of the sturdier trees. Aluna could just make out his long dark hair and pale desert clothes near one of the higher branches.

Aluna quietly pulled herself to Calli's side and peered over the edge of the ridge. A dozen meters below, a group of Humans slowly made their way along the path, a massive striped rhinebra lumbering behind them. The beast's shuffling feet kicked up so much dust that Aluna could barely make out the figures through the cloud of particles.

"What do you see, Calli?" Aluna asked. The Aviars had far better eyesight for distances.

"There are five in the group there, although more may be scouting ahead," Calli said.

"I thought I saw something glint. Metal, maybe?" Hoku asked.

"Oh, they're definitely Upgraders," Calli said. "There's one with two metal prongs instead of feet, and another with what look like horns jutting out of his head. I haven't seen any swords or flame shooters, but they could be hidden."

Aluna squinted, but the figures remained vague. "At least they don't have a dragonflier. That improves our chances of speaking to them without being killed from a distance first."

Dash shimmied quietly down the tree and dropped to his stomach next to Aluna. Dirt smudged his tunic, and a gnarled twig stuck out of the cloth tie binding his hair. He smelled like horse, and he probably always would.

"We could simply follow them," Dash said. Aluna used to think his accent was strange, but now, after months of living with the Equians in the desert, she couldn't imagine him speaking any other way. "They travel the same direction as all the other groups we've seen. Perhaps they will go straight to Karl Strand."

"More likely, they'll just join his growing army," Aluna said. When she'd suggested they take the fight to Karl Strand, she'd had no idea it would be this hard to locate him. Then again, Strand had been around when all the LegendaryTek splinters were created; he knew the value of hiding. "We have to convince the Upgraders to take us to Strand himself. It's our only chance of finding him."

"I still don't understand why Dash and I can't go by ourselves, since we can pass as Upgraders," Hoku said.

Calli shoved Hoku in the shoulder. "We're just supposed to stay safe and let you two have all the fun?"

Hoku snorted. "Infiltrating a group of Upgraders sounds like fun to you? You've obviously been friends with Aluna for too long."

"They won't take you to Strand without a reason, and there's no better reason than valuable prisoners," Aluna said. "Besides, we need to stick together." She looked at each of them in turn. Hoku, Calli, Dash. Kampii, Aviar, Equian.

They'd never have freed HydroTek from Fathom if Hoku and Dash hadn't found a way to win the Dome Meks to their side, or if Calli hadn't distracted Fathom at just the right moment, or if Aluna's sister, Daphine, hadn't helped her pin the monster to the ground until High Senator Electra arrived.

And at the Thunder Trials, Aluna had lost her fight against Strand's clone Scorch. Scorch should have killed her, and the desert Equians should, even now, be marching to join Strand's army. Except that Hoku had put himself in harm's way. He'd stepped between Aluna and a vicious killer, and he'd convinced the High Khan that honor was worth fighting for. When Calli and Dash and the Equian herds had joined him, the whole battle had turned. That one act of courage — not on Aluna's part, but on Hoku's — had changed everything.

Asking for help was sometimes the bravest thing a person could do. The lesson had taken Aluna a long time to learn, but now she clung to it as if it were the last bubble of air in the ocean.

"We're about to walk into the middle of our enemy's army," Aluna said. "I don't know what dangers we're going to face, but we'll have the best chance of succeeding if we stay together."

"If we stop Karl Strand, then we stop his army," Calli said.

Aluna had been thinking the same thing, yet the words sounded so strange coming from Calli. In her mind, Aluna still saw Calli as the innocent bird-girl cowering in her mother's throne room. But Calli had grown braver and stronger during their travels. She'd been poisoned and almost killed. Innocence couldn't survive in a world gripped by Karl Strand.

"Calli's right," Aluna said. "The Equians are preparing for an all-out war. If we can get to Strand first, then maybe we can end this before thousands of people lose their lives. It's worth the risk."

Dash sat up and Aluna's gut twinged. He moved so effortlessly, with so much hidden strength. She used to be like that, too, although she was never so graceful. Now she felt clumsy all the time. Her body seemed to delight in defying her.

"I will follow the Dawn-bringer, even into the heart of the enemy," Dash said. He wiped his palms on his shirt, stood, and offered Aluna a hand.

Aluna's stomach fluttered again, but in a warm,

happy way. Dash pulled her up and steadied her elbow while she got her crutches in place.

Calli stared at the Upgraders disappearing down the path. "They'll camp soon. We can take our time and approach them in the morning."

"No," Aluna said. "We go tonight. I don't want to risk losing them. And Hoku and I can see in the dark."

"I'm sure several of them have night vision, too," Hoku said. "It's a very common Upgrader modification. Rollin told me they don't even need medteks to add the lenses to their eyes."

"Okay, so we won't have an advantage, then," Aluna said gruffly. Hoku knew more than she did about Upgraders—he'd studied with Rollin for months in the desert. "But I still want to go soon. Now, even. Before . . ."

"Before I lose my courage," Calli said quietly. Aluna saw Hoku squeeze her hand.

Dash pushed his way through the shrubs back toward the horses. Hoku and Calli followed, and Aluna tried not to hear the sweet words Hoku whispered to Calli as they walked.

Aluna went last, trying not to catch a branch in the eye. When Khan Tayan of their new Flame Heart herd had renamed Vachir, she'd also given Aluna a new name: *Dawn-bringer.* But was she leading them to a new day—to a new world without Strand—or to their early deaths?

Vachir met her at the edge of the scrub. Aluna leaned on her friend and watched Hoku and Dash pull their disguises from their horses' saddlebags.

Hoku donned a mask that covered half his face and one eye in shiny silver and circuits. It wrapped around his neck for protection and hid his Kampii breathing necklace. The neck cover had been Rollin's idea, if Aluna remembered correctly. Weeks of planning meetings back in the desert now blurred together in her mind. But Aluna had been the one to insist that Hoku wear the force shield he'd made for her for the Thunder Trials. It had already saved her life; maybe it would save his, too.

Calli touched Hoku's metal cheekbone and shuddered. "I don't like it," she said. "I miss your freckles."

Aluna agreed, but said nothing. She'd known Hoku her whole life, and yet the mask had transformed him into someone she barely recognized. She turned away, reminded of the hideous scope that Karl Strand's clone Fathom had attached to her sister's eye.

Dash slipped a crude metal skeleton over his left forearm. He'd lost that wrist and hand in the battle at the HydroTek dome. The medteks had replaced it with a mechanical limb, but the tech wasn't obvious enough. The new external piece glinted dangerously in the amber dusk. Aluna hopped over and helped Dash strap his retractable sword to his other forearm in the hopes that it would look built into his flesh when he extended it.

It had taken so long to convince Tayan and the other Equians that this was the best plan. If they'd stayed in the desert and joined the Equian army, they'd be just five more swords among thousands. By going after Strand himself, they had a chance to make a difference.

Tayan had hated Aluna's plan. "Bravery is honorable," she'd said, "but this? It is merely foolish."

High Khan Onggur had disagreed with Tayan, and so had Khan Arasen of Shining Moon. Aluna hadn't needed the Equians' approval, but it certainly helped to have their supplies and Rollin's tech, and a place to stay while they prepared. Eventually, Tayan had come around, and she had even granted them the sun's blessing when they'd left. Nothing would ever be easy between Aluna and Tayan—not even when they were fighting on the same side.

After Hoku and Dash finished adjusting their new upgrades, they slipped behind the horses and traded their desert clothes for patchwork leathers and a few mismatched pieces of armor. When they emerged again, Aluna gasped. Her friends had become Upgraders.

"We're ready," Hoku said. "Only one thing left to do."

Calli looked at Aluna, her face pale but resolute. Aluna nodded. They were already dirty enough, and Aluna had a large scratch over one eye that she'd allowed to crust over with dried blood. Now she attached her crutches to Vachir's saddle, hopped up, and secured her tail.

"Hands," Hoku said.

Aluna held them out and watched Hoku wrap his custom-made cuffs around her wrists. "Remember, you can struggle all you want in these. If you need to break out of them, twist out with both arms at the same time and they'll pop open."

She gulped and stared down at the shackles while Hoku bound Calli's hands. "Don't leave me," she whispered to Vachir. "You're my secret weapon."

Vachir threw her head back and whinnied, clearly pleased to be a weapon of any sort.

Dash looped a rope over Vachir's neck and another over Calli's horse. He kept the ends loose in his hand and mounted his mare, Sandwolf.

The world seemed to fall silent around them, the only noises the distant caw of birds, the swish of the horses' tails and the shuffle of their hooves as they shifted their weight.

"The word is *Zorro*," Aluna said. "Anyone says it and the mission is over. We get away as fast as we can. If we get separated, we meet up again at the HydroTek dome."

Aluna lowered her chin to her chest and let months of travel sweep over her body. She and Calli needed to look like prisoners: hungry, exhausted, and defeated.

They were ready to meet the Upgraders.

CHAPTER 2

Hoku touched his cheek and felt cool metal instead of flesh. He didn't mind it nearly as much as he probably should have. The faceplate felt slick and dangerous under his fingertips. No one could see it and think he was still an ignorant youngling who only understood books and tech.

"I wish Rollin had changed her mind," Dash said quietly. He rode next to Hoku and pulled Aluna's and Calli's horses behind him. "I would feel safer if we had an actual Upgrader with us. Someone who knows their customs."

"She said she'd be more trouble than help," Hoku said. "I know she was afraid of being recognized; I just don't know why."

Dash huffed. He sounded just like a horse. "Well, it would be unfair of me to condemn someone for keeping secrets. Perhaps she was exiled, just as I was."

Hoku said nothing. He knew Rollin better than anyone, and he knew it wasn't just the Upgraders that Rollin was avoiding, but Karl Strand himself. She'd gotten twitchy when Strand's name came up during their planning meetings, and she had been far more likely to punch someone soon after. But they all had their scars, and Rollin's were none of his business. Maybe someday she'd trust him enough to share.

Up ahead, the Upgraders had started a campfire, and Hoku could see hazy forms clustered around it like fish at feeding time. Their rhinebra had settled itself into a slumbering mountain nearby. "We're close enough. Are you ready?" He wasn't sure whom he was asking, Dash or himself.

"Yes," Dash said. "Walk us between worlds, friend."

Hoku smiled. After the Thunder Trials, Khan Tayan had given him the name *Sun-strider, he who walks between worlds.* Time to see if she was right.

He glanced back at Aluna and Calli. Their faces were grim but determined. He sucked in a big breath and tried to remember how Rollin talked. Mostly he remembered her throwing things.

"Yo," he called out. His voice came out softer than he wanted, so he tried again. "Yo! Got room at your fire for a couple of Gizmos with a . . ." What should he call Aluna and Calli? *Prisoners? Prizes?* "With some cargo?" He winced.

"Good," Dash whispered. "This is a game. We must play our parts."

"Don't say 'parts' when we're around Upgraders," Hoku said.

The Upgraders around the fire stood and one took a few steps toward them.

"You on horses, then?" a man called. "Just two of you?"

"Two of us and two prisoners," Dash said.

"We don't want blood," the Upgrader said. "But we'll spill it everywhere if we have to."

"Not necessary," Hoku said, probably too quickly. He forced himself to stay calm. "We just want a seat at the fire."

"He is posturing," Dash whispered. "They are a small group, too. He tries to assert his dominance to make us think they are stronger than they are."

"It's working," Hoku mumbled. He pulled his horse Sunbeam to a stop while they waited. The silence stretched and stretched while the Upgrader conferred with his group.

"Can you hear what they're saying?" he asked Dash.

Dash shook his head. Hoku saw him twitching his

right arm, the one with the expandable sword sheathed under his sleeve.

"Steady," came Aluna's quiet voice from behind them, and Dash settled.

The Upgrader called, "Come closer. We want eyes on you."

"Yeah, sure," Hoku answered. He nudged Sunbeam. His heart seemed to beat louder with each clomp of his horse's hooves. He squinted, trying to count the shapes taking form amid the smoky campsite. Calli had said there were five, but he only counted four.

Two Upgraders stepped forward, close enough to see. The one they'd been talking to was a burly man with goggles over both eyes and a long shock of red hair spiking out from the center of his otherwise bald head. The hair fell in a scraggly braid over one of his muscled shoulders. The other Upgrader was slight and possibly female, although her body was hidden beneath a thick leather coat that went all the way down to her feet. Her dark hair bobbed around her head like a shadowy nimbus, somehow defying gravity.

"Close enough," the man said. "I'm called Odd. This here is Mags. We speak for the kludge."

"I'm Hawk and this is Dash," Hoku said.

Rollin had told them that most Upgraders named themselves, picking words that matched their upgrades and the identities they had built—or were trying to build—for themselves. Hoku was pretending to be a trader, so they chose "Hawk" for him, since he was always hawking goods. Dash could be their hunter, their warrior, so his name worked fine as it was.

When Hoku had asked Rollin what her name meant, she'd only snorted and told him to keep his wiggly fingers out of other people's heads.

"And what you towing behind you, Hawk and Dash? Most cargo don't have tails and wings and ride horses," the woman Mags said. Her voice seemed sharp as a gull's cry over the ocean.

Calm as Big Blue, Hoku thought. *They either believe our story, or we run.*

"We got prizes for Karl Strand," Hoku said. "Some trinkets he wants. He wants them bad enough to take to war in order to find them. Think we can make out good in a trade."

Mags walked toward them, the hem of her long coat drifting just above the ground, making it look as if she were floating. She didn't focus her gaze on him, but on Aluna and Calli. He forced himself to keep staring at the man Odd, to not let his eyes trail her and show how worried he was.

Behind him, Mags said, "What are these, scales? Can think of a dozen who would pay for some of these shinies. And the feathers, too."

Thwack.

Mags laughed. "The one with a tail isn't broken, I see. Still got spirit and a good strong arm. We can help with that." She rejoined Odd and whispered something in his ear. Hoku relaxed slightly. She hadn't hurt Aluna, and Aluna hadn't pulverized Mags. A good start.

"Is there room at your fire or not?" Dash asked.

"We can just as easy make our own," Hoku added. "In fact, maybe we should. Come on, Dash. Let's take our . . . cargo . . . and find another spot."

He started to turn Sunbeam when Odd called out, "Wait. Yeah, we got room. Room for you and extra feed for your animals. Our beast won't mind sharing. Only one catch."

Hoku kept his face still. A catch. Of course there'd be a catch. "Name it," he said.

"While you share what's ours, you fight for our kludge," Odd said.

So that's why Odd and Mags had been sizing them up. They wanted to know if Hoku and Dash could fight.

"Only in defense," Hoku said. "You start a fight, and you're on your own."

Dash nodded. "I agree to this."

"Then get over here," Odd said. "We got ourselves a tasty little pact."

Hoku had almost been hoping the Upgraders would say no and the plan would fail. Then they could all go back to Mirage or HydroTek and think of another plan. Something less dangerous.

Odd and Mags led them into camp. Hoku kept his eyes forward even though he wanted to stare at the other Upgraders. *Look like you don't care,* Rollin had said. *Pretend you've seen their gizmos and buzzy-bits a thousand times before.*

"You can tie up your horses and cargo here," Odd said, pointing to a metal spike that had been driven into a huge rock. A single rope looped around it trailed off toward the sleeping rhinebra.

While Dash fed and watered their horses, Hoku dismounted and stood next to Odd, who seemed even larger up close. Or maybe Hoku just felt smaller. He squared his shoulders and tried to imagine he was one of Aluna's warrior brothers or a fierce winged Aviar, instead of merely himself.

Dash helped Aluna down from Vachir and carried her to a position facing the campfire. Aluna hated being carried, but that was part of their plan, too. If the Upgraders didn't think she could walk, then they'd never see her as a threat. If she needed to fight, she'd have the advantage of surprise.

After everything was settled, Hoku and Dash followed Odd to the campfire and accepted strips of stringy meat. They met two more Upgraders named Pocket and Zeelo. Pocket was Hoku's age and had a pair of twisty animal horns sprouting out of his head. Zeelo seemed old and crusty, and when she smiled, Hoku saw row after row of sharp metal teeth.

At least none of the Upgraders had named themselves "Instant Death" or "Annihilation."

"What about the one watching us from the cliff?" Dash said calmly. "What is that one called?"

Odd glared up at the cliff, but Mags chuckled. "That scamper is Squirrel, and she'll be down when she's ready. Might want to keep your packs secure while you're here, though. Sparkly bits have a way of disappearing lately."

Once Dash pointed her out, Hoku could see Squirrel clearly. She was small, hunched, and had metal extenders attached to her feet. Wait, no. Those metal devices *were* her feet.

"Who chops off their own legs?" Hoku muttered.

"I've known a few who've done it," Mags said, "but not our Squirrel. No, someone else did that for her."

The world seemed to spin. Hoku swallowed, his mouth suddenly as dry as desert sand.

"Young as your years, are you?" Mags said, shaking her head. Her hair bounced around her face. "Seen worse than that my first year of medtek apprenticing."

Odd grunted and settled down by the fire. Hoku, Dash, and the Upgraders followed his lead. "We'll see much worse soon," Odd said. "War makes a mess of things."

"Are you really taking those people to Karl Strand?" the boy called Pocket asked. He had skin darker than Aluna's and eyes like deep ocean. Hoku loved the way his horns slid out of his temples, curved back toward his face like a nautilus shell, then poked out to the sides. Had it hurt to attach them? Even if it did, the effect was worth it.

"We are," Dash said, gnawing on a stick of meat Zeelo had offered him.

"Strand will give us whatever we want for them," Hoku added. "That winged one is an Aviar. Her people killed Strand's Sky Master. The one with a tail is a Kampii. Hers killed Strand's Sea Master." They didn't really kill Fathom, they just disassembled him, but the Upgraders didn't need to know that.

"Haven't met Strand myself. Haven't even seen him," Odd said. "But I hear he's a dangerous man to play. You could sell those pretties to us and go on your way, richer and alive."

Hoku pretended to consider the offer. "It'd take more than you have to buy our cargo."

Odd stared at the fire, then laughed. "Yeah, true."

"Shut it," Mags said. "We do fine." She pulled a clump of her springy hair and rolled it between her fingertips. "Could always do better, though. You maybe up for a deal?"

"We're listening," Hoku said.

Mags looked at Odd, but he was still staring at the fire. "We take you to Strand, we split the reward," she said. "You only got two. There's no way you make it that far without a fight and someone bigger and badder taking your prizes. Together, we got seven. Enough to make other kludges wary."

There it was, the offer they'd been hoping for. No one could refuse the potential reward that turning Calli and Aluna over to Strand might bring.

"How many warriors do you have?" Dash asked.

"Warriors?" Odd grunted. "Don't hear that word much. At present, we have no slayers. But don't think that makes us weak. No, we got hidden skills. Right, Pocket? Hidden skills."

Pocket smiled. The boy wore a cloth shirt with blue sleeves and leather vest. Hoku couldn't see any other tech mods besides his horns. But his name was Pocket. Maybe he had weapons hidden in his skin.

"No slayers at all?" Hoku said.

"Well, we have Odd here," Mags said. "He can bash skulls as good as any other sword-brain. Looks the part more than you two."

"What are you good at, then?" Hoku asked. "What are we getting besides one Gizmo who looks dangerous?"

"Best medtek in the zone," Mags said, raising her

chin. "No infections since I joined the kludge, and I aim to keep it that way."

Of course, Hoku thought. Upgraders probably needed healers more than any of the splinter tribes. And their healers had to know tech, flesh, and how they worked together, too.

"And Odd here is lucky," Pocket said. "Finds us good caches. Knows when we need to hide. Never lets us go hungry."

So they were tech hunters, this kludge. Rollin said a lot of Upgraders survived by scavenging old tech — using metal detectors and old bits of map to find ancient cities, then digging up what they could. She said that sometimes kludges would meet and form temporary towns. They traded food for tech or upgrading services, shared news, fell in love, or even swapped members. The towns lasted days or weeks or even a month or two, then they broke down and each kludge went off on its own again. Unlike the LegendaryTek splinters, Upgraders were nomads.

Then there were the kind of tech hunters who did horrible things.

"Do you take your tech from living things?" Hoku asked, afraid of the answer. He'd seen the damage other Upgraders had done on the Humans and the Deepfell near the City of Shifting Tides.

"No," Pocket said easily. "We got tools for finding and digging. Safe tools. Squirrel keeps them whirring, good as new."

"We traded our last stash of shiny in the horse city. Kept some of the choicer bits for bribes and trading along the way," Odd said. "Make better time to the army without dragging sacks of metal behind us."

"Not all of us wanted to join the army, mind you," Mags said, glaring at Odd. "Some of us just yell louder than the rest. But even I can't spit on a turn of luck as good as this one." She nodded toward Calli and Aluna.

"Seven is lucky," Odd said. "A good sign. Maybe with seven, Karl Strand will give us what we want and let us live. Better chance of that than if you go with just two."

Hoku grabbed another stick of meat from the tiny pile by the fire. "Seven it is. But we go straight to Strand, fast as we can. No scavenging along the way."

Odd scratched his head, making his red hair bob back and forth. "Not like I know where the man is. Not exactly," he said. "Ask as we go. Best we can do."

Hoku shared a look with Dash. So much for their brilliant plan. Not even the Upgraders knew how to find their leader. Still, traveling with Odd's kludge gave them a better chance than they had by traveling alone.

"Eat up," Odd said. "Tomorrow we head north."

CHAPTER 3

ALUNA SAT NEXT TO CALLI, her back against a rock, and watched Hoku and Dash pretending to be Upgraders. Odd and the others had welcomed them quickly. Maybe too quickly. Were they just excited about the possibility of a big reward from Karl Strand, or was there something else going on?

"We need to take turns keeping watch," she whispered to Calli.

Calli pressed her lips together. "I was thinking the same thing. I don't want to wake up and find my throat slit. Not that I'd wake up if it was, but you know what I mean."

"You sleep first," Aluna said. "I'm not sure I can anyway." Her mind felt like a whirlpool, all other thoughts sucked into the swirl of their mission. "I hope I haven't led us all to our deaths."

Calli leaned over, shuffled her wings out of the way, and rested her shoulder against Aluna's. "We followed you willingly. Whatever happens, the decision belongs to all of us now."

Aluna stared down at her hands and toyed with the fake bindings. "How does your mother handle this? She's led warriors into battle. She's watched them die because of her orders. How does she live with herself?"

Calli was quiet so long that Aluna wondered if she'd fallen asleep. Finally, Calli said, "I don't know. I just hope I figure it out before it's my turn." A moment later, her breathing slowed and her head drifted to the side.

Aluna settled against the rock and studied the Upgraders. They sat around their fire about a dozen meters from the stone where she and Calli were anchored. Far enough away that she couldn't hear what they were saying unless they raised their voices, but close enough for them to keep an eye on their prisoners.

The Upgraders ate and laughed and passed a canteen around their circle. When it got to Hoku, he stood and offered a toast.

"To Karl Strand and the world he's building!" His

words sounded directly in her Kampii ears and sent shivers skittering across her skin in the cool night air.

Odd raised his cup and bellowed, "To the new king, bringing peace and shiny bits to us all!"

Some of the Upgraders cheered, but not all of them. Aluna could hear an argument rising in their voices and strained to make out their words. Mags stood suddenly and stomped away from the fire, the hem of her coat dragging in the dirt behind her. As she stalked passed Aluna, she mumbled, "Empty-headed idiots."

Odd watched her go, then took another swig of his drink. "Don't mind her," he said, loud enough for Mags to hear him. "She hasn't seen the blood and tumble, not outside her med training. Hasn't got used to doing whatever it takes to keep the kludge safe."

Aluna whispered quietly, so only Hoku could hear. "So they're not all loyal to Karl Strand. We could use that."

Hoku couldn't respond, not with Odd passing him drinks and asking him questions, but she saw him nod once and reach for more food.

She stayed awake far into the night, wishing she were back among the Flame Heart or Shining Moon herds, where she could listen to the Equians weave their stories around a bonfire until morning. She even missed her spongy bed back in the City of Shifting Tides. The darkness here was empty, despite a sky full of stars. Critters and creepy-crawlies darted around the rocks and through the bushes, but the world still seemed too quiet. Too lonely.

Aluna awoke to find a hand tugging at the breathing shell embedded in her throat. She opened her eyes and saw stringy brown hair, a face smudged with dirt and sweat, and dark kelp-green eyes.

The Upgrader girl Squirrel.

Aluna grabbed for her but Squirrel jumped out of the way like a desert jackrabbit. The girl didn't run, but stayed crouched three meters away, just beyond the length of the rope tying Aluna to the rock. Squirrel had a good eye. And good instincts.

"You can't steal my necklace," Aluna said to her. "No more than I could steal one of your feet."

Squirrel—she looked about ten years old—stared down at the curved metal prongs attached under her knees. Her long hair fell around her face and clung to her cheek.

"You're Squirrel," Aluna said.

Squirrel looked up sharply and narrowed her eyes.

"I don't bite," Aluna continued calmly. "Not when you're smart enough to stay out of my range." The girl wore a bulging satchel over one shoulder and a thin blade strapped to her thigh. "Do you talk?" Aluna asked.

"No," the girl answered.

Aluna stifled a smile. By her side, Calli started to stir. "You keep watch over everyone," Aluna said to Squirrel. "You're the eyes of the whole group."

Squirrel didn't answer. She seemed fascinated by Calli's yawning and the way her feathers were twitching in the wind.

"I bet you see a lot," Aluna said. "Have you ever been to Karl Strand's base of operations? His lair?"

The girl narrowed her eyes again, then shook her head once.

"Too bad," Aluna said. "You could have told us what to expect."

"You're better off in ignorance." Mags walked toward them carrying two bowls. She handed the pasty white grub to Aluna and Calli and squatted down a few meters away from Squirrel. Not even Squirrel's kludge got close to the girl.

"I've seen what Strand and his maggots can do, and it's nothing I want a piece of," Mags said. "I spend my whole life fixing things. Making things better. He claims to do the same thing, but all I see are broken bodies in his wake. Things I can't even make sense of, let alone put back together."

"But you've agreed to take us to Strand," Calli said, wiping the sleep from her eyes with the back of her hand. "Why?"

Mags looked back at the camp, at the dusty lump that was Odd's sleeping body still snoring by the fire. "Everyone's got to survive. Right, Squirrel? We do what it takes. Whatever it takes."

Squirrel's small hand went to the hilt of her knife. Her mouth and brow pressed into grim lines. Her nose flared.

Mags smiled. "That's right, girl. Never trust anyone. Not even me."

"That's no way to live," Aluna said. "You have to trust your friends."

"Is that what landed you here, all wrapped up like a present? Did you trust someone you shouldn't have? How did that work out for you?" Mags asked. "No. I'll take my way and saw off the arms of any Gizmo who tries to make me do something I don't want to do."

Squirrel seemed to quiver in agreement, her eyes shining bright through that veil of thin, dirty hair.

"Don't count us out yet," Aluna said.

Calli lifted her chin. "We've faced worse and come out on top."

"Well, seeing as how it's partly my job and Squirrel's to make sure you stay tied up until we deliver you to Strand and his grunts, I'd say it's over for both of you. Right, Squirrel?" Mags said. "We take our jobs seriously, and we need what Strand has to offer."

"What does Strand have to offer?" Aluna asked. "Power?"

Mags snorted. "Not power. Safety. Security. Knowing that you can go a whole span of days without someone or something trying to kill you or yours. Shinies and power can be fun, no doubt, but they can mean safety, and that's the true end. A space to breathe in a deadly, suffocating world."

Mags tilted her head and her mass of black hair bobbed. She glanced back at Odd and Pocket, still asleep, and lowered her voice. "Might be that we can work out a deal, though. You see, we could make a lot of good trades—powerful trades—with those scales and feathers you two got in abundance. Maybe not make as much as Karl Strand will offer, but enough to keep us safe, buy us some more muscle, get us someplace better."

Squirrel frowned and shifted on her sproingy metal feet.

"You promise me some of your scales and feathers—and those glinty-glowy necklaces you're both wearing—and I'll give you poison." She patted the pocket of her long coat. "I got tricks that can take you out quick. Painless. Be a mercy to end it like that, compared to what Strand will do to you." Mags leaned in. "You believe anything in this whole wide world, you believe this: Any death is better than living under Karl Strand's control. That's no life at all."

Mags stood abruptly. "What I'm offering is a kindness," she said quietly. "You think on it. You think on it long and hard, and you let me know how you want this to go."

Squirrel's head turned suddenly, but not toward the fire. She was looking down the path behind them.

The corners of Mags's mouth twitched. "You see something, girl?"

Squirrel shook her head, then sniffed.

"You smell something, then. I'll go wake the others." Mags turned and walked to the fire. She started kicking the sleeping boys and men and cursing at them until they stirred.

Squirrel kept her eyes on the horizon behind them. "Be here soon," she said in a soft voice. "Got to be ready."

"Ready for what?" Calli asked.

"Who? How many?" Aluna said at the same time.

"Been following us a few days," Squirrel said. "Not talking, just following. Odd thinks they're looking for the right time to pounce."

Aluna breathed deep. So that's why Odd and Mags were so quick to take in their group. It wasn't just the promise of reward from Karl Strand, but the addition of Hoku and Dash to help strengthen the kludge. Maybe Odd had been hoping that whoever was following them would lose interest. But they hadn't. That meant they were either much stronger or much too desperate to give up.

Squirrel stood up and bounced on her springy feet. "You have a funny horse." And then she was off, bounding meters with each long stride.

"A funny horse? What did she mean by that?" Aluna asked.

Calli pointed. "Look."

Aluna followed her finger and saw Vachir munching scrubby grass in the shade of a large rock a dozen meters away, the frayed end of a rope dangling from her neck. Apparently Vachir hadn't felt like playing a captive this morning.

"Hey!" Aluna called. Vachir's ear twitched, but she didn't look up from her breakfast. Aluna picked up a small stone and threw it at her flank. Her aim was true. Vachir raised her head and huffed air out her nose.

Aluna pointed to the rock where Vachir's rope was supposed to be tied. Vachir sauntered back slowly, still chewing grass, clearly unrepentant.

"Who would be following the kludge?" Calli said. She scooped out the last of her goopy white breakfast and set her bowl on the ground.

Aluna pushed herself up and started to stretch. She had a small knife hidden under her Serpenti skirt and her talon weapons tucked into her sleeves. But she wanted a spear. And a sword. And maybe a harpoon, too.

"Another kludge, I'm guessing," Aluna said. "Probably a bigger one."

"Do they all live like this?" Calli asked. "Like they don't know if they'll live through the next day? It's exhausting!"

"When I was growing up, I was almost never afraid," Aluna said. "We had hunters and defenses and healers and *rules*. I worried about being bored, not about being killed."

"And I worried about disappointing my mother," Calli said with a sigh. "Guess we had it easier than we thought."

Aluna thought about Squirrel's muck-streaked face and wild eyes. "If I'd been born out here, maybe I'd want someone to bring order, too. Maybe I'd be fighting *for* Karl Strand, instead of against him."

CHAPTER 4

Hoku helped the upgraders break camp. Odd's face held no humor this morning, Pocket seemed focused on his duties, and Zeelo had stopped telling horrible jokes and belching. He didn't mind that last one so much. What he did mind was the idea that they were apparently being stalked by another kludge.

Only a few minutes after they'd eaten breakfast, they were packed up and heading north in a tight cluster. Hoku walked his horse next to Odd and Dash. He kept lifting his fingertips to the metal plate attached to his face and tracing the sleek curve over his cheekbone. It stayed cool and smooth no matter how much grit and grime covered the rest of his face.

"Stupid rhinebra," Odd grumbled. "Could make twice the distance if that dumb animal wasn't so blasted lazy."

"I can talk with the creature, if you like," Dash said. "I have a way with . . . dumb animals."

Odd raised an eyebrow. "Do you, now? Well, give it a go, boy. Beat the idiot beast, if you want. Makes no difference to me, as long as it puts one foot in front of the other with more speed than a sun-blasted turtle."

"Yeah, go take care of it," Hoku said, trying to sound as impressive as Odd. Another ninety kilos of fat and muscle would have helped.

Dash nodded and just barely stopped himself from bowing like an Equian before turning his horse to tend to the animal.

"He's a strange one," Odd said. "Talks strange, too."

"Can't argue with you about that," Hoku said. He glanced back at Mags, Pocket, and Zeelo. The Upgraders were watching the road behind them and whispering. At least Aluna and Calli were in the middle of the kludge, safe on Vachir and Nightshade and ready to run if they needed to. Although, getting Vachir and Aluna to run *from* a fight instead of *toward* it would probably require a miracle.

"Strand is good for us," Odd said suddenly, as if he were answering a question. "People should be able to muck about their lives however they want. Shouldn't need to pay slayers to keep you from getting sliced in half every day. Shouldn't need to glue swords to your arm or turn your skin to stone, neither. Karl Strand will beat some order into the world. Set some rules. Then maybe a person can walk from one place to another without getting killed or stole from or beaten into pulp and bits."

"I hear you," Hoku said. "I think—"

But Odd wasn't done. "Young ones like Pocket and Squirrel should be allowed to grow up with enough food to eat and a medtek when they need one, and other people to count on when they're sick or tired or feeling broken." He shook his large head. "Most days all we can do is wait for the fist to fall and hope we survive the hit."

So Odd was conflicted about aligning with Karl Strand, too—maybe even as much as Mags was. But Odd was responsible for the whole kludge, and he clearly saw Strand as a path to a safer world. Not necessarily a happier world, but one where the kludge had to worry a little less about surviving each day.

Hoku's mind spun like gears. If they stopped Karl Strand, nothing would change for the Upgraders. And clearly something *needed* to change, or Strand wouldn't have found so many followers, so many people willing to risk their lives for the hope of a brighter future.

Aluna wanted to rid the world of Strand, and Hoku agreed with her. But maybe they had to do more than that. Maybe instead of just removing Strand, they needed to give the Upgraders another choice. A *better* choice.

"I had a family and a safe home once," Hoku said, surprising himself. But it was true, he had. Back in the City of Shifting Tides, his mother and father had worked hard every day of their lives to give him those things.

"What happened?" Odd asked.

Hoku shrugged. What happened? The Kampii necklaces started failing. Aluna burst the illusion that everything was okay. But he couldn't tell Odd that. He settled on: "The world changed, and we either had to change with it, or die."

"They still alive?" Odd asked. "Your family, I mean."

Hoku's gut clenched like a fist. He wanted to say, "Of course they are," but . . . were they? He'd never really thought about it before. He'd always just assumed they were fine, that they were still working and eating clams and taking care of Grandma Nani. But what if they weren't?

Odd's meaty hand landed on his shoulder, heavy as dead fish, but the Upgrader said nothing.

A cheer went up behind them as the lumbering

rhinebra suddenly bolted into a jog. Dash stood on its head and held its reins, looking as comfortable as if he were standing on flat ground.

Odd whooped. "Get your feet moving, you great globby kludge! Let's put some meters between us and them gutless Gizmos behind us."

Hoku patted Sunbeam's sweaty neck and glanced back at Aluna and Calli. Pocket walked next to them and seemed to be plying them with questions. Vachir could certainly handle such a small Upgrader on her own if Pocket decided to start trouble, but Hoku didn't want to take any chances. He pulled on Sunbeam's reins and sat back, slowing the horse down so he could join his "cargo."

"I wasn't messing with them," Pocket said as Hoku approached. "I was just seeing if they needed anything."

Hoku looked sharply at Calli and saw her trying to suppress a smile.

"They're prisoners," Hoku said. "You don't have to be nice to them."

Aluna grunted and scowled, and if Hoku hadn't known she was acting, he'd probably have kicked Sunbeam and gone back to walking with Odd.

"Well, they're still people, too," Pocket said. "They got wings and scales and they come from places we can't even go, but they were like us once."

"They're nothing like you," Hoku said, then corrected himself. "They're nothing like us, I mean. We're tougher and more dangerous and we're going to rule the world."

Bizarrely, Pocket laughed. "I'd trade my horns for wings," the boy said. "I'd probably trade my pockets, too."

Calli's chin raised proudly.

"Never met a bird-woman before. Or a fish-woman," Pocket said. He stared up at Calli. "Can you tell me what it's like to fly?"

Hoku could see Calli warming up to the boy, and it wasn't good. Not if they wanted to keep their cover.

Calli began, "It's the most—"

"Be quiet," Aluna said gruffly. "We won't talk to the people who are turning us over to Karl Strand."

"Oh, right," Calli said brightly. Too brightly. She twisted her face into an adorable scowl. "The mermaid is right. We won't talk to you."

Pocket's shoulders hunched. He seemed to fold in on himself. "Wouldn't be my choice," he said softly. "I don't get to choose."

"Come on," Hoku said. "Let's leave the prisoners alone before . . . before I have to hit one of them." He cringed at the idea, but Pocket didn't seem to notice. The boy followed him meekly.

In the back of the kludge, Mags called out, "Twenty!"

Pocket picked up the pace of his walking. He was still young, his head barely up to Sunbeam's shoulders.

"Does twenty mean there are twenty people coming to attack us, or that they're twenty minutes away?" Hoku asked him.

"Does it matter?" Pocket answered. "Have to fight them no matter what. Nowhere to go, nowhere to hide."

Hoku frowned. "Is there any chance they want to talk, or are simply passing through on the same route?"

"No," Pocket said. "They would have announced themselves already, like you did, if they wanted to talk. If they were passing by, they would have done the same. Maybe stayed a night at our fire to swap stories and goods. No, they've been sizing us up, counting our blades. They think they can take our tech and our beast without losing too many of their own. Not all kludges scavenge from the old, dead places. Some think the living places are a lot easier."

Hoku looked at the force shield strapped to his wrist. If only they were easier to make, then he could outfit Odd's whole kludge with them. "Can you fight?" he asked Pocket. "Your name—does it mean you've got weapons hidden somewhere?"

Pocket chuckled. "I've got food. Tools. Some nice shells and a few shiny bits of tech I picked up here and there. I keep a ball that Squirrel and I toss around, and a little stuffed thing she likes to hug when she sleeps."

"Your horns look dangerous," Hoku said. "Can you hit people with them?"

"I can store water in them," Pocket said proudly. "Most of the time that's a lot more useful."

"How have you survived this long?" Hoku asked. He felt an unfamiliar outrage growing in his mind. "Your kludge doesn't even have any warriors!"

"Used to," Pocket answered. "They signed up with Strand. Mags convinced Odd to hold out a little longer, but then you and Dash came along. Looks like we'll all be part of his army before long."

Not if we can stop Strand first, Hoku thought.

Squirrel bounded out from behind a rock and leaped in front of Sunbeam. Hoku barely managed to hold on to the reins as Sunbeam jerked his massive body to the side.

"They didn't like that we sped up," Squirrel said to Pocket. She acted as if Hoku weren't even there, as if Sunbeam hadn't almost trampled her to death. "I heard the big one say they needed to attack now, before we got too far ahead."

"How many are there?" Hoku asked.

"All my fingers," Squirrel said. "Plus one."

"Eleven coming," Hoku said aloud so Aluna could hear.

Squirrel bolted away, her springy feet carrying her to Odd in three quick strides. A moment later he yelled, "Circle up! Pocket, Squirrel, and the prisoners on the beast. Everyone else, get ready for blood."

Pocket headed for the rhinebra. Hoku paused to grab the reins of Vachir and Calli's horse, even though Aluna and Calli were already moving to where Odd wanted them. Calli's hands were still bound, but he could see Aluna toying with her ropes.

Dash made the rhinebra sit, a defensive pose intended to protect its more delicate underbelly. Not that the other kludge would try to hurt the beast; the rhinebra was more valuable than tech to a bunch of nomads. Dash slid down the rhinebra's side and joined their group.

"Do we run?" he asked Aluna, his dark eyes darting down the path, to the sides of the valley, and back again. "We must make sure we survive."

"We'll know what we're up against in two flashes," Aluna said. Her eyes seemed brighter now that a fight was close. "It may be too late to run."

"Good," Dash said. "I would not abandon these people to a slaughter unless we had no other choice."

As he spoke, the world around them seemed to burst into blades and flames and battle cries.

CHAPTER 5

ALUNA PULLED HERSELF to the top of the rhine-bra's saddle so she could get a better view of the fight. She thought Pocket had already climbed up, but when she got there, she found only the saddlebags and supplies strapped to the animal's side. *Good.* She didn't have to worry about playing prisoner in the middle of a crisis.

"More Upgraders," Aluna said. She knew Hoku could hear and would share her words with the others. "The girl was right. There are eleven. No beasts of their own, as far as I can see."

The attacking Upgraders had come from the south, so at least they hadn't had time to surround the kludge. She watched Odd wade into a cluster of men and women and metal and start swinging his massive, armored arms. The Upgraders dodged and taunted him, but he didn't falter. He'd seemed focused and methodical, as if he were merely a farmer pulling in his fish nets or a gardener weeding his kelp beds.

Aluna spotted Mags and Squirrel working together. Squirrel darted in and out of combat, grabbing a satchel off one woman and pulling another Upgrader's shirt over his head. She was a tiny blur of chaos, too quick and unpredictable to be hit.

Mags, on the other hand, approached the fight with calculated precision. Aluna watched her load a needle full of red liquid into a tube, then lift the tube to her mouth. She blew sharply, sending the needle shooting through the air. It lodged itself in the fleshy leg of a huge Upgrader trying to race past Odd. He stumbled to the ground and twitched in the dirt.

Zeelo, who Aluna had assumed was nothing more than a crotchety old woman, wielded her two walking sticks with deadly force and far more speed than seemed possible. Aluna could have watched her forever. She'd never seen someone turn such simple objects into weapons of such incredible power and versatility.

The kludge may not have had any "slayers," but they were clearly no strangers to fighting for their lives. Even so, they were outnumbered. The attackers were going to win.

"There are too many," Aluna said to Hoku. "We have to join in to give them any shot of surviving."

"Dash already decided that for himself," Hoku said.

Aluna scanned the battle until she found him, a dark-haired figure holding off two Upgraders who'd tried to sneak around the side. Dash's sword blade flashed, sending a spray of red across his mismatched leathers and robes. The Upgraders—a man with a blackened helmet and a slender woman with silvery fists—were in for a tough day.

She felt another sharp pang in her chest. She wanted to leap into the fray, talons spinning, and fight by Dash's side. She'd been named the Dawn-bringer, after all, not She Who Watches from a Safe Distance.

Reluctantly, Aluna tore her gaze from Dash and surveyed the rest of the fighting. Most of the attackers were still clustered around Odd, trying to break through his wild, vicious swings. An Upgrader barked an order and three others detached themselves from the pack and ran straight for the rhinebra.

"Three on their way," Aluna said to Hoku. "You and Calli get up here!"

"No," Hoku said. "If I hide, our plan is over."

She looked over the rhinebra's side and saw Hoku searching in the packs for a weapon. Calli tugged at his arm, but Aluna couldn't hear what she was saying. Probably something about certain death, because that's what Hoku was walking into. It was one thing to be brave, but surviving fights also took skill and practice, and he didn't have either.

"Wait," Aluna said. "I have a plan."

The rhinebra had clearly been trained to sit and do nothing during battles; it was too valuable a treasure to be harmed by either side. But a motionless rhinebra made a great barrier—not between them and their enemies, but between Aluna, Calli, Hoku, and the rest of Odd's kludge.

"Vachir!"

Vachir looked up from where she was standing with the other horses. Her tail swished, her front hoof pawed at the earth. She wanted this almost as much as Aluna did. Without another command, she cantered over and stood by the rhinebra's side, right under Aluna.

Aluna maneuvered herself off the rhinebra's saddle and slid down its flank. She grabbed Vachir's saddle and twisted it onto her back. In two flashes Aluna had her tail wrapped around the front saddle horn and the end strapped to Vachir's side. Vachir's hair bristled. They were ready.

"What are you doing?" Hoku said. "You can't go out there! If the attackers don't kill you, Odd or Mags will when it's over."

"Hoku's right," Calli said. "But maybe I can fly us away, one at a time. I'll start with—"

"No," Aluna said. "We stay here and fight . . . . We just don't let Odd and Mags know we're fighting. We can use the rhinebra for cover. Hoku, can you bring them to us?"

It took Hoku a moment to figure out what she was asking. "I'm the bait?"

"If you're up for it," Aluna said.

He grinned. "Anything is better than actually fighting!"

"Don't forget to use your shield," Calli said. She pulled a retractable spear from Vachir's saddlebag and expanded it to its full two meters.

Hoku bolted out from behind the rhinebra and yelled, "You Gizmos want a fight? Come and get one!"

Aluna saw him twist his wrist to turn on the force shield. A shimmering wall appeared just in time to deflect one of the Upgrader's daggers. His bravado wavered slightly, but he recovered. "Nice shield, right? You'll have to kill me to get it!"

"That's enough," Aluna said. "Get back here!"

She maneuvered Vachir to the side, frustrated that they had to stay hidden behind the rhinebra. She could see the three Upgraders charging at Hoku: a large, dark woman wearing scaled armor over most of her body; a lighter-skinned man with an animal's muzzle jutting out of his face; and a person completely hidden in bulky robes, but wielding huge swords in each hand.

"Faster!" Aluna called to Hoku. She released Spirit and Spite, her newly repaired talon weapons, from their hidden spot in her sleeves and started to swing them. In a flash, the two thin chains were whirring in deadly circles at her sides. Vachir danced beneath her, a storm barely contained.

"If it goes badly, you fly Hoku away," she said to Calli.

Calli gripped her spear tighter and did a few slow figure eights. The girl had been practicing regularly, but still wasn't ready for this kind of fight. Aluna preferred to handle the enemy herself and use Calli as backup.

Hoku ran between them and there was no more time for thinking, no more time for wondering if they should have done something else.

Aluna sent her right talon at the large woman's eyes and sent her left for the woman's arm, hoping to either blind her, immobilize her weapon hand, or both. The woman yelped and dodged, batting the talon out of the air with her armored limb.

Vachir spun and kicked, landing two powerful hooves in the woman's chest. She went sprawling backward with a grunt—and hopefully some broken ribs.

"Like a thunderbolt," Aluna said. Vachir shook her head proudly and spun to face their next victim.

The battle became a blur. The attacker with swords managed to land a cut across her forehead. She blinked the warm blood out of her eyes and managed to wrap a talon around his throat. When his hood fell back, she almost dropped her weapon in surprise. The Human underneath had been burned so badly that she couldn't even make out his features. All she saw were two bright-orange eyes glaring out from a ravaged landscape of angry flesh.

One of the burned man's swords burst into flames while the other crackled into blue ice. He plunged them both at Vachir's flank, thinking she'd be frozen in place by her rider's shock. But Vachir had a mind of her own and danced easily out of the way.

Aluna yanked the talon she'd wrapped around his neck and he fell face-first to the ground with a strangled cry. Vachir reared, ready to bring her hooves down on the back of his head or his spine.

"No!" Aluna shouted. "Just an arm. Or a leg."

Vachir screamed her frustration but shifted her body and landed on the man's shoulder. The ground muffled his cries.

After the third attacker fell, knocked unconscious by a vicious hit from the butt end of Calli's spear, Hoku ran off to fetch more of them. Aluna scanned the battle and saw Dash helping Mags and Squirrel, saw Odd fighting three opponents and still holding his own. Zeelo seemed to be cursing more than fighting, but her old bones and incredible skill were keeping her up and alive.

"Last two!" Hoku called, racing toward them with his shield activated.

"Bring 'em in," she answered.

Aluna could hear her heart beating through her body, could see the glow of her breathing necklace as it pulsed at her neck. Sweat dripped down her forehead and down her back. Vachir's body was too warm under Aluna's tail, her gray horse flank slick and darkened with moisture.

Tides' teeth, she felt *alive*. Maybe for the first time in weeks. She wanted to whoop and yell, to scream at her enemies and run, fast as sunlight itself and as far as she could go. And maybe a few months ago, she would have. But now she harnessed the battle rush, channeling it into her strikes, her precision, her technique.

She watched Hoku running toward their spot, two Upgraders gaining ground right behind him. One of them shot a gout of sickly green liquid from a weapon in his hand, and Hoku twisted, flicked his wrist, let his force shield take the damage.

But in that moment, in just a flash, his foot hit a rock and he fell. It seemed as if the entire world slowed down as his shoulder crashed into the hard ground and he slid, suddenly obscured by a cloud of dust and grit.

"Hoku!" Calli screamed.

The Upgraders would be on him before he could get back up. One raised her ax above her head, ready to strike. But Hoku hadn't made it to the rhinebra. If Aluna went for him, everyone would see.

"Go," Aluna told Vachir. The horse leaped forward eagerly, out into the open.

Even on the ground, Hoku had the brains to activate his shield for the first of the Upgrader's attacks. The ax bounced off it with a shower of sparks. The Upgrader took the sudden recoil, spun the ax, and went for a second hit.

And then Aluna was there, spinning her talons and wielding Vachir like a weapon.

She heard someone behind her and assumed it was Calli, coming to pull Hoku out of the battle. "Get him out of here," she said.

"We will," said a boy's voice.

Aluna turned and saw Pocket helping Calli drag Hoku back to the rhinebra. There was no time to argue. No time to figure out what this meant for their survival or their hopes of finding Karl Strand. Her enemies were still up, and in this moment, they were all she had time to see.

CHAPTER 6

HOKU WATCHED ALUNA dispatch the two remaining Upgraders with the efficiency of a shark. She used to be angry when she fought, full of a wild rage that drove her strength. Their time with the desert Equians had changed all that. Now Aluna possessed a battle calmness that seemed far more deadly. If her family could see her now, they'd be astonished at the change.

"You okay?" Pocket asked. Calli poked Hoku's arm, looking for a break.

"I'm fine," Hoku said, trying to sit up. "Aluna, get back here! Maybe they haven't seen you yet!"

Vachir whirled and thundered back to their safe spot beside the rhinebra. Aluna unhooked her tail from the saddle and slid down Vachir's side until she was balanced on her tail sheath.

Quick as an eel, she grabbed the front of Pocket's shirt and pulled him toward her. "If you say anything about this, we'll have to kill you."

Pocket tried to scramble away, but Aluna's grip held him in place.

"Wait," Hoku said. "Don't hurt him. He helped us." He climbed to his feet, ignoring the sharp pain in his shoulder and the warmth soaking through his shirt.

"He knows too much now," Aluna said. "Calli, what would your mother do?"

"Break his fingers if he talks," Calli said, far too easily. "Or worse."

Pocket cringed.

"He won't say anything," Hoku said quickly. He didn't know if Aluna and Calli were pretending to threaten Pocket, or if they were serious about hurting him. He hoped they weren't, but he couldn't take the chance. The sounds of battle were dying down and he could hear Odd giving orders to tie up the attackers that were still alive. "Pocket, get these Upgraders secured before they regain consciousness," Hoku said. "I'll tie up the prisoners again."

Aluna stared at Hoku, her dark eyes searching his. He kept his own gaze even and calm. He didn't look away. Finally, she released Pocket. The boy scrambled backward like a crab, his eyes wide.

Hoku bound Aluna's and Calli's wrists, wiped the

blood from their wounds, and stored their weapons. Pocket did as he was told—all five of the enemy Upgraders were bound and groaning by the time Hoku was done.

"You another kludge, or you something else?" Pocket asked Hoku quietly. He cast a fearful glance at Aluna.

Hoku wanted to lie, to stick to their story about prisoners and rewards and his life as an Upgrader. But his shoulder ached, his body was covered in sweat and grime, and instead he said, "Something else."

The energy of the fight started seeping out of Hoku's body, leaving him tired and shaky. But if he'd learned one thing in all these months, it was that the work wasn't over when the fighting stopped. He and Pocket dragged the bound Upgraders into the center of camp where Odd and Squirrel had brought the others. Dash and Mags were still off to the side, crouched over what looked to be a bundle of rags on the ground.

"Zeelo," Pocket said. "Zeelo!" He dropped the last Upgrader and raced over. Hoku followed more slowly, a deep chill creeping over his skin.

Zeelo lay on the ground, panting like an animal. Dash held her head in his lap and smoothed the hair out of her eyes. She snapped at him like a wild thing, but he simply removed his hands and tried again after she had calmed.

"Give me something to sop blood," Mags said.

Dash ripped off his leather vest and pulled his shirt over his head.

"Press it there," Mags said, pointing. Dash gently lowered Zeelo's head to the ground and shifted closer to her gut. Hoku couldn't see the wound because of Mags's puffy hair. He made no effort to move.

Dash bunched his shirt into a ball and shoved it against Zeelo's skin. The old woman hissed and let out a stream of curses.

"Good," Mags said. "That means you still have some spit inside. You haven't let all of it leak out on the dirt."

"What can I do?" Hoku asked. "Give me something to do."

"Water," Mags said. "Make a fire. Get it hot. Pocket, you help him."

Hoku left without a word, eager to be away from the stench of guts. How could Dash sit there and watch it all?

While Pocket gathered wood, Hoku went through the packs until he found a basin and enough water to fill it halfway. He piled the wood, then watched as Pocket opened a compartment on his calf and pulled out a tiny firestick. So that's what "pocket" meant. What else did the boy have hidden?

They got the fire blazing and set the water heating.

Instead of bringing the water to Zeelo, they helped Mags bring Zeelo to the fire. For the warmth, Mags said. Zeelo cursed the whole time, which Mags took to be a good sign. Then Mags got to work. She demanded tools, and each one had to be cleaned in the hot water, dried, and handed to her before she lost her temper. Luckily, Dash was fast and good with his hands, and Mags got what she needed.

Odd sat by Zeelo's head and berated her. Hoku would have been appalled, except he was friends with Rollin and had seen her behave the same way. Insults and projectiles were apparently signs of affection in some Upgrader cultures.

Hoku, Pocket, and Squirrel did everything else. They tended to one another's wounds, built another fire to cook dinner, and kept an eye on their prisoners. Five of the attackers were dead, three felled by Odd, one by Mags, and one by Dash. Hoku wanted to bury them, but Pocket shook his head.

"Not until we divvy up their shinies," he said.

Parts, Hoku thought, his mouth dry. *Of course.* Maybe he could pretend to be generous and give his share to the others. Would that look suspicious?

"No!" Mags yelled.

Hoku looked over and saw the medtek hunched over Zeelo's body. Odd had been talking to Zeelo, trying to keep her mind distracted from the pain, but now he fell silent, the flickering fire reflecting in the lenses of his goggles. Hoku walked toward them slowly, not quite wanting to get there but not quite able to stop himself, either.

"She has entered eternal night," Dash said. "She is gone." He wiped his crimson-stained hands on the ground.

"No," Mags repeated. "She hasn't gone anywhere yet." She leaned over and slapped Zeelo in the face. The old woman's head fell to the side.

"Stop it," Odd said. "Don't need her ghost coming back for revenge."

Mags sat back on her haunches. Her hands hung at her sides. A moment ago they'd been useful—sewing rips and cleaning out muck. Now she didn't seem to know what to do with them.

"You did good," Odd said. "You gave her a chance. She chose not to take it. Always was a stubborn Gizmo."

Hoku looked back to where Aluna and Calli were waiting by the rhinebra. Calli's brow was furrowed, her lips compressed with worry. Aluna's face was blank. Unreadable. Calculating. Maybe she was thinking Zeelo's death meant one less Upgrader she'd have to take out later.

Odd stood slowly, a hand pressed against his chest where he'd taken a bad hit in the fight. "Bring the dead near the fire and make sure those prisoners are tied tight. Maim 'em some more if you have to. Then take your naps, find your wind, and get cleaned up. Tonight we see to Zeelo's 'cycling."

'Cycling? Hoku had no idea what that meant. He didn't know the Upgraders even had rituals. He couldn't risk asking Pocket about it, not if he was supposed to know already.

At least they had time to rest before the event. He watched Mags treat a growing bruise on Dash's face. One of his enemies had landed a heavy punch and broken his nose. Mags pressed the bones back in place without a word of kindness. Dash gritted his teeth and let the tears fall from his eyes, but stayed still while she worked.

"Walking twig, you're next," Mags called.

It took Hoku two flashes to realize she was talking to him. He took Dash's spot on a low, flat rock and prepared for pain.

"Took a dive into the ground, did you?" Mags said as she prodded his shoulder. "Can you lift it?"

He raised his arm, winced, and let it drop again.

"Messed up your joint, I'd say," Mags said. "No more rough and tumble while it heals."

Hoku tried to look disappointed while Mags immobilized his shoulder with cloth strips. She'd looked so upset when Zeelo died, but here she was, back to her normal get-it-done expression. Maybe her eyes seemed a little more red and puffy, but nothing else was different. Her hands moved with speed and confidence and he tried not to think of the deadly needles she had hidden in her coat.

After Mags finished tying the ends off, she started poking around for other injuries. "What else hurts?" she said. "No way you could take out five Gizmos with no more than a bum shoulder as your prize."

Hoku started to pull away, but forced himself to stop. "I, uh, got lucky," he said. "They must have sent the weakest ones to me."

Mags snorted and started prodding his jaw and nose. "A Gizmo who doesn't puff up when he has the chance? Next you're going to tell me that rhinebras can fly." She got to his faceplate and stopped, her fingers poised near the edge.

"I'm fine," Hoku said. This time he did pull away, but not far. He could feel his breathing necklace pulsing fast under his metal collar. His disguise could never fool a medtek. He should have known that. After the whole battle, he'd managed to ruin their plan after all.

But Mags just started rolling up her extra cloth strips and storing them in her bag. When her head was turned, all he could see was her mass of black hair.

"You aren't the first I've seen," she said quietly.

"First of what?" he said. It came out with a croak.

"The first one trying to look like he's got more whiz-bang than he actually has," she said. She wiped off her tools next, although they already looked clean. "No one takes a basic seriously, but not everyone can pay for more."

"I . . . I don't know what you're talking about," Hoku said. His fingers were on his face, feeling along his metal cheekbone, before he could stop them.

Mags chuckled. "Sure you don't."

"You going to tell the others?" he asked.

She cinched her bag and tied it closed. "Don't see the point," she said brusquely. "But if you ever want to trade that bit of pretty for something that actually does something, you come to me. Got it?"

He nodded once, and she smiled. He hadn't seen her do that before.

"Good," she said. "And who knows? You took out five of them today. Might win yourself a little whir and fizz tonight. We could turn you into a real Gizmo before we even make it to Karl Strand."

Hoku didn't respond. He couldn't. His brain was too busy whirring and fizzing, too full of hum and shine.

CHAPTER 7

ALUNA DOZED NEXT TO CALLI while the kludge
bustled around camp, cleaned themselves, and gathered wood for the night's fire. She could hear them
talking as they piled the sticks and blew the embers
into flames. Apparently Odd wanted his prisoners close
enough to watch whatever ritual he'd be performing.

As the sky started to darken, Dash brought them
bowls of food. Then he pulled out a coarse brush from
a saddlebag and began to groom Vachir. Vachir huffed
and pranced, clearly enjoying the extra attention.

"How is your head?" Dash asked quietly.

"It hurts less than your broken nose," Aluna said.

Dash had done a decent job washing the red off
his hands in the dirt, but his shirt was gone and blood
and grime matted his usually perfect hair. The bandage

on the bridge of his nose did little to hide the deep bruising across his cheeks.

Dash ran his hand down Vachir's neck. "I killed one of them," he said. "It was not my wish, but his hit disoriented me. Ending a life . . . It never gets easier."

"You helped protect us," Calli said. "You did the right thing."

Dash rested his forehead against Vachir's neck. The horse leaned in to him, offering support. "This is harder than I thought it would be," he said. "I thought the Upgraders would be evil. I thought I might even enjoy killing them. Karl Strand has earned our hate."

"Your people thought the Serpenti were evil," Calli said.

"And the Kampii still think the Deepfell have the blood of demons," Aluna added. "We're all good at hate."

"And blood. And death," Dash said. He pulled himself away from Vachir and continued to brush her, although his heart clearly wasn't in the task.

Aluna stared at Squirrel and Pocket and Hoku poking at the fire, at Odd and Mags talking quietly near Zeelo's body.

"It will all be over soon," Aluna said. "We've gotten so far. We just need to hang on a little longer. You can do this, Dash."

Dash sighed. "I *will* do this."

As the sun set, Odd called his kludge to the fire.

The Upgrader prisoners had gags in their mouths, but every one of them was awake and watching, too.

"Zeelo's gone and died," Odd said.

Aluna had been expecting something more poetic, but she blamed the Equians for that. The horse folk were practically born being majestic.

Odd continued. "Zeelo fought hard. Served the kludge well. Was loyal as a . . . well, whatever you think is a loyal thing, she was as loyal as that." Mags and Hoku chuckled. "She cursed better than any old Gizmo I ever knew, and she drank better than most of them, too."

"To Zeelo!" Mags called.

"To Zeelo," Dash and Pocket answered. Pocket nudged Hoku, who added, "Yeah! Zeelo!"

Squirrel stayed silent, her eyes alternately scanning the fire and the falling darkness, but no one seemed to mind.

"Now, let's see what Zeelo says about her 'cycling," Odd said. He pulled out a small silver stick and pressed a button on the side. An image of Zeelo appeared above the device, flickering and tiny, but moving around as if she were alive.

"So you're watching this, meaning some blasted Gizmo got the best of me," Zeelo's tiny voice said. "Or maybe some coyote or a cough or one of you stuck me with something in the night. No matter. I'm gone, and you get my stuff."

What stuff? Aluna wondered. Even the woman's weapons had been just two gnarly old sticks. Nothing fancy or worth anything, except as a remembrance.

"My ears go to Odd," Zeelo said, "so maybe next time he'll hear whatever it was that sneaked up and killed me." She chuckled then, even though the joke wasn't funny, and Odd smiled. "My left cutting finger goes to Mags, if she wants it, and to Pocket if she doesn't."

"It's yours," Mags said to Pocket. The boy nodded grimly.

"And my best of best, my beautiful teeth"—Zeelo smiled, showing off rows of pointed metal fangs—"my beautiful babies go to Squirrel. She doesn't need them now, but later on, she might want more bite." Zeelo laughed again, and this time the other Upgraders joined her.

"No sad faces," Zeelo's video-self continued. "I'm older than most Gizmos, and a lot more handsome, too. About time I had a rest. You all go on with living. Curse my name at dinner, and I'll know you're thinking of me. You want my mark, then make it red. A flower. Something delicate and sweet smelling, just like me."

The video disappeared and the night suddenly became a little darker and a little quieter. Only the fire dared to crackle. Aluna studied Dash's and Hoku's faces, but found them still and unreadable. Either they were getting better at playing their parts, or they didn't find this whole vile tech transfer nearly as disgusting as she did.

"I'll see to the 'cycling after dinner," Mags said. "Can't do all the upgrades while we're on the move, but I'll get you your parts for safekeeping until I can."

"I'll do the marks," Pocket said. "Got enough red for Zeelo's flowers, as long as you don't want them too big on your skin."

Aluna thought of the tattoos she'd seen on some of the Upgraders. Odd's arms were covered in pictures so dense that they blended together and made it look like he was wearing tight, brightly colored sleeves. Did every tiny image represent a person who had died?

Odd walked over and clapped Mags on the shoulder. "We did well today, my fellow mess-ups. We owe thanks to the two new slayers who joined us. I submit that they get first choice of spoils from those they bested."

"Tech cannibals," Aluna muttered to Calli. "Scavengers."

Calli shrugged. "We don't make a lot of new tech nowadays." She touched the gold necklace wound around her throat, the one that let her breathe in the thin air of the mountaintops, and Aluna wondered who it used to belong to. "We all rely on the work of the ancients, don't we? The only difference is that we're given our tech when we're born, or during our ceremonies. The Upgraders have to take theirs wherever they can find it."

"From one another?" Aluna said. She glanced at the Upgrader prisoners tied up nearby. Their metal bits glittered in the firelight.

"It's life," Calli said. "It's not always about honor and friendship. Sometimes it's just about surviving."

Aluna looked at Calli, wondering when this hardened warrior had replaced the shy girl Aluna had met all those long months ago. Probably at the moment Calli had gotten stabbed and poisoned and almost killed in the Shining Moon settlement.

"Does anyone want to argue with me?" Odd asked the Upgraders around the campfire. "Any who feel Dash and Hawk don't deserve what I say?"

Aluna looked at Pocket. That boy knew the truth. He'd seen everything. But he kept his head down, seemed to study some crack in the earth by his feet. She'd been expecting him to betray them, especially now when it was safe.

"I don't want any spoils," Hoku said. "You lost a member of your kludge. You choose first. You need the strength." Only Aluna heard him mumble afterward, "No *parts*. Not yet."

"I, too, will pass," Dash said, his expression dark. Aluna suspected he found the idea of profiting from a kill repellent. Dash only killed to survive, and for no other reason.

Odd shrugged, his massive shoulders barely moving. "More for us, then. This is the order we're choosing: me, Mags, Squirrel, Pocket, and back 'round again."

Hoku and Dash came over and sat a few meters in front of Aluna and Calli. Close enough so they could talk, but far enough away to make it look as if they were simply guarding their prisoners.

They watched as Odd and his kludge divvied up their spoils. The list seemed long. Longer than it should have been. When one of the Upgrader prisoners nearby started to grumble, Aluna realized why. Odd was giving away everything—even the tech that belonged to their prisoners.

"Oh, sweet currents! They didn't list the parts that are still attached," Hoku breathed.

"What do you mean?" Aluna asked.

Hoku pretended to talk to Dash. "Odd is giving away the prisoners' weapons and the tech that can be taken without injury. I thought . . . I thought he might be planning to kill them and take everything."

"He intends to let them live," Dash said. "That is a great relief. I am not ready for another fight."

Aluna glanced at the helpless prisoners who'd tried to kill them only a few hours earlier. "Strand's Upgraders would have slit their throats, just because it was convenient." Her brothers and the other Kampii hunters might have done it, too, but she didn't say that out loud.

"The kludge puts itself in more danger by letting them live," Dash said, "but it is an honorable decision."

Aluna watched Odd's kludge take their new tech and weapons and store them in their packs. There would be no gloating tonight. Instead, they returned to the fire and started telling stories about Zeelo. Some were funny: her loudest fart, her best curse, the time she beat an arrogant young man who'd tried to rob her. Others were heartbreaking. Mags told them all about Zeelo's three children and how they'd each died. Zeelo had worn their symbols on her chest, drawn directly over her heart.

Sleep came like a whirlpool, trying to drag Aluna under. She fought it as long as possible, not wanting to miss any of the Upgraders' stories. They didn't talk like the Equians, but they clearly understood the power of sharing words and memories around a crackling fire.

Hoku said they couldn't just stop Karl Strand, that they needed to replace him with a more appealing option, or another person bent on world domination would simply rise to take his place. Not for the first time, she was beginning to think that Hoku was right. She was beginning to think that these people deserved better.

CHAPTER 8

HOKU WATCHED THE MOUNTAINS to the north loom a little larger and closer every day. The dry earth beneath his feet grew moist and dark and turned to soil. Hoku loved the cool feel of it beneath his head at night. He loved how *green* the plants were that grew from it—foliage the rich color of kelp instead of those poor faded shrubs in the desert. Deep in his heart, it made him feel closer to water.

But getting closer to the mountains meant they were getting closer to Strand's army amassing in the foothills. Hoku liked traveling with Odd's kludge— at least on the days they had enough food to eat and weren't under attack. Everything would change when they got to the army, and he worried that by using the kludge to get close to Strand, they were putting Odd, Mags, Pocket, and Squirrel into far more danger than they knew. It ate at him, this worry, but he kept it to himself.

When they reached the edge of the vast forest that sprawled between them and the mountains, Odd paused.

"Hate this place," Odd said. "Knew a man came through here once. Stepped into the forest on the south side and they found his body three months later on the north side. Dead. Throat sliced. Propped up against a stump, like a message."

"A message from who?" Hoku said, eyeing the trees.

Odd took a swig of his water. "Someone smart enough to leave messages. Someone who doesn't care if they make enemies."

Hoku spotted a squirrel racing up a tree trunk and three bright-blue birds gossiping on a nearby branch. Odd could wade into battle against five foes at one time, and he was scared of a *forest*?

"If the trees bother you, we could find another route," Dash said. He tried to make it sound like he had no preference, but Hoku knew that Dash had no love of enclosed spaces. "The forest cannot extend forever. We can go around."

Mags pulled off her wide-brimmed hat and wiped her forehead. "Yeah, sure. Let's go another way," she said. "Had enough of these bugs. My boots weren't made for mud. Don't even know what manner of poisonous creatures live in there, waiting to snack on us."

Mags, too? Hoku eyed the forest with new respect.

"Can't go around," Odd grumbled. "Unless you want to arrive at Strand's after he's old and buried. Take us weeks, maybe months, to go around woods this size. They follow the mountains in both directions. We go through, or we give up."

"Then we go through," Hoku said quickly. He glanced at Aluna and saw her face tight with worry.

Mags muttered a colorful string of words. "Fine. We go through. We're not the first band of Gizmos trying to make our way to the army. Maybe whatever lives in here got itself killed by now."

"Double up on the watches from now on," Odd said. "Hawk with Pocket, Mags with Squirrel, Dash with me."

Hoku urged Sunbeam into the woods, expecting the horse to resist. Instead, Sunbeam clomped ahead, oblivious to their discussion. Hoku tried to follow the horse's example.

The trees grew thicker and taller and closer together as they traveled. The sun disappeared behind the thick canopy of leaves for hours at a time. Their progress slowed as Dash scouted ahead, trying to find paths wide enough for the rhinebra. The animal grunted and whined each time it had to squeeze between the rough bark of two ancient trees.

Branches rustled. Birds chittered and called. Strange things howled and barked and sometimes growled. At night, it seemed as if the entire forest were alive and plotting to kill them.

Days blurred into a series of Upgrader stories told while they walked, insect bites, and a variety of stringy, charred rodents eaten over the campfire. Hoku spent his time with Aluna and Calli when he could claim to be checking on them, and with Pocket when he couldn't.

Sometimes Pocket rode with him on Sunbeam. Hoku had heard the stories behind every one of Pocket's tattoos, and he had watched Zeelo's red flower fade from angry red to deep crimson on Pocket's arm. Whenever he saw it, he thought of Zeelo's sharp teeth and wicked humor.

One overcast evening, Hoku started to ask about Pocket's horns again when the boy suddenly sucked in his breath and pointed into the trees.

"Did you see that?"

Hoku scanned the darkening patch of trunks and foliage. "I don't see anything but trees. Maybe —"

A face. In the bark of a tree. Two brown eyes staring back at him. Hoku gasped.

"You see it, too!" Pocket said. "Maybe my gears aren't rusty after all."

Bark. Now all Hoku could see was bark. But how was that possible? He hadn't stopped looking. He hadn't even blinked.

"Tides' teeth," he muttered.

"Tides what?" Pocket asked.

"Nothing," Hoku said quickly. "The face is gone now. I swear, I saw it, though. Like it was part of the tree."

"Shut it," Odd called. "Whatever lives here decides to come for us, we'll know soon enough. No use getting yourselves riled over shadows. Keep your eyes ahead."

"And your hands on your swords," Mags added.

Hoku looked back and saw Aluna squinting at the tree. She shook her head and shrugged. Calli mouthed, "Sorry!"

Pocket whispered, "I know what we saw."

That night the air was so cold that Hoku could almost feel the chill through his thick Kampii skin. Pocket shivered under a blanket and poked at the fire with a stick. Not much in the wet forest would burn, but they kept their blazes small just to be safe. Traveling for weeks through a dense forest was bad enough; if the trees caught on fire, they'd have nowhere to run.

Hoku scanned the treetops, letting his dark vision show him animals scurrying from their nests and bats swooping at insects. He saw a raccoon climb up a tree and his heart ached for Zorro. He pictured the little guy following Liu the Dome Mek around HydroTek, growing fat on apples and doing tricks for scruffles.

The owls were talkative tonight, calling to one another from the treetops.

"What do you think they're saying?" Pocket asked, inching closer to the fire.

"I think they're flirting," Hoku said. "Bragging about their feathers, or how fast they can catch a mouse."

Pocket laughed. "I always imagine they're talking philosophy. Meaning of life, and stuff like that."

"Owls with a lot on their minds," Hoku said.

A branch rustled, and then another one. Hoku scanned the area, but couldn't find the source. He'd never had that problem with his dark vision before.

"I don't like this," he said. He pushed himself slowly to his feet. "Aluna, wake up."

"What?" Pocket asked. "Oh. You're talking to the fish."

"She's not a fish, she's a —"

And then the trees came alive. A dozen Human-shaped figures dropped out of the sky and landed around camp without making a sound.

Hoku blinked. His eyes thought they were trees, kept tricking him into thinking they weren't people at all. He caught glimpses of rough, bark-like skin and long, gangly limbs dotted with tufts of leaves. He thought they were wearing strange capes at first, but the voluminous material hanging from their arms seemed connected to their flesh.

One of the invaders hooted to the others and made a motion with its hand. Hoku and Pocket hadn't been listening to owls at all. They'd been listening to battle plans.

CHAPTER 9

SOMEONE SCREAMED. Aluna bolted awake, her hands already reaching for weapons.

"Wake up!" Pocket yelled again. "The trees are attacking!"

But it wasn't trees. Strange people darted through camp, thin Humans moving fast as eels but making no sound. They swarmed over the Upgraders' camp in misshapen clusters, grabbing, yanking, clawing. The kludge was completely overrun.

Except . . . no one was attacking her or Calli.

"Who are they?" Calli asked. "Oh, no. Hoku!"

Aluna scanned the battle until she found Hoku. *There*. Struggling against an attacker determined to pull him to the ground with a choking wire. She snapped off her wrist bindings and used her arms to drag herself toward him, fast as a seal on dry land.

"They've got Dash, too!" Calli cried. "I'll help him. You save Hoku."

Calli's wings unfurled with a snap, and for a moment, it seemed as if everyone in the clearing stopped to look at them.

Aluna felt a tug on her tail. She turned and kicked one of the Humans away. It let go without a fight. What was going on? Aluna started toward Hoku again, but one of the creatures now knelt in front of her, less than a meter away, blocking her way to Hoku.

The skin on its face seemed rough and craggy, like the bark of a tree. Twigs and leaves jutted from its wild hair. Without her dark vision, she may not have been able to pick out the creature from the forest behind it, even this close.

Aluna shifted her weight to her arms and swept her tail around to knock the Human off balance. It hopped up and over her tail as if it were playing a game.

"Wait," the creature said, holding out its hand. "We come to rescue you. You and she, the winged one. We will take you to the fluttering heights! We will save you." Its voice came out raspy, as if it hadn't spoken in a long time and it barely remembered how.

"Don't kill the others," Aluna said. "They aren't enemies!"

The creature was blocking her view of Hoku, but she could hear him grunting and gasping inside her ear. He was still alive, and his Kampii necklace would help him breathe even while he was being choked. But what if the creature decided to stab him instead?

"Go limp," she whispered, hoping Hoku could hear her despite his panic. "Breathe through your shell. Let them think you're dead."

"We have no understanding," the creature replied. "We will save you. We will kill to save you."

"No killing," Aluna said. "No killing!" Her muscles quivered. Her body wanted to fight. It wanted to snap every one of these creatures in half like twigs. No one was allowed to hurt her friends. No one. Not even if they were trying to help. But wading into the fray herself would only make things worse.

Aluna rolled onto her back and vaulted herself up to her tail. "Stop fighting!" she yelled. "Everyone stop or they'll kill you!"

Hoku had already stopped struggling, but a creature loomed over him, poking him in the chest. Aluna scanned the camp until she found Dash and Calli, too. Dash had blood dripping down his face and his sword in his hand. His gaze darted everywhere. His nose flared. Equians couldn't see well at night; poor Dash was fighting blind.

"Stop, Dash. Please!" She rarely used the word,

and it had power. Dash's eyes widened. He lowered his sword.

"It's a trap!" Odd bellowed. "Prisoners are working with these devils! Fight, you Gizmos, fight!"

"No!" Aluna yelled, but it was useless.

Mags had three of them on her, but was twisting and turning, managing to stab them with her needles. Aluna heard a creature squeak and saw it leap away, an empty needle dangling from its neck. Squirrel fought beside Mags, jumping this way and that, slashing her attackers with something small and shiny clutched in her hand. Odd seemed indomitable, flinging his attackers off of him as if they were small as rats and bellowing into the night. Only Pocket was down, pinned to the ground and surrounded. And even so, the boy struggled and kicked.

The tree creatures hadn't killed anyone yet, but if the Upgraders kept fighting, they would, even if just by accident. Odd and Mags and Squirrel would never stop, not until their bodies had lost every last bit of fight. If this battle continued, the kludge would be destroyed.

Aluna tried to slow her breathing and clear her head. She could stay and help the kludge fight. With her and Dash and Vachir, and even Calli and Hoku, maybe they could turn defeat into victory. Not without casualties, she knew, but they'd still have a small chance of surviving the forest and making it to Strand's army, and then to Strand himself somehow.

But if she fought, she'd be choosing her desire to find Karl Strand over the lives of the Upgraders in Odd's kludge. A week or two ago, it would have been an easy decision to make. But now they weren't Upgraders, they were people. People she'd begun to respect. The fact that she'd ever thought they were expendable overwhelmed her with shame.

Karl Strand had a plan, and he didn't care how many lives were lost while he achieved it. If Aluna wanted to make a better world than the one Strand was offering, then she needed to make better choices. No plan was worth the senseless death of good people, regardless of its goal.

"Take us," Aluna said to the creature. "Calli and I will go with you right now. Take the horses and those two as well." She pointed at Dash and Hoku. "Leave the others alone. Do not kill a single one of the rest, or there will be blood on both sides, I promise you."

The Human stood in one smooth motion and emitted a series of birdcalls. It sounded so much like a night owl that Aluna would never have known the noises were made by a person unless she'd seen it herself.

A cluster of tree people surrounded her. She ground her teeth together as their rough hands grabbed her. She smelled moist soil and bark. "Hoku, Dash, Vachir—don't fight them!"

"Fight them!" Odd countered. "Break them! Set them on fire!"

The creatures carrying her moved as one being, graceful and quick. In a flash they had maneuvered her to the base of an ancient tree and started climbing. She thought they would struggle with her weight, with the awkwardness of her body and her tail. Instead, they continued to move smoothly, tiny hooks on their feet and elbows giving them easy purchase up the tree trunk.

Calli, Dash, and Hoku were being carried up other trees.

"I can fly," Calli said. "Just let me fly!"

But the creatures continued to hold her, and Aluna understood why. Branches and leaves clotted their path. Calli couldn't even open her wings up here, let alone find the space to flap them.

On the ground, the Upgraders continued to fight. She saw Odd smack a tree person and it flew across half the campsite. But the creatures were leaving now, breaking off when they had openings and making their way up the trees and into the darkness again.

The horses. The creatures hadn't taken the horses.

"Vachir!" Aluna called.

Vachir looked up from the ground, her huge eyes searching. The horse cried out, and Aluna felt the sound deep in her chest. Vachir's massive body was no bigger than an ant, and getting smaller and smaller.

"I'll find you!" Aluna yelled. "Stay safe! Stay with the kludge! I'll find you no matter what!"

Tears welled in her eyes and she blinked them out, not caring if the creatures saw. She tried to find the person who had bargained with her originally, but she couldn't tell her rescuers apart. "I told you to take the horses," she said, her hands squeezing into fists. "Rescue them, too!"

"No. Too big, too heavy. The wrong shape," one of the people said. "They splinter if they fall."

Aluna closed her eyes and swallowed. She couldn't think about Vachir falling from a treetop. Her legs, so strong when they ran, were inflexible, fragile even, in other circumstances. No, horses did not belong in the treetops.

"Vachir," she said again, her voice tired and broken.

She should check on Calli and make sure that Dash and Hoku were uninjured. She should find out where the things were taking them. Find out who their leader was and what they wanted.

But all she could do was say Vachir's name over and over again and hope that this whole thing was a nightmare, an evil vision concocted by her brain to punish her and break her heart. It was better than facing the truth.

The creatures carried her higher than she thought possible. She began to see platforms stretched like cobwebs between the branches. Some were small, single sleeping hammocks, and some were large enough to hold huts with webbed roofs. Large glowing bugs the size of her head clung to the trees and the webbing and provided a faint light, just like the glowfish did back home. Without them, she'd have been blind up here. The tree people were almost invisible to her dark vision.

She watched one creature jump from a ledge and spread its arms. She'd thought it was wearing a loose cloth shirt, but the folds weren't fabric—they were a membrane. A *flying* membrane. A thin layer of skin extended from the creature's wrists down to its ankles on both sides. Another membrane opened between its ankles. The membranes caught the air and the creature glided gracefully down to another branch of the tree.

The creatures talked more up here, but only in their bird voices. Answering calls came from every direction, filling the air with a cacophony of whistles and chirps and small melodies.

Eventually they reached a wide, hanging stairway. It swung side to side as the creatures carried her up it, toward a vast area inside the trees. Leaves and branches created a canopy overhead, not unlike the curved walls of the domes back in the City of Shifting Tides. Dozens upon dozens of tiny webs surrounded a single, round platform in the center. They'd been brought to an arena.

The creatures deposited her in the center area. She tried to balance on her tail, but the shifting webbed ground made it impossible. She toppled over and braced herself with her arms. A fish in the desert was bad enough; a fish in the treetops was simply ridiculous. At least the webbing under her palms felt thick and coarse and sturdy, and not sticky and fragile as she'd suspected.

Hoku, Calli, and Dash were dropped with equal ceremony by her side. Dash helped her stand again so she could hug them and check for injuries. Blood covered Dash's face, but he waved it off.

"I am fine," he said. "The old wound reopened. Nothing more."

"We'll go back for Vachir," Hoku said quietly.

Calli nodded. "We'll find her, Aluna. She's smart and brave, and she'll be okay until we do."

Aluna wanted to say something. Anything. She could only manage to nod.

The arena filled with tree people. They sat two or three to each small web, some dangling their feet over the edge, some crouched, some leaning against each other. Some moved like squirrels, others like insects. Aluna couldn't tell how old they were, or if they were male or female. They all wore the same sort of muddy bark clothes plastered to their torsos and upper legs, and they all seemed perfectly comfortable despite the fact that they lived a hundred meters up in the sky.

A hunched tree person limped onto their platform with the help of a walking stick. Tattered and worn membranes hung under its arms, and deep ridges etched the skin of its face, making it look like the bark of an ancient tree. When the creature looked up at them, Aluna could barely see its eyes under the protruding overhang of its woody brows.

"We rescued you from the glints," it said, and smiled. "A brave rescue. A good rescue!"

"Yeah," Hoku muttered. "Just great."

CHAPTER 10

ALUNA STARED at the creature's grinning face, her heart heavy, her hands starting to clench, and tried to remember that these people had risked themselves to save her and Calli from what had seemed like a terrible fate. She should be grateful. She should thank them. She should try to recruit them for the war. But she really just wanted to punch this one in the nose. A few months ago, she probably would have.

"Thank you," she finally managed. "Thank you for rescuing us."

The air filled with hoots and whistles and caws. The tree people were cheering.

The leader emitted a series of notes, a birdsong, and the crowd settled back down. Aluna had thought that the tree people's speech seemed simplistic, but suddenly she understood: their primary language was their birdsongs. They were actually quite well-spoken for a language they probably rarely used.

"I speak as Melody," the leader said. He motioned to the group. "They sing as Harmony. Together we are Silvae."

Calli gasped. "Silvae! One of my Aviar teachers mentioned them once. They're one of the secret LegendaryTek splinters!"

"There were secret splinters?" Hoku asked.

"The ones LegendaryTek hid best of all," Calli said. "No one even knows what they are, or how many. But my teacher's grandmother had met a Silvae."

"How many other secret splinters are there?" Aluna asked. They could also use more people to fight against Karl Strand.

"I don't know," Calli said. "That's why they're secret."

The Silvae leader in front of them coughed politely. "I speak as Melody," he repeated. "You speak as?"

"I'm Aluna. Calli has the wings. Hoku and Dash are the ones dressed as Upgraders," Aluna said.

Melody, who Aluna was almost certain was male, repeated each of their names in turn. "Glints smash and burn, tromp and crush," he said. "Good rescue from glints. Last rescue, not as good."

"Last rescue?" Aluna said. "What happened on the last rescue?"

Melody shook his head slowly from side to side. "Glints with flames, trees on fire. Prisoners too big. Not shaped for treetops." He motioned to another Silvae. It dropped down to its hands and pranced around on its webbing.

"A horse," Dash said. "Your last rescue attempt involved horses?"

"That's why they couldn't take Vachir," Calli said, laying a soft hand on Aluna's arm. "It was too dangerous."

"No," Melody said. "Not a horse."

Another Silvae joined the first in its pantomime. Aluna couldn't tell if they were wrestling or just goofing around, but whatever they were doing, it wasn't helping.

"Equians!" Dash said. "You tried to rescue the desert horse people!"

"Yes," Melody said, grinning. The old man was clearly enjoying this game. "Horse people. Equians. Two people, eight legs."

"Two," Dash said. "Was one of them dark skinned and bald with a brown horse body? The other was the same color as me, short brown hair, with a black flank?"

"Who are you talking about?" Hoku whispered.

"I don't remember anyone who looked like that from Shining Moon."

"Because they were gone before we got there," Aluna said. Her breathing necklace pulsed faster. "Erke and Gan. Dash's fathers! They left Shining Moon to look for him when Dash was exiled and didn't return."

She looked at Dash, wanting to see her own hope reflected in his face. But Dash didn't look at her. He stared straight ahead at Melody, his jaw clenched, and waited for his answer.

Melody whistled to his people and listened as they answered with trills and hoots of their own. "Harmony says yes," Melody said eventually. "Horse people were as you say."

Dash closed his eyes and exhaled. "And what happened?" he asked. "How did the rescue go badly? Did you drop them? Did you . . . break them?"

Tides' teeth. Aluna wanted to reach over and take his arm, to remind him that she was there if he needed her. But she could tell by the way his whole body had started to quiver that he needed answers, not kindness. If she offered comfort, it might burst the fragile bubble he'd suddenly become.

"Break?" Melody said. He tilted his head to the side and whistled again. His people chirped back. It only took two flashes for this exchange, but it felt like years. "We could not rescue horse people," Melody said, "but we did not break them. Glints took them to join glint swarm."

"They're alive," Aluna said to Dash. "The Upgraders wouldn't have kept them alive unless Karl Strand wanted them that way. There's still time. We'll find them."

"I hope you are right," Dash said, his voice a painful mix of hope and despair. "Erke is strong. He once survived a full month in the desert by himself after a sandstorm. But Gan . . . Gan is not like that. I fear for him." He looked at Melody. "Do you know where they are? Does *swarm* mean they are with Strand's army?"

"Army swarm, yes, but where? Swarm is huge, sprawling, hungry," Melody said. "Swarm started small, used to nibble at Song's edge, a caterpillar snacking on a leaf." He shook his head angrily. "Now swarm has grown vast. Swarm devours. Trees fall, animals flee, birds fly away. Song shrinks, curls up on itself, starts to die."

The Silvae keened when Melody stopped speaking, their birdcalls anguished.

"Join the Equians and Aviars against Karl Strand," Aluna said. She spoke in a loud voice, trying to sound like the leader she wanted to be, not one who'd recently watched her plans crumble around her. "Help us fight

Strand and his glints. Help us save our people, and the Song. We want to stop the war before it even starts, but if it comes to fighting, you would add much strength to our side."

"No, no, no. We have Melody and Harmony. Song needs no other voices," Melody said. "When glints enter Song, we hinder and poke, trip and rescue. When glints leave Song—these trees, this sky, that breeze—we do not follow." He motioned to all the people around him. "Silvae do not leave Song. Silvae do not fight wars."

"You're already fighting a war," Calli said. "You're just not acknowledging it."

"Harmony defends Song and Song only," Melody said. He pointed a twiggy finger at each of them. "When war is done—fields of dead, red rivers, weeping young ones—Silvae and Harmony will remain."

Aluna clenched her fists and looked away. Melody was almost as closed-minded as her own father. The Silvae had survived on their own for hundreds of years, and even now, faced with the destruction of their beloved forest, they insisted on fighting alone. And probably dying alone, too.

But the Silvae had rescued them and had left Odd's kludge alive. They clearly valued life. If she spent a few days here, maybe she could convince Melody to see things a different way.

"You will go now," Melody said abruptly. "We take you where you want."

"What? Take us where?" Calli asked.

Melody pointed east, west, south. "Wherever, but not to swarm," he said. "You pick and we take you to Song's edge."

"They'll take us to the edge of the forest in any direction we choose," Hoku translated. "Except the one direction we want to go — toward the army."

"Even if we got to the army, we would not pass as Upgraders without Odd and his kludge," Dash said. "They would take Aluna and Calli and we would not be strong enough to stop them."

Hoku plucked a twig off his shirt and broke it in half. "Dash is right. We can't find Strand on our own, and walking into the army by ourselves would be suicide."

"Can we just go back to the kludge?" Calli asked. "We could tell them that you and Dash stole us back from the Silvae."

"Odd is too smart," Hoku said. "He thinks we can fight, but he'll know Dash and I aren't strong enough to win you both back ourselves. I couldn't even beat the Silvae choking me at the camp." He rubbed the angry red welt across his neck. "And Pocket knows our secret. With us gone, there's no reason he wouldn't tell the kludge everything he knows."

"I agree," Dash said. "Odd and Mags do not fully trust us even now. If we came back without injury and with our prizes . . . they would never take us in."

Aluna's tail ached. She'd been balancing on it for a while, leaning on the others when she needed to, but trying to stay upright by herself. And none of them had slept yet, not after a full day of hiking through the forest and a full night of being lifted into the treetops.

"Melody, we're too tired to travel tonight. Will you let us sleep?" she asked. "We will know which direction we want to go in the morning."

The old Silvae's face twisted, and Aluna feared he might say no. But then Melody mumbled, "Bad rescue," and began calling to his people.

"But my fathers," Dash whispered to her. "We need—"

"We need rest," she said firmly. "We can't be smart if we're too exhausted to use our brains. Tomorrow we'll figure it all out. I promise."

"The Dawn-bringer speaks, and I will listen," Dash said.

Aluna sensed an odd hitch in his voice. He would do as she asked now, but for how long?

Melody led them to a cluster of webbed hammocks nestled under a massive branch. "For sleep," he said.

"Thank you, Melody," Aluna said wearily. "And . . . please, think about what we said."

Calli and Dash helped her hop onto the closest hammock, but she couldn't balance, even with their help. She fell, grateful that the thick fibers of the web were softer than their strength implied.

"Are you okay?" Calli asked.

Aluna nodded. Her hammock swayed in the breeze. "I'll be okay if I never have to move again."

"Not for a few hours, at least," Calli said. She put her hand on Aluna's shoulder, then jumped easily over to the next bed.

Dash took the hammock farthest away. He always did this, always distanced himself from them when he was upset. Or—her chest tightened—was he angry with her for making them sleep? She couldn't blame him if he was. She'd been so furious when she'd found out that Fathom had her sister, Daphine. Hoku and Dash had argued for reason and strategy, and she'd ignored them. She'd rushed off to fight her battles by herself and almost gotten them all killed.

She'd made the right decision tonight; she just hoped Dash would be able to forgive her for it.

When Aluna awoke, she found darkness still clinging to the trees and Dash sitting a meter away, cleaning the blade of his sword. Calli and Hoku were still asleep, and at least one of them was snoring.

"I did not mean to wake you," Dash said quietly. He was wearing his Upgrader leathers, the fake metal splint around his mechanical arm still in place.

"You didn't," Aluna said. She could hear her pulse echoing in her ears. She sat up and dangled her tail over the edge of her bed. "Are you going somewhere?"

"Yes," he said. He finished wiping down his sword and hit the button that retracted the slender blade into the hilt. "I'm going back to the kludge."

"We talked about this last night," Aluna said. "We can't go back. They'll never believe you and Hoku could extract us from so many Silvae."

Dash stowed his weapon in his satchel and secured the latch. He didn't seem to know what to do with his hands, so he plucked a leaf from a nearby branch and began to shred it.

"They will not believe all of us could escape, but they might believe that I could," he said. "Just me. Alone."

Aluna swallowed, her mouth suddenly dry. "You . . . want to leave us?"

He looked up at her, his dark eyes barely visible in the faint light. "No, of course I do not *want* to leave . . . all of you. But think about it—"

"Your fathers," she said.

"The location of Karl Strand."

"And Vachir."

"And Vachir," Dash agreed. "I could save people we both care about and perhaps finish our mission. Your plan was a good one, Aluna. I would see it to its end."

She looked away, pretended to study the dirt and grime stuck in her fingernails. "It wasn't a good plan if it leads to this. To us not being together. We're stronger as a team."

"We are an infinitely impressive team," Dash said. "But my fathers left the desert to save me. I must do no less for them."

Aluna put one of her dirty hands up to her forehead and closed her eyes. Everything was unraveling so fast. Their plan was ruined. Vachir separated from the group, and now Dash. Losing him felt worse than losing her legs.

"Please tell Vachir that I would have come back for her myself," Aluna said quietly. She felt tears form in her eyes and kept her hand in place to hide them. *Weak. Useless.* This was not how she wanted Dash to remember her.

"I will tell her, but she already knows this," Dash said. "She trusts you with her life." Aluna looked up in time to see a small smile form on Dash's face. "I know how she feels."

"I won't ask you not to go," Aluna said, her voice gruff.

"I know," Dash said. "You have honor even when you wish you did not."

He leaned over and for one endless moment, Aluna thought he might kiss her. Tides' teeth, she wanted to kiss him. To kiss him and hold him and never let him leave her side.

She leaned toward him and pressed her forehead against his, felt his warmth soak into her skin, let wisps of his cool hair brush against her cheeks.

"Be safe," she whispered.

"I will if you will," he said.

She stared into his eyes and felt the rest of the world wash away. If they saw each other again, she would kiss him. When their friends were safe, when Karl Strand was gone, when there was time for such a selfish thing.

They pulled apart slowly, as if they were fighting the tide. Aluna watched him secure his bags and smooth down his hair, pleased that he seemed as flustered as she felt. When he was finally ready, she nodded just once and he was gone.

CHAPTER 11

HOKU SHOVED A PILE of acorn mash into his mouth and almost spit it back out again. Not even mustard could have saved him from the bitterness. He forced himself to swallow and took another, much smaller bite. Over their heads, Silvae moved from branch to branch, partly jumping and partly gliding on the membranes attached to their limbs. Morning sun snuck through the dense leaves and covered their platforms in dancing pinpricks of light.

"Dash will be okay," Hoku said. "Odd likes him. Mags likes him. Tides' teeth, even the rhinebra likes him."

"Vachir will be happy to see him," Aluna said. "I'm grateful she won't be alone. That neither of them will be."

"He didn't even say good-bye," Calli said. "I would have liked to wish him blue skies."

Hoku watched Aluna blink in the sunlight, her shoulders slumped, her face emotionless. He could tell she was only half listening to them, that part of her was still with Dash. Hoku stole a glance at Calli. She stretched her left wing and plucked twigs and leaves from her feathers, and he felt like the luckiest Kampii in the world.

"We could wait for Dash to come back," Calli said. "Or maybe follow the kludge from the treetops."

"We'd have to watch out for Squirrel," Hoku said. "That girl sees everything."

"No," Aluna said. "Odd's kludge may not even go to Strand now that they've lost their prizes. We could lose valuable time by following them. If Dash and Vachir somehow manage to locate Strand, they'll have to find a way to let us know." She poked at the nut mash on her leaf but didn't eat any. "My plan failed. We can't keep trying to save it. It's time for a new plan."

Hoku frowned. *Failed* was not a word he heard often from Aluna, and he didn't like it. "Let's go to HydroTek," he said. "Fathom must know where Karl Strand is. He's only a brain in a box since we disassembled him, but maybe the Dome Meks and Zorro have found a way to read his thoughts by now."

"Even if the Dome Meks get access, they probably

won't find anything," Calli said. "Fathom was smart enough to wipe the important memories once he knew he'd been defeated. I'm guessing he uploaded them to Strand before he did it, too."

Aluna continued staring. "HydroTek . . ."

"HydroTek has a comm room," Hoku said. "I didn't recognize it last time, but now I know what to look for. Maybe we can warn the Aviars and help coordinate things with the Equians and Serpenti. HydroTek would be a great base of operations for all our . . . strategies and stuff."

"A command center," Calli said. "Maybe Aluna could run the whole war from there!"

Hoku saw Aluna's face twitch, but she smoothed it over quickly. Losing Vachir, losing Dash, losing the last few weeks of work on their plan . . . Of course she needed time to recover from all of that. But he knew her. The sooner they could get her mind out of the past and focused on moving forward again, the sooner Aluna the Dawn-bringer would be back and ready to lead them.

"What do you think, Aluna?" Calli asked. "Should we go to HydroTek?"

"That's where we said we'd meet if something went wrong," Hoku added. "If Dash and Vachir need to find us, that's where they'll look."

Aluna nodded.

Hoku wiped his hands on his pants and stood up. "I'll tell the Silvae to take us to the ocean, to the west. I'm sure they're eager to get rid of us."

"Are you ever going to take off that metal plate?" Aluna asked. "You're not an Upgrader anymore."

Hoku froze, as surprised that Aluna had decided to speak as by her words. His hand went to his face. He could have taken off the faceplate last night, when they'd agreed not to return to the kludge. Or this morning, when Aluna had told them about Dash. Or . . . he could take it off now.

"Let me find Melody first," he mumbled, and headed off before Aluna or Calli could say anything.

Barnacles. Why was he clinging to a piece of metal that didn't even do anything? Maybe he should have taken Mags up on her offer and gotten the real thing. Some tech embedded in his flesh that would let him analyze heat patterns or see great distances like Calli, or monitor his blood so he could tell if he'd been poisoned.

The Silvae collected water in thick leaves and carved wooden bowls they hung from the branches. Hoku found one, drank, then stared at the water as the ripples faded. He felt under the edge of his shirt and unhooked the collar's binding. He rubbed his throat and wiped away the grime that had collected on his breathing shell.

"Look at that," he muttered. "Still a Kampii."

He pried off the faceplate next, grimacing at the extraordinarily pale skin underneath, visible even in the tiny patch of bowl water. One side of his face was rough and gritty from weeks of traveling with the Upgraders, while the other side felt smooth and soft. It seemed impossible that both sides belonged to the same person, and inconceivable that the person was him.

Hoku cleaned his Upgrader parts in the basin and stored them in his pack, then went to find Melody. But the old Silvae would not speak to him; he merely pointed one long, twiggy finger at a young Silvae female and said, "Flicker, go."

Flicker looked like a sapling, tall and thin with smooth, unwrinkled skin the color of dry sand. She wore leafy twigs at her shoulders and atop her head, almost like armor. Hoku liked her immediately, though he didn't know why.

"Come," Flicker said, and joined Hoku in one graceful stride. "I will show you how to pack your things for tree jumping."

Hoku followed her as best he could, and Flicker did her best to slow down and match his pace, although it clearly annoyed her.

"You speak our language very well," Hoku said. "Do you practice it?"

She smiled and said, "Later."

Flicker was brisk but efficient. She helped Aluna stand and fasten her pack without a single word about Aluna's tail and how difficult it was going to make their trip. She modified Calli's pack to fasten around her waist instead of her back, to accommodate her wings. She even managed to smile and tell Hoku he'd done a good job with his things.

Neither Aluna nor Calli commented on Hoku's face now that he'd removed the faceplate, and he was grateful.

Finally, Flicker pronounced them ready to depart. She whistled four different phrases and four Silvae dropped from the trees to join them. Flicker pointed and said, "Thistle, Blade, Petal, Brook. Now, we go."

Hoku had expected a farewell ceremony, or at least a good-bye from Melody, but there was nothing. They may have been rescued in triumph, but they certainly weren't leaving that way.

He'd wanted to talk to Flicker as soon as they left the Silvae tree city, but the travel itself required his full concentration. His hands slid over rough bark. Tiny branches whipped his cheeks and tried to blind him. A Silvae had been assigned to help each of them navigate the larger jumps between trees, but it was still terrifying. One misstep and he'd be plunging to his hideously painful death.

They traveled for hours until Flicker called for a break. Hoku was grateful for it, but anxious, too. They couldn't have covered more than a few kilometers at most, which meant they had some long, terrible days ahead of them.

"Ow," Calli said, wrapping another cloth bandage around her hand. "I thought the skin on my palms would last longer."

"At least you didn't almost poke yourself in the eye three times," Hoku grumbled. "I should have left my faceplate on. I would be less of a danger to myself."

He looked over at Aluna. She'd managed to keep up with everyone for the first few kilometers, using her strong arms to swing from branch to branch and swinging her tail to keep up her momentum. But some of the gaps required them to jump with their legs or to shimmy around tree trunks, and she'd had to let the Silvae help her. Now she sat on a branch and stared to the west toward the sea.

"Want some food, Aluna? Calli dosed my mash with some magic spice and it doesn't taste as bad now. Almost good, even." Hoku walked over and held out a small pile of acorn goop stuck to a leaf.

Aluna pulled herself back from wherever her mind was and smiled. She took the leaf and nibbled some mash. "Mmm. You work miracles, Calli."

"She does, doesn't she?" Hoku said. "She'd make

a good cook if she weren't already a brilliant scientist and the future leader of her people."

Calli sighed. "Some days 'cook' sounds a lot more appealing."

The Silvae busied themselves with gathering more supplies and trilling little songs, and then Flicker joined them. She moved with such ease, like a Kampii underwater.

"You travel well," Flicker said. "We expected more complaining."

"We're just good at hiding it," Calli said.

"Do not push yourselves past recovery," Flicker said easily. "Our saplings often dislocate their shoulders when they first learn to swing between trees. One must respect one's limits."

"Why don't you talk like Melody?" Hoku asked, hoping it wasn't a rude question.

Flicker squatted, her knobby knees sticking out to both sides. "Melody speaks of Harmony as if we are all of one mind and purpose, but it is not so. Many of us—mostly in younger generations—see value in understanding the world outside Song."

Hoku expected Aluna to perk up at Flicker's words, but she was still sitting motionless, her gaze distant, her shoulders slumped.

"Are there any among you who would stand with us against Strand?" Calli asked.

"We want to know more," Flicker said. "The four I have brought with us can be trusted. Tell us what there is to know, and we will spread the word. Some have been looking for a chance to leave Song, even though Melody has forbidden it. A purpose might give them the strength to defy him."

"We'll tell you everything we can," Hoku said.

Flicker nodded. "Not here. We are too close to Melody and Song's Heart. But there will be time on our journey when your bodies refuse to work. We will hear your stories then. Right now, we must make more distance. Finish your meals and prepare." She stood up and leaped into the trees.

"Did you hear that, Aluna? Maybe there's a chance to salvage something good from all of this," Hoku said, then instantly regretted his words. He didn't want to keep reminding Aluna that her plan had failed. "I'm sorry. I didn't mean—"

"No, you're right, Hoku," Aluna said. She seemed to wake up from her daze. Her eyes seemed troubled but sharp. "Things haven't gone how we wanted, or how I said they would." She paused, wet her lips, swallowed. "Back in the desert, Khan Tayan called me Dawn-bringer. She said I would lead us to a new world, and you may have even believed her. Tides' teeth, even I believed her that night."

She ran her hand through her short hair. "You

agreed because you trusted me. You all thought I knew what I was doing. But I don't. I keep making mistakes. I keep taking chances and losing. I didn't even beat Scorch in the Thunder Trials. I *failed*. If it hadn't been for all of you and the other Equians, the desert would be lost."

Hoku wanted her to be angry. He wanted to see that familiar rage roil up inside of her and propel her into action. Instead, she seemed . . . *tired*.

"I don't know what I'm saying," Aluna said with a little laugh. "What it comes down to is this: I don't want to lead anymore. Not you, not Calli, not Dash, not even myself. If don't trust myself, I can't ask anyone else to trust me, either. I'm sorry."

CHAPTER 12

TRAVELING THROUGH THE TREETOPS required all of Aluna's focus. Except for the incessant birdcalls, her grunting as she grasped for branches, and an occasional snide comment from Hoku, their group moved in silence. Even so, Aluna knew that something was wrong. Her speech last night had broken something between her and Hoku and Calli. . . . She just didn't know what.

When the Silvae weren't listening to their stories and asking questions about Karl Strand and his clones, they were off gathering food or scouting routes through the trees, leaving Aluna alone with Hoku and Calli. They talked to her at meals like nothing was wrong. Hoku counted his scrapes and bruises and made fun of himself. Calli commented on the weather or wondered how Dash and Vachir were doing. But these were surface motions, merely the waves on top of deep ocean. And for the first time, Aluna couldn't see what was beneath.

Maybe they were angry at her. She was making their lives harder, after all. They couldn't sit back and wait for her to make all the decisions. They'd have to go stumbling out on their own now, the same as her. Maybe after they'd made as many mistakes as she had, they'd finally start to understand.

Aluna dropped her forehead into her hand and sighed. This — whatever was happening to her — wasn't about Hoku and Calli. She looked over and watched Calli dig a twig out of Hoku's hair. He plucked it out of Calli's hands and put it back.

She could hear Hoku's voice in her ears, but their conversation still felt muffled and distant, as if they were both on dry land and she was deep underwater.

Calli had been poisoned. Hoku had offered to die by Aluna's side when Scorch was going to kill her. They'd pretended to be Upgraders and prisoners and had lost Vachir and Dash, just like she had. But here they were, laughing. Being themselves. Trying to make the best of a horrible world filled with cruel people like Karl Strand. Why couldn't she do the same thing?

The one thing she'd never doubted was her willingness to fight for what she believed in. But that Aluna—the *real* Aluna—felt oceans away. Lost or trapped, or maybe dead. The impostor Aluna, the one stuck in the trees, felt helpless without her. It took all her strength just to keep moving.

Day after day, through rain and sun, they dug their way through the treetops. The Silvae's bark-like skin kept them safe from cuts and scrapes, but Aluna, Hoku, and Calli looked as if they'd been dragged across a beach made of sharp stones. Even with their thick Kampii skin, droplets of dried blood clung to their noses and cheeks like Hoku's freckles. Aluna's hands had blistered and bled and blistered over again. She tried wearing leather guards to protect them, but couldn't get a strong enough grip.

"The ground," Hoku said. "It was practically made for walking. Why don't we give that a try?"

Hoku might as well have suggested walking on the moon. Flicker laughed, patted him on the back, and said, "Fish people are funny."

"I never thought I'd say this, but I miss Sunbeam," Hoku grumbled. "Even a horse's disdain is preferable to this exercise in pain and suffering."

"Imagine how I feel," Calli said. "I have wings, and I can't even use them! Sometimes I wonder if the

Silvae are doing this on purpose. Like, maybe there's a perfectly good path to the ocean somewhere, and this is their idea of a joke."

"This is their ocean," Aluna said. Her own voice surprised her — how long had it been since she'd used it? Two, three days? "Kampii swim *through* the water; we don't walk on the bottom. The treetops are their open ocean, their open sky."

"I wonder if LegendaryTek made any splinters that live in active volcanoes," Hoku grumbled. "We should go find them next."

Calli laughed and ruffled his hair. A breeze shifted directions and a new scent drifted through their makeshift treetop camp.

"Ocean," Aluna said. "Do you smell it? Ocean!"

Hoku leaned toward the west and closed his eyes. "I've never smelled anything more glorious."

The ocean's scent somehow eased the pain in her hands. *Water! Waves!* Her whole body longed to submerge itself. Had the Ocean Seed done that when it had given her a tail? Had it implanted a physical desire for the sea into her blood?

No. This urge, this calling, was something every Kampii was born with, just like dolphins knew how to migrate, or how sea turtles crawled out of the sand and found their way to the surf. The ocean had always been a part of her.

Leaves rustled and Flicker appeared out of the branches. Everything the Silvae did was abrupt and graceful, and Aluna envied her for it. "Song ends here, and so does our journey. You have given us much to think about. Harmony will hear of Strand, we promise you."

"The Equians, Serpenti, and Aviars will welcome you," Hoku said. "Even if your numbers are few."

Flicker nodded. "Song's Heart may not be ready for the wider world, but there are those among us who dream of it. They might be willing to fight for that dream."

"Swift currents," Aluna said, and managed a smile.

"And blue skies," Calli added.

Flicker granted them a rare grin. "Soft landings, friends of the trees." She and the other Silvae jumped away, leaving only the gentle rustle of branches in their wake.

Aluna watched them go, wondering if she'd ever see another Silvae again.

"I kind of wish they'd helped us get back down to the ground," Hoku said.

Aluna laughed. Then she looked down and watched the ground blur and spin far beneath her. "I think it's time for Calli to break out those wings again. And quickly, or I might try diving for the ocean from here."

"Aluna first, then," Calli said. She hopped over to

Aluna's branch and wound her arms under Aluna's. "Keep still, please!"

Aluna released her grip on the tree just as Calli stepped back off the branch. For one quick flash, it felt as if Aluna's stomach were going to fly out her mouth. Then Calli's wings opened and caught air, and their plummet slowed.

The space between the trees opened as they approached the ground, and Calli flapped her wings a few times to slow them even more. By the time they reached the solid earth, Aluna's tail sheath barely impacted at all.

"Perfect landing," Aluna said. "You're getting stronger." She felt strangely shy around Calli now, embarrassed by the shadow of herself that she'd been the last few days. And ashamed that Calli had accepted her anyway.

Calli's face dripped with sweat, but the girl glowed. "Let's see how I do with Hoku."

The second landing wasn't quite as perfect, but neither of Hoku's legs broke, so it was still a success. Hoku stood, brushed himself off, and gave Calli a quick kiss on the cheek. It was the first time Aluna had seen either of them do that in weeks. Calli blushed and turned away fast, apparently concerned with a leaf stuck in her wing.

"What was that for?" she asked quietly.

"Payment for the ride," Hoku said. "And because we're not in the stupid treetops anymore, where trying something like that might have made me fall to my death."

"I would have caught you," Calli said. "At least, I would have tried."

Aluna dragged herself around the clearing until she found two decent branches about the same size and shape to use as walking sticks. They didn't have straps to secure around her biceps like her old crutches, but they'd work well enough to get her to the water.

Within an hour, the massive trees of the Song had shrunk to shorter trees more used to sandy earth than rich, dark soil. Sweet sea breezes toyed with Aluna, taunting her and urging her to move faster. At the first sign of open sky, Calli was up and away, soaring high and laughing, her wings stretched wide.

When the first white-capped wave came into view, Hoku whooped and broke into a run. Aluna hopped faster until the soft sand of the beach made it impossible. She abandoned her walking sticks, dropped to the ground, and removed the leather sheath binding her tail. The sand felt hot and gritty under her wounded palms as she dragged herself toward the surf, and she loved it anyway.

Hoku hit the water first and dove. Aluna wasn't far behind. A wave crashed in front of her and slid up the sand. The churning froth hit her forearms and chest and splashed her face. She laughed and tumbled into the surf, letting it pull her into the sea. Within two flashes, the water enveloped her. Hugged her. Spun and twisted and tossed her around like a youngling with a new toy.

She wanted to swim deeper. To feel the pressure of the water all around her and see the sun's power dwindle into darkness. The last time she'd been in the ocean, she'd had legs. Now . . .

Her tail glistened. In the Above World, it had been like a parched desert tree, pale and fragile and aching for water. But underwater, colors emerged: lush kelp greens, vibrant blues, warm golds. She reveled in the way the pattern changed with every angle. Her tail fin unfolded and splayed open, a full meter of diaphanous, shimmering membrane, sleek and strong.

Aluna floundered, trying to force her new body to move the way the old one had. But soon she found it, the rhythm of muscle movements she needed to propel herself through the water.

Hoku splashed up ahead, his legs kicking in their erratic, undisciplined way as he swam. She zoomed past him. Crabs scuttled out of her way. Fish darted for cover. Eels retreated to their hidey-holes.

Swift as a seal, fast as a dolphin.

She dove, giddy with the power her new tail gave

her. When she reached the sea bottom, she somersaulted, fast, and shot straight up toward the surface. The sun welcomed her back. She broke the surface of the water and flipped into the air. Her tail spun over her head once, twice, three times. She crashed back down with a victory yell bigger than any battle cry.

Aluna's breathing shell throbbed at her throat. She closed her eyes and drifted. The salty water had erased every last bit of the desert from her skin.

With her tail, she could swim fast and far and never get tired. She could leave everything and everyone behind and become like the Deepfell, a creature of the ocean in mind as well as body. Digging mussels, hunting fish, catching crabs, and exploring citywrecks. She'd never wanted that life more than she wanted it right now.

"Aluna!" came Hoku's voice in her ear. "Come quick. Calli saw something."

"I'm here," she said. She rolled in the water, amazed at the way it buoyed her. She was so tired of crutches and pain, of her own tedious slowness on land. "I'm coming."

She rode the waves back toward the beach until she found them. Hoku stood waist-deep in the water, obviously reluctant to leave it. Calli hovered a few meters above him, her hands clasped nervously in front of her chest.

"What is it?" Aluna asked. "What's wrong?"

"I scouted down the shore looking for HydroTek, and I found what's left of it," Calli said. Her hands wound around each other like a pair of eels. "HydroTek has been destroyed."

CHAPTER 13

"**D**ESTROYED?" Hoku asked, fighting off a wave of panic. "Completely?"

"The dome is broken," Calli said. "The buildings are smashed and there's smoke billowing into the sky. It must have been recent. I saw two tiny things flying around. Maybe dragonfliers. I think at least some of the Upgraders are still there."

"Did you see any Dome Meks scurrying around trying to fix everything?" Hoku asked, thinking of the crab-girl Liu. "No small, furry raccoon-shaped pieces of tech?" He already missed Zorro more than he could even admit; the idea of losing him forever was simply unbearable.

"It's too far away to see, even with my distance sight," Calli said. Her voice softened. "But I'm sure Zorro and the Dome Meks escaped somehow. They must have."

Hoku shook his head. "The Meks wouldn't have left the dome. Not even if it was crumbling around them. They were built to protect and preserve it. Remember the SkyTek dome? Those poor Meks were still there, trying to put the pieces back together."

His throat constricted painfully. He tried not to think about that little bundle of tech and fur, and the more he tried not to, the more he did.

Aluna gasped. "Tides' teeth! Our breathing necklaces!"

Hoku's hand went to his throat. "They fully recharged the last time we were here, but without HydroTek continuously beaming more energy. . . ." He did some quick calculations in his head. "They've already started to drain, especially because we left the ocean and went to the desert for so long. We might only have weeks—or days, or just hours—before they stop working for good."

"What about the rest of the Kampii in the City of Shifting Tides?" Aluna said.

"Their necklaces were being charged until the moment HydroTek was destroyed, so some of them might have months," Hoku said. "But not every breathing shell is the same. Some don't hold their energy as well as others, and some Kampii use more power than others when they breathe. I bet a lot of necklaces have already failed."

Aluna punched the surface of the water. "After everything we did—after everything we sacrificed to defeat Fathom—our people are going to die anyway! Hoku, what if Daphine . . . ? What if your parents . . . ?"

"Stop it," Calli said. She dropped into the surf and held her wings above the water. "Both of you, stop it. This is terrible, but we can't start guessing. It won't help anyone. And besides, the Kampii aren't ignorant now. You told them how their necklaces work. If their tech started to fail, your Elders would at least know why."

"You're right. Daphine was at the battle," Aluna said. "She promised to tell the Elders everything. Maybe they listened."

"It doesn't matter if they listened, because they can't fix anything," Hoku said, and the invisible hand clenching his chest squeezed tighter. "Elder Peleke won't know how to generate the energy they need— despite the fact that the sun and waves and wind are right above him—and even if he did, he wouldn't know how to transfer it to the necklaces. I need to get down there. *Now.*"

Aluna's tail churned the water. "HydroTek first—or at least the shore closest to the dome. If there are survivors, they might have escaped into the woods. Maybe they rescued the generator, or some tech that might help us fix the necklaces. The Dome Meks were charged with protecting the Kampii, not just HydroTek itself."

Hoku itched to dive into the water and swim for the City of Shifting Tides, but Aluna made sense. He couldn't let panic make him stupid. Recovering any bit of tech might help him find a solution faster. "HydroTek, then," he said.

"You swim. I'll fly," Calli said, and she vaulted into the air. "The dome is south, not too far. I'll meet you on the beach, but be careful. The Upgraders circling HydroTek might have better eyesight than I do."

Aluna dove into the water and Hoku saw the tip of her ocean-slicked tail for the first time. She looked powerful, but in a whole new way. His best friend was finally a real Kampii.

Just like old times, he dove after her. Aluna had always been a better swimmer than he was, but the ocean was still his home. His legs remembered how to kick, his arms remembered to how to form a wedge over his head to cut down on his drag.

Tail or not, he was a real Kampii, too.

He stayed close to the surface in case his breathing

shell decided to fail, and tried to pace himself. In the old days, long-distance swimming would have meant hacking and wheezing and stopping repeatedly for breaks. But his body seemed to have no trouble with the distance now. After months of hiking through the desert and the forest and the treetops, maybe the weakling he used to be was gone for good.

After a few kilometers, Hoku started to dodge debris. Plastic, tree branches, metal casings held aloft by their foam interiors. He surfaced and saw the HydroTek dome in the distance, just as Calli described it: broken. Smoking. He couldn't see any Upgraders from this far away, but he trusted Calli that they were there.

Hoku swam on until he found Aluna and Calli searching the beach and the threshold of the forest for signs of survivors. They'd both gotten there long before him. He stood in the surf, shook the water from his ears, and spit the ocean from his mouth. "Anything?"

"If there were footprints, they've long since washed away in the tide," Calli said. "Or they were carefully erased."

Hoku walked out of the water and scanned the beach. "It looks like the Upgraders came through the forest over there," he said, pointing. "See the snapped branches and the opening in the underbrush? They probably had rhinebras pulling their boats, or whatever it was that they used to get to the dome."

A twig snapped. Hoku turned just in time to see a small gray creature emerge from the tree line and race across the sand, directly at him.

"Zorro!"

The raccoon squealed and leaped into Hoku's arms. Hoku tried to brace for the impact, but it was no good. Zorro barreled into him with all the power of Big Blue. Hoku tumbled backward onto the sand. Zorro, obviously unconcerned, stood on Hoku's chest and licked his nose.

"Zorro, did you miss me?" Hoku asked. The raccoon's eyes glowed green. Hoku scruffled his ears and laughed. Zorro was a mess—dirt and dried blood matted his fur, his normally puffy tail was missing large tufts, and the tip of his left ear had been sliced off. Hoku examined the little guy's wounds and was relieved to find them all healing. Well, everything except his ear.

Hoku thought Zorro's front leg had been damaged, but the missing patch of fur turned out to be a small scrap of paper wrapped around the raccoon's leg and tied with cord.

"What's this, boy?" He unknotted the cord and smoothed out the wrinkled, muddy paper. Only one word was written on it, in hasty black letters: PLAY.

"What does it say?" Aluna asked. "Who is it from?"

"Come over here," Hoku said. "I think Zorro's about to tell us something." He sat up and waited for Aluna and Calli to join him. Zorro circled three times and then settled into his lap.

"Here we go," Hoku said. "Zorro, play."

The raccoon's eyes glowed green again, but only for a flash. They quickly changed into small projectors, emitting a cone of pale-green light. A familiar face took shape: Liu the crab-girl, the Dome Mek who helped him and Dash win the battle of HydroTek.

"This message is for Aluna and Hoku," Liu said. "If you've found this raccoon and managed to play this message, find my friends and give it to them, or else."

Liu looked behind her, then back at the camera. Her pale head was still bald, but the bundle of wires sticking out the back bobbed like hair as she talked. "Don't have much time, so I'll make this quick. HydroTek has been overrun. Karl Strand's forces came to get Fathom, and they destroyed everything else in their path . . . including the Kampii generators. We tried to save them, but we couldn't. I'm really sorry, Hoku.

"A few of the Meks escaped into the dome's tendrils and flooded the passageways to stop Strand's armies," Liu said. "I'm joining them as soon as we're done here. We'll start rebuilding as soon as we can, but the repairs will take a long time. Several generations for your people, at least, and that's assuming the Upgraders leave and we can fabricate all the parts we need from the salvaged metal and—"

Liu stopped herself. "Never mind that now. What's important is that the Upgraders took Fathom. We set off some sort of security alarm when we tried to extract information from his brain. That's probably what brought Strand's army. Either that, or he managed to send a message before we shut off his communications. But we do know where most of the Upgraders are headed next. . . ." She paused. "They're headed for the Aviars."

Calli gasped.

"Aluna's sister, Daphine, escaped yesterday. At least, I helped her through the tunnels and saw her dive into the water myself, only I don't know how far she made it. I guess she could be dead." Liu's eyes widened. "I shouldn't have said that, should I?"

A clang sounded and Liu's picture shuddered.

"Upgraders! I've got to go," Liu said. She looked to her right and hefted a heavy wrench. "Hoku, I've made some changes to Zorro. Most important, I sealed him up so he can travel wherever you do—underwater, through the desert, up the mountains . . . He'll probably outlive us all now."

"Thank you," Hoku whispered, and stroked Zorro's back.

"I don't know what you can do about all of this," Liu said. "But then, I never thought you'd manage to defeat Fathom, either. I like being awake. If you've got another miracle in your pocket, now's the time to use it."

The projected picture disappeared suddenly. The air in front of Zorro's eyes—so full of sound and motion a moment ago—now felt painfully empty.

"I'm sure they're safe," Hoku said. "Liu is really good with that wrench, and Daphine is smart. She has more common sense than the rest of us Kampii combined."

Aluna nodded, but said nothing. Her brow hung heavily over her eyes, her jaw clenched.

"Skyfeather's Landing is next," Calli said. "Strand's army may already be there." She started to pace along the water's edge. "We need to go there right now. We need to help with the fight."

"No, we go to the Kampii," Hoku said. He placed Zorro on his shoulder and stood. "Our people are probably dying already. I have to help them recharge their breathing shells."

"But Skyfeather's Landing is where the fight is," Calli said. "If we want to stop Karl Strand once and for all, we need to be at the heart of the battle!"

Hoku kicked the sand. "Our families are down there! So saving the lives of Kampii isn't important?"

Calli walked up to him and put her face just centimeters from his. Her nostrils flared. "Of course it's important. It's just not *more* important than saving the lives of Aviars. Or *my* family."

"I didn't mean—"

"No, of course not," Calli said. She waved her hands in the air. "Don't you see? Maybe Dash was right to leave. We all want to stop Karl Strand, but maybe we need to do it in different ways. You and Aluna need to save your people, and Dash wants to save his. Is it so wrong that I want to save mine, too?"

Hoku had never seen her like this before. Her cheeks burned with anger, her wings twitched. He felt his own rage rising just as fast, like a wave carrying him higher and higher. "Your people are fighters. They can defend themselves. The Kampii are practically helpless!"

"The Kampii have *chosen* ignorance, and that's not a good enough reason to let my people die," Calli said coldly. "I'm going to Skyfeather's Landing—with or without you."

CHAPTER 14

*C*ALLI'S RIGHT," Aluna said quietly. She wasn't sure if they'd hear her over their own yelling, but both Hoku and Calli stopped to look at her. "Calli, you should go help your mother at Skyfeather's Landing, and Hoku, you and I should return to the City of Shifting Tides."

Hoku crossed his arms in front of his chest. "I can't believe I'm hearing this from you two. I thought we were friends. I thought we were a team!"

"We *are* a team," Calli said, her anger dissipating. "But sometimes a team has to split up to accomplish its mission. The Aviars have scouts and strategists and medics and warriors—everyone plays their role in battle. Our roles are just taking us in different directions right now. Dash understood that, and now I do, too."

"Besides, it's not like Calli can join us underwater anyway," Aluna said. "Hoku, you were the one who said the water pressure would snap her delicate Aviar bones."

Hoku dropped his head into his hands and groaned. "It would. Of course it would. I don't know why I didn't think of that."

Calli put a hand on his shoulder. "Because you want us to stay together, even when it doesn't make sense. That's . . . not a bad thing."

Hoku dropped his hands from his face and nodded.

"When you get home, Calli, turn on Skyfeather's Landing's commbox and have someone monitoring it at all times," Aluna said.

"I will," Calli said. "I'll make sure it's never turned off again."

"Tell High Senator Electra to stay out of trouble," Aluna added. "Tell her . . . that I'll be irritated if I have to come rescue her."

"And let Senator Niobe know that I'm out of mustard," Hoku added.

Calli laughed and bent down so Aluna could hug her without jumping up and balancing on her tail.

"Wishing you blue skies, sister," Calli said.

Aluna dove into the water and swam out to sea,

wanting to give Hoku and Calli a moment of privacy to say good-bye. She was still in range when Hoku said, "I'll miss you," but after that, she heard nothing.

When she returned to the beach, Calli was a distant speck of white in the vast expanse of sky. Hoku sat cross-legged on the sand holding Zorro, his face mashed into the animal's fur.

She dragged herself over and sat behind him, back to back, like they used to do when they were younglings.

"Remember when all you used to want was an apprenticeship with Elder Peleke?" Aluna said. "Every time we found a three-clawed crab, that's what you wished for."

Hoku grunted. "What a waste of wishes."

"Well, we both know what to use them on now." Aluna leaned her head back, so it was touching his. "Calli will be okay."

"So will Dash and Vachir," he said. "Now all we need is a beach filled with mutant crabs."

She laughed. "Are you ready for this? Are you ready to go home?"

"No," he said with a sigh. "But they need us." He started to stand up when Zorro jumped out of his lap, squealed, and raced toward the tree line. "Zorro, come back here!" Hoku called. It was a direct order, but the animal didn't so much as slow down.

Aluna dragged herself up the beach. Sand clung to her wet tail and arms, but she didn't mind. She'd be back in the ocean soon enough, and such Above World irritations would be forgotten.

Hoku jogged past her. "There he is! He's digging."

By the time Aluna reached them, Hoku had dropped to his knees beside Zorro and the two of them were pulling sandy earth out of a hole.

"There's something buried here," Hoku said. "A box, maybe? Zorro, dig around the edges, boy."

The hole wasn't big enough for all three of them, so Aluna dropped down to her elbows and watched. Within a few minutes, Hoku lifted a very muddy but familiar object from its hiding place. Even though it was dirty, Aluna could make out hints of silver and pearl.

"The water safe!" she said.

"This is Liu's doing." Hoku blew sand away from the locking mechanism, entered the combination, and popped open the box. "Karl Strand's letter, the carved dolphin . . ." He pressed the hidden latch. "Even Sarah Jennings's secret tech. It's all here."

"Good raccoon," Aluna said. Was it her imagination, or did the raccoon lift its chin a little higher?

Hoku closed the water safe and stowed it in his satchel. "Grandma Nani is never going to believe what we found inside."

"I don't know about that," Aluna said. "Sometimes I think your grandmother knows everything."

"Only one way to find out," Hoku said. "Race you to the water!"

He ran, his feet kicking sand in every direction, Zorro bouncing on his shoulder. Aluna pulled herself after him with much more speed than he clearly expected. They got to the water at the same time and dove.

Aluna swam ahead, unable to resist using her tail for as much speed as possible, and circled back every few minutes to make sure that she and Hoku stayed in range. Hoku still had terrible technique, especially with the raccoon creating so much extra drag, but he was taller and stronger now. Faster in the water.

She counted sharks as they swam, an old childhood game. Most were small, under two meters, and far too smart to attack prey as large as her and Hoku. Even the large ones stayed away from Kampii, especially in this area of the ocean. But soon she lost track of the number.

"Too many sharks," Hoku mumbled.

Normally she'd laugh at him; even one shark was too many for Hoku. But this time, she agreed with him. "They're heading northwest. Maybe something died and they're following the blood scent. It must be something huge."

"The City of Shifting Tides isn't that far north," Hoku said. "But that doesn't matter, does it? You want to know where the sharks are going."

"Am I that obvious?"

"Only to everyone," Hoku said. "Go. Follow the sharks. I'll meet you in the city when you're done. I need to start work immediately."

Aluna swished over and hugged him, careful not to dislodge Zorro from his shoulder. "I'll see you in a few hours."

Aluna watched Hoku swim off, then found a smiler—a shark with a curved mouth that made it look like it was grinning. She matched the shark's speed, then calmly grabbed the animal's dorsal fin with one hand and its pectoral fin with the other. The shark ignored its new parasite and kept on swimming.

The shark dodged through kelp and around growing columns of coral. Aluna could tell they were approaching the vast reef that hid the City of Shifting Tides, only they weren't near the city itself. She studied every hermit crab and shiny-blue they passed, letting the ocean soak back into her bones. The number of sharks swimming with them grew, but Aluna still couldn't see what they were hunting.

Eventually the smiler changed direction and headed up, toward the sun, and Aluna's ears filled with noise.

"No attacks on the south," a male voice said. "Is the western flank secured? Good. Let me know if that changes."

Aluna released her shark and swam up until her head broke the surface of the water.

Dozens of adult Kampii lay scattered across a kilometer of shallow reef, looking more like a herd of sunning seals than people. A few younglings stood and squatted among them, not yet old enough to have their tails. All around them, the water churned with sharks.

The Kampii on lookout spotted Aluna immediately. "You! Unless you're in the hunting party, get back to the reef!"

"Who's in charge here?" Aluna asked. "Is it Elder Kapono?" Her stomach twisted as she said her father's name.

The lookout snorted. He was young, maybe just twenty, with sun-yellow hair and thin scars covering his arms and tail. "An Elder? Up here? You've spent too long in the sun."

Aluna couldn't stop staring at the Kampii. Something about him looked strange. *Wrong*. What was it? "His necklace," she whispered. "He's not wearing a breathing shell!"

Of course, since Aluna was close enough to hear the lookout, he was close enough to hear her, too.

"You've got a breathing shell." The lookout's face

no longer held any concern for her safety. "You don't belong here. Go back down to the city."

"No one here has a breathing shell?" Aluna asked.

"You think we're up here because it's fun?" The guard spat into the water. "We don't have any Elders up here. Not much shelter or food, either. You want a nice sticky bed or a safe place to sleep, then go home."

"If there aren't any Elders, then who's in charge?" Aluna asked.

The lookout pointed back along the reef. "You'll find her over there," he said. "She used to be the Voice of the Coral Kampii, but now she's stuck with us."

Daphine.

Aluna closed her eyes and breathed deep, too overwhelmed to even thank the guard. She made herself swim slowly through the shallow water covering the coral reef, careful not to agitate the sharks.

Daphine sat at the center of a group of Kampii, just like always, but instead of politely accepting compliments from her suitors, she was barking orders. Leadership seemed to run in the family.

When Daphine saw Aluna, she squealed. Aluna couldn't keep a grin from spreading across her face. She sped across the reef's surface and tackled her sister in a hug.

"Watch the scope," Daphine said, laughing. "You'll poke your own eye out with it, if you're not careful."

Aluna refused to let Daphine go. She buried her face in her sister's stupidly long hair and squeezed. The ocean made almost everything smell the same, but there was something about Daphine's scent that would always remind Aluna of being a youngling and feeling safe.

"I missed you, too," Daphine said. "You were gone so long in the desert, and then when the attack on HydroTek came . . . We were all so worried."

Reluctantly, Aluna released her hold on her sister and pulled back. Daphine's face had once been considered perfect, but Fathom changed all that. He'd replaced her left eye with a scope of black metal that protruded a dozen centimeters from her eye socket. Now Aluna had to work to see anything else: Daphine's sun-cracked lips, the new scar on her cheek, the frown lines framing her sister's mouth.

"You're wearing a breathing shell," Aluna said. "I thought if you were up here, it meant your necklace had failed."

"Mine still works, but I wasn't about to abandon all these people, no matter what the Elders ordered me to do." She traced the tiny seahorse design on the shell with her fingertip. "I still use it when I go down to talk to the Elders, although I don't know why I bother. They've got working necklaces for themselves and their families, and that's all that seems to matter to them.

When Anadar's breathing shell failed, Father gave him a new one — despite the fact that so many other people were in need. He wouldn't even tell Anadar where it came from."

"So Anadar is still down in the City of Shifting Tides?" Aluna asked. She touched her own necklace, wondering how many minutes or days or weeks she had left. Or maybe it was already depleted and she'd never taste deep ocean again.

Daphine smiled. "No. Anadar gave the new necklace to a woman so she could stay with her family. He lives up here now, and leads the hunting parties."

"Still the same Anadar, then," Aluna said. She should have known. He was the one who'd taught her how to fight even though it was forbidden. Only her brother could teach her a lesson in selflessness when he wasn't even here.

"Yes, he's the same," Daphine said, her thoughts obviously swimming in the same direction as Aluna's. "I don't know what I'd do without him."

"What *are* you doing?" Aluna asked, her gaze sweeping across the Kampii clustered on the reef. "You can't protect yourselves up here, and you certainly can't build any kind of shelter. This isn't a long-term solution."

Daphine's scope whirred and spun as she stared at her people. "We can't go to the shore, or we'll be useless. Unless we do it for the younglings who still have legs. At least they have a chance for a life in the Above World."

"I'm going down to talk to the Elders," Aluna said. "Maybe after we've told them about the desert and Karl Strand's growing army, they'll agree to take action. They should at least be bringing you supplies and helping you stay safe."

Daphine put a hand on Aluna's shoulder. "If you can make the Elders see reason, then I'll do all your chores for three tides."

Aluna laughed. They used to make those sorts of bargains all the time, back before the world fell apart. "And if I can't, then I'll let you braid my hair whenever you want."

"Deal!" Daphine said. "But you're getting pearls and shells woven in, too."

"I'll go to the city now, but I'll be back," Aluna said. "If the Elders won't help you, then I will. For what it's worth."

Daphine hugged her. "It's worth everything."

CHAPTER 15

HOKU SWAM into the City of Shifting Tides with his fingers pressed against his breathing shell, convinced it would fail. Is this how the Kampii had been living—terrified that they might start to drown at any moment?

To stave off his panic, he focused on his surroundings. Anemones grew everywhere, covering the outskirts of the city in a patchwork blanket of brilliant reds, yellows, and purples. Some had been grown in patterns, creating living mosaics depicting Kampii swimming or fighting or singing. Fish snuggled among them, adding movement and surprising sparkle.

The city was familiar in so many ways, but Hoku felt as if he were seeing it with new eyes. Now he noticed the simple tools the Kampii used for hunting and gathering and the way all their food was eaten raw and without flavoring. Compared to the other LegendaryTek splinters, the Kampii barely used any tech at all.

He should have gone straight to Elder Peleke to see if the old tech master was working on a way to fix the breathing necklaces, but he let his heart lead him to the sand-side of the coral reef instead. To his family nest. His father and mother would be home from their work duties by now, and Grandma Nani would be there, too, since she was far too old to dig mussels or mend nets. He couldn't bear the thought of waiting one more minute to see them.

He swam through the opening to his family's modest nest, and into the kitchen. Everything was the same as he remembered, except smaller, as if the whole place had been magically shrunk. Had they really all crowded into this tiny room for their meals? Had they actually invited other families over to join them?

"Mom? Dad? Grandma? I'm home! I'm back from the Above World!"

No answer, not even inside his ear. He could hear some of their neighbors squabbling over dinner, but nothing more.

His parents' room was empty. Well, empty but messy. His father never bothered to tuck his things back into the cubbyholes in the wall. Zorro squeaked and shook his head. Hoku pulled himself out of his parents' room and swam across the hall.

"Grandma Nani?"

She wasn't there. Her bed and her resting stick were gone, replaced by a sticky bed far too small for his grandmother's old body. Zorro swam off Hoku's shoulder and paddled through the room with his four small paws, smelling everything with his twitchy raccoon nose.

Hoku examined the items in one of the cubbyholes. Instead of the supply of special kelp that Grandma Nani ate to help her sleep, he found toys. Bright shells on a string for counting, a little Kampii doll made from sand and cloth, and a tiny shark carved from white coral.

Baby toys.

"Hoku? Is that you?"

He turned and found his father's arms around him, felt his dad's wiry beard crushed against his cheek. His mother waited for them to separate before taking her turn. Hoku stared at her, amazed that she could look both so familiar and so strange at the same time. Her hair was pulled back from her face and she wore a billowy white shirt that almost hid her wide, round belly.

She laughed. "You've come back just in time, little one. You're going to be a brother!"

"A brother?" he said, extending his hand. She pulled it to her stomach so he could feel the tiny creature rolling around inside.

"This will be the baby's room," his mother said. "She's coming any day now."

"A sister!" he said, amazed. Until the rest of their words sunk in. "But where's Grandma Nani? Is she sleeping in my room?" He'd be sad if they'd given his room away, but he didn't blame them. Their nest was small and he'd been lucky to have his own room for as long as he did.

His dad pulled Hoku into a hug again. "Your grandma left us, Hoku," he said gently. "She went quietly in her sleep. There was no pain."

Hoku felt tears form in his eyes and twisted his face to stop them. He pushed himself away from his father. "She would have hated going quietly," he said. "She would have wanted to die on an adventure, or in an explosion, or cursing and yelling in order to irritate the neighbors."

"She was proud of you," his father said, and Hoku could see the pride in his father's eyes, too.

"She never stopped talking about how you went to the Above World," his mother said. "We were angry and hurt when you left. Your father wanted to go after you. But your grandma yelled at us. She told us to have more faith in the boy we'd raised."

Hoku buried his face in his father's shoulder.

"She was right about everything," his father said. "But especially about how brave you've become."

"The baby!" Hoku said suddenly. "The breathing necklaces are failing—do you know that? Have the Elders told you? The baby won't be able to live underwater. And what about you? Your shells could stop working at any time!" He pictured his mother a full nine months pregnant, struggling as she swam for the surface. "You're not safe here anymore."

"We know, Hoku," his father said, putting a callused hand on Hoku's arm. "Kaila's necklace went last week. She had a few hours to make it to the surface and find that colony that the Voice started." Hoku remembered Kaila, a young Kampii who lived alone nearby and refused to have children, but who would swim over and watch Hoku when his parents were working extra shifts. He hoped she had made it to the surface in time.

"The Voice. You mean Daphine, Aluna's sister? She's somewhere Above World?" Aluna would be so relieved when he told her.

His mother kept a hand on her belly, as if she were protecting the baby inside. "Daphine made sure to spread the word so we'd all know where to go if something happened. She told us to have emergency sacks ready. We'll go the instant there's trouble."

"Good," Hoku said. "But what about the baby? They can't be giving out new necklaces when so many are failing."

His parents shared a dark look with each other. "We've kept your grandma Nani's passing a secret from the Elders," his father said quietly. "Her breathing shell was still working, so we didn't turn it in to the city. The sand-siders—all of us—have made a pact. More of our necklaces break than the moon-siders', but the Elders don't give us as many shells. We've started to take care of our own."

Hoku winced. Hoarding breathing devices had been a crime even before they'd started breaking. If the Elders found out, his parents would be in terrible trouble.

"Best not tell your friend Aluna," his mother said. "We trust her, of course, but her father . . ." She raised an eyebrow. "He's no friend to the sand-siders."

Hoku nodded. Of course he could tell Aluna. She'd never betray his family to her father. But his parents didn't know that, and he didn't want them to worry. "Grandma Nani may not have died the way she wanted, but she'd be happy that she turned you both into lawbreakers on her way out. I guess I'm one now, too."

"These are dark times, son," his father said. "I hope you understand why we have to do this."

"I do," Hoku replied.

He let his parents feed him clams and mussels and tell him about their lives since he left. His mother patched a hole in his shirt. Eventually, he told them about his travels, too. Not everything—they were his parents, after all, and he didn't want to scare them with how close he'd repeatedly come to dying. But he told them enough . . . and probably too much about Calli. Maybe someday he'd figure out a way for them to meet her.

"From what you've told us," his mother said, "we've got even more to worry about than drowning, with this Karl Strand person trying to take over the world."

"Aluna and I came here to talk to the Elders," Hoku said. "Maybe when they know what happened in the desert and at HydroTek and about the war, they'll start to see. We have to try."

His mother handed him another mussel. "Yes, try. But don't be too disappointed if it doesn't work, little one. You've seen a world far greater than your years, but to the Elders and most of the moon-siders, the world down here still looks very much the same."

Hoku looked around the room. "No, it doesn't. There's no Grandma Nani."

His father reached out and took his hand, pulled him into the cramped hallway and toward the front of the nest. One of the curved walls in the gathering room was pitted with tiny cubbyholes. In each one was a single, crudely carved figurine. His family's ancestor wall.

A new statue sat in a center cubby, its body and tail hewed from dark stone.

"Grandma Nani," Hoku said. He gently touched the statue's head.

"We'll throw her another feast tonight," his mother said. "In honor of your return, and for her. She'd be so happy that we're all together again."

No, she wouldn't, Hoku thought. Not while Karl Strand is still out there.

"I . . . want that," Hoku said. "I want that very much. But I've got to go find Elder Peleke. I'm the city's best chance for finding a way to recharge the necklaces. I shouldn't have stayed as long as I did." He wondered if any Kampii had been forced to flee for the surface while he'd been enjoying his reunion with his parents. He couldn't bear the thought.

"Of course," his mother said. "We'll save you some clams."

He didn't recognize his mother's tone at first, and then suddenly he did. Patronizing. She didn't believe he could do anything about the necklaces. Then again, why should she? He'd been barely tinkering with tech before he'd left for the Above World. Even so, her doubt stung like a scorpion. He barely managed to mumble a good-bye and escape out into the city before he let her see exactly how much.

He found Elder Peleke hunched over a workbench in the main research dome, his tail wrapped around a worn resting stick. Jars of doodads, spools of wire, and heavy, well-worn tools dangled from the desk.

Hoku used to sneak into the dome and stare in wonder at such a glorious array, but now that he'd been to Skyfeather's Landing and trained in Rollin's cluttered tent, Elder Peleke's tools seemed as simplistic as a youngling's toys. This was not the place for serious technological creation or discovery.

Hoku had last seen Elder Peleke less than a year ago, but in that time the man seemed to have aged ten years and shrunk ten centimeters. Peleke bent over his work, cleaning a tiny device with an even tinier tool. "You're late with my dinner," he snapped. "Bring it here and get out."

Ah, now, there was the Elder Peleke that Hoku remembered.

"I don't have your dinner and I'm not one of your apprentices," Hoku said quietly.

Peleke's head whipped around. He studied Hoku through a deep squint. "No, you aren't. Weren't smart enough to be an apprentice, if I remember rightly."

Even in the cold water, Hoku felt his cheeks burn. He mumbled, "Not connected enough, you mean."

"What was that?"

Hoku lifted his chin. "I came here to talk to you about the breathing devices. I have ideas about how to recharge their batteries and—"

"I hardly think I need ideas from a youngling." Elder Peleke snorted. "Go run off with that trouble-maker friend of yours and play your silly games. I have real work to do."

Hoku swam closer, trying to get a glimpse of what Peleke was working on. Strangely, medical equipment littered the table—scalpels and sponges and something large enough to be . . .

. . . *a head.*

His stomach twisted and churned. He wanted to flee the dome and Peleke and find something cute to stare at for a few hours. But he didn't. He stayed.

The object was definitely a head, severed low on the neck. Hoku recognized the gray smooth skin, the wide black eyes, and the gills. The name escaped before he could stop it.

"Deepfell."

CHAPTER 16

ALUNA SLOWED as she neared her family's nest. Maybe she could turn back now and return to the surface colony. Daphine and Anadar were all the family she needed.

Yet her tail propelled her forward, through the familiar maze of coral, past the openings to her neighbors' moon-side nests. Her body knew the way and she let it take her. Is this how dolphins felt when they were migrating? That they were the prisoners of their own instincts?

She'd thought there would be time to swim through the nest, to remind herself of her old life and prepare for the inevitable reunions. But when she entered the dining area, she ran smack into Pilipo, Ehu, and her father having dinner.

They were huge, even bigger than she remembered. Her brothers cried out. She felt their massive arms wrap around her and squeeze her gently. Ehu twirled her in the water and laughed.

Aluna had never spent much time with either of them, but her heart warmed anyway. Pilipo with his gorgeous dark hair curling around his rugged face. Ehu with his jutting cheekbones and dark-brown eyes that made the girls swoon. They both seemed older now, like real Kampii adults. She saw new scars on their faces, arms, and tails. Scars that marked their prowess and experience, that made them even more desirable matches in the colony.

"Good to have you back, little sister," Ehu said. "Daphine abandoned us and Pilipo can't even prepare mussels without mangling them."

Aluna bit back a retort.

"Glad you're home," Pilipo said. "The nest feels colder without you and Daphine. I'm tired of Ehu's incessant talking about his love life. Listening to him is your job now!"

Aluna frowned. "Well, I'm not sure how long—"

"Pilipo. Ehu. Leave us," her father said.

Kapono had been waiting motionless on his resting stick in the far corner of the room, and Aluna had been doing her best to forget he was there. Maybe if she ignored him completely, they could continue living in separate worlds, the way they did before she left home.

Ehu nudged her in the ribs. "Let him get it all out, Aluna. He's been bottling it up for months. It'll be better after that—you know how it goes." Then Ehu and Pilipo swam out, taking most of the mussels with them.

Aluna looked up at the dark, seething person in the back of the room. At her father.

"You have a tail. That means you stole the Ocean Seed and used it, against the express orders of the council of Elders, and against *my* wishes." His voice was low, gravelly, dangerous. She hated the way it sounded in her ears, as if he were too close.

"It's nice to see you again, too," she said. Aluna could feel her defenses building, layer after layer, like the thickest armor imaginable. She hadn't needed the armor in months, but she remembered how to wear it. "Glad to see you're still focusing on me, your disappointing daughter, instead of trying to find a way to save our people."

"We are nothing without our traditions, and we are no more than barbarians if we ignore the rules of our society," he said. "You disgrace us all."

"I don't mind being a disgrace if I'm saving lives at the same time," she retorted. She felt the anger surge inside her. No one could trigger it as quickly as her father.

"Your time in the Above World hasn't changed you, I see," he said. "Still the same selfish girl who left here without even telling her family where she was going."

Oh, don't pretend you were hurt, she thought. "You knew where I was going. Or you would have, if you'd been listening to me at all. I was right about Makina's necklace—about the necklaces failing in general. I was right about going to the Above World."

Her father unwound his tail from the resting stick and seemed to grow a meter taller as he swam closer. Sharks had the same dark eyes as he did, but she preferred their lifeless cruelty to her father's intelligent, thoughtful disdain.

"We would have found a solution from here, without risking the colony," he said. "You brought the Above World down on us. You put everyone in the entire city in danger."

"What about the surface colony?" she asked. "Your own son and daughter are up there right now, exposed and in danger. Is this how the Elders' plan was supposed to work?" She tried to make herself taller, bigger, more imposing. She'd never have Pilipo's size, but she'd definitely grown in the last few months.

"Daphine and Anadar would be here, safe, if they'd

listened to me," Kapono said. "I will protect this family with my last breath." His mouth twisted into an unfriendly smile. "I will even protect you, should you ever let me."

She could see the rage swirling through him, begging for release. His fists clenched, his jaw twitched. He'd been angry as long as she could remember. Had it started when his wife died, or had it always been there, even a million years ago when he'd been young? Some days it seemed like fury alone propelled him.

Aluna understood anger; she'd let it rule her, too. But rage was demanding. Greedy. Overpowering. It left no room for other emotions like happiness or joy. Like love.

Karl Strand had a son once. Tomias. He'd gone insane when his son died, after Sarah Jennings left him. He'd figured out how to live forever so that if he ever had another child, they wouldn't know death. Strand had even sent his army to HydroTek to rescue Fathom.

Somehow Karl Strand managed to love his children, and yet Aluna's own father couldn't find a way to love her. The realization should have made her angry all over again, but it didn't. It made her sad.

Well, if she couldn't reach him as a daughter, maybe she could reach him as a Kampii citizen.

"Elder Kapono . . . " She winced at how awkward it sounded, but kept going. "I've seen a lot of things. I traveled to the mountains and the desert. I've been to the dome that used to power our breathing shells. Please . . . won't you just listen to me?"

Her father stared at her with hard eyes. After what felt like hours, they softened slightly. He swam slowly back to his seat and wound his tail around his resting stick.

"Speak."

A surge of hope washed through her body, but she knew better than to smile. Instead, she found a resting stick of her own and began to talk. She told him everything that happened after she left the city—her encounters with the Deepfell, the Aviars, the Upgraders, the Equians, the Serpenti, the Thunder Trials. A friend would have stopped her, asked questions, offered hugs. He did nothing but sit and listen.

It felt like the biggest victory she'd ever won.

And then her stomach grumbled. She clutched it and offered an embarrassed smile. "Guess I forgot to eat."

"Stay," her father said. He swam into the food preparation area and came back a moment later with a net of mixed delicacies: mussels, clams, shrimp, and crab. Far more than she could eat in two days, let alone one meal.

"Thank you," she said, and took the offering. She'd never tasted anything as good as that first crunchy bite of shrimp. It reminded her of scorpion, but sweeter.

Her father studied her while she ate. If she hadn't been so hungry, it would have made her nervous. He used to do that when Aluna was a youngling, just float in the shadows and watch Daphine crack open Aluna's mussels for her, or pretend not to pay attention while Daphine braided her short hair. Daughters had always confounded him. Apparently they still did.

When she'd polished off the last of the shrimp and started on the crab, her father spoke. "I appreciate your telling me of the Above World," he said. "It is . . . useful . . . to know what is happening to our breathing necklaces." His tail swished. "However, I do not think a war with Strand is in the best interests of the colony at this time. We must see to the protection of our own people first. Elder Peleke has devised a solution to our breathing-shell problem, and we don't need to break our vow of isolation in order to accomplish it."

"A solution?" Aluna said. "What solution?"

A voice rang in her ears just two flashes before Hoku appeared in the room's archway.

"The Deepfell," Hoku said, out of breath from swimming. His freckled face burned red. "They're going to kill the Deepfell and rip the breathing devices from their throats."

CHAPTER 17

ALUNA TUGGED on Pilipo's sealskin shirt. "You don't have to do this."

Her brother brushed her away with a smile. "No worries, little sister, we'll be fine. Ehu and I have faced worse than a pod of Deepfell before. A good victory will give the colony something to celebrate."

"I could use a feast," Ehu said. "It's been months since we've had one."

Aluna watched dozens of hunters secure their armor and sharpen their weapons. A cluster of Elders watched from a few meters away, but Aluna and Hoku had already been banished from their presence.

"This is ludicrous," she said. "We need to be fighting Karl Strand and his armies, not each other!"

"The Deepfell are on our side," Hoku said.

"Prince Eekikee helped us rescue Daphine from HydroTek." Aluna looked back and forth between her two brothers. "Doesn't that mean anything to you?"

Ehu snorted. "Didn't help rescue her *before* she got that hideous scope attached to her face."

Aluna turned to Hoku. She'd been angry before, but now she felt numb. "Am I really related to these two?"

"Not in any way that truly matters," Hoku said. "I thought the Upgraders were bad, but at least they honor the people they kill before taking their tech. They don't treat it as some sort of contest or game. As a reason to have a *feast*. Maybe I was wrong. Maybe the Kampii don't deserve to be saved."

"What's that, little guy?" Ehu grabbed Hoku in a neck hold and mussed his hair.

Hoku went limp, like he'd done as a youngling. It was the fastest way to escape the cruelty of his bullies.

"Let go of him," Aluna said, gritting her teeth.

Ehu laughed. Aluna had put up with Ehu's teasing her entire life, but she couldn't bear to see Hoku subjected to it. She darted behind Ehu, wrapped her forearm around his neck, and applied the same hold on him.

"I told you to let him go," she said.

Ehu gasped and released his grip. Hoku bolted away like a fish from a net.

"Where did you learn this trick?" Ehu asked, trying

to pry Aluna's arm off with his fingers. He wasn't even using his full strength. Even in a choke hold, he underestimated her.

"Not from you," she said. If she'd had a knee, she would have driven it into the small of his back and forced his body to contort. She wasn't sure how to do that with a tail—and no kneecaps.

Ehu twisted and flipped, an easy thing to do in the water. Aluna hadn't experienced the maneuver in the Above World. In a flash, she found herself facing Ehu, her hold broken.

"You have a lot to learn, *little fish*," he said. Aluna silently promised to never use that nickname on Hoku again.

"I'm not used to fighting underwater," she said. "Give me a few days to get used to it again, and I'll be whipping your tail from one tide to the next."

Pilipo, who had been ignoring them up until now, said, "Such ridiculous talk was fine when you were a youngling, Aluna, but you're an adult now. Try to behave like a woman."

Hoku grabbed her arm. "Come on," he said. "We're never going to convince your brothers that they're idiots."

"Let me know if you want a rematch," Ehu said. "I'll tie both arms behind my back and wear a blindfold."

Aluna started for him, intending to punch the smile off his jeering, condescending face, but Hoku held her back. "Your brothers have a senseless, brutal war to start, and we have an entire city to save." He raised an eyebrow and pretended to whisper, "Someone down here needs to use their brain, and your brothers have clearly opted out of that responsibility."

Aluna snorted. *Tides' teeth.* If it weren't for Hoku and his sense of humor, she'd spend the rest of her days fighting Pilipo and Ehu instead of Karl Strand.

She let Hoku lead her away from the hunting party and the Elders. The run-in with her brothers had jumbled her insides, made her anxious and angry. It also made her feel helpless. She could scream at them with every ounce of her strength, and they'd either not hear or laugh. In all her travels, she'd never encountered anything more frustrating than her own family.

"I don't want my brothers to die," she said, "but a part of me hopes Prince Eekikee and his Deepfell teach them a lesson. That makes me a bad Kampii, doesn't it?"

"Maybe, but it also makes you a good person," Hoku said. "Don't you remember when you wanted to save Eekikee, and I wanted you to kill him? Nothing is ever as simple as we want it to be."

She thought Hoku had been leading her away from her brothers, but he'd actually been taking her somewhere specific: to Sarah Jennings's memorial. The familiar white stone rose out of the sand, strong and still, impervious to the currents. Aluna swam over and pressed her palms against a smooth side, just as she'd done a hundred times in the past.

"I thought things would be different when we came back," she said quietly. "I thought after everything we'd been through, after everything we'd done . . . that we would have earned some respect from our own people. But nothing has changed. We're still the same younglings we were when we left."

"No, we're not," Hoku said. "We've been to the mountains and the desert. We've made powerful enemies and truly terrifying friends. It's this place that has stayed the same, not us." He looked off, toward the distant kelp forest. "Then again, my grandma is gone and I'll be a brother soon. So maybe some things have changed, after all."

Aluna circled the monument until she found Sarah Jennings's profile etched into the stone. She traced a finger down the slope of Sarah's nose.

"Sarah Jennings tried to protect us," Hoku said. "And for a long time, it worked really well."

Aluna's other hand went to the worn pouch still hanging around her neck. Someday, she'd take out her mother's ring and actually wear it.

"I've got to do something," she said. "If I can't stop

the Elders or my brothers from hunting the Deepfell, then I've got to warn them. Prince Eekikee and his people saved us from the Upgraders. They helped me rescue Daphine. I owe them at least a warning."

She thought Hoku would argue with her, but when she looked over at him, he nodded, his face serious. "You've got some time," he said. "You know where their secret cave is, and your brothers don't. You can get there first."

Her stomach clenched. "You're not coming with me?"

"No," he said, swimming closer. "Calli was right. Sometimes a team has to split up to accomplish its mission. I can't help you with the Deepfell or your brothers, but I can go to Seahorse Alpha. If Zorro and I can get inside and interface with the old tech, maybe we can find a way to power the Kampii necklaces." He ran his hand through his short, spiky hair. "And if I can access the records, maybe I'll figure out Karl Strand's weakness, or where he's commanding his army from, or, I don't know, his favorite color."

"Green," Aluna said. "Definitely green." She smiled. "It sounds like a good plan, but what if Great White is still hanging around the outpost? And the glowfield is probably still up. Maybe I should come with you."

"No," Hoku said firmly. "I can do it by myself. Well, by myself with Zorro. I'm thirteen now, old enough to get my tail. This will be my rite of passage instead."

Her eyes widened. "Your birthing day! I forgot!"

He grinned. "We've had other things to worry about."

"I need to give you a present." He always wanted tech or food, and she didn't have access to either.

"Just come back safe," he said. "We'll celebrate when all of this is over. I'm sure Calli, Vachir, and Dash won't want to miss out on the fun."

She laughed. "The Aviars probably give each other weapons. And the Equians' best gift is a canteen of water."

"I'd prefer those presents to anything from Vachir."

"I'm sure Vachir's bite or trample would be full of love and affection," Aluna said. Then she remembered why they'd started talking about his birthday in the first place, and her heart grew heavy. "So we're really going to split up?"

Hoku nodded. "You're going to save the Deepfell and stop our people from doing something horrible, and I'm going to go find some way to save the Kampii, even though some of them don't actually deserve it right now."

She swished her tail, and the remaining distance

between them disappeared. She wrapped her arms around Hoku and hugged him hard.

"Be swift as a seal," she said.

"Be deadly as . . . an Aviar," he answered back, his mouth curled up at the corners.

CHAPTER 18

SEAHORSE ALPHA was exactly as Hoku remembered: a cluster of ancient domed buildings hidden behind a glowing barrier of deadly jellies. The jellies had been coaxed to grow together, their tendrils woven into a tight web that could easily paralyze even the strongest of intruders. Half-eaten fish stuck to the glowfield, along with two dolphin carcasses and the undulating remains of a long-dead squid.

Hoku swam under an outcropping of rock on the ocean's floor and scanned the water for Great White. If Strand had been watching Seahorse Alpha months ago, when Aluna and Hoku had first found it, then he was probably watching it now.

Zorro shifted on his shoulder. "I know," Hoku said quietly. "Just a little bit longer. We have to be sure."

The goldenrods Hoku had brought squirmed and thrashed in their small net, seemingly aware that he planned to use them as bait. Hoku adjusted his grip on the short spear in his other hand, but the stupid thing felt awkward no matter how he held it.

When his muscles started to cramp and Zorro had shifted his position for the tenth time, a lazy school of shiny-blues swimming near the glowfield suddenly scattered. A heartbeat later, the hulking mass of Great White glided into view.

The shark's mouth hung open, and old, decaying meat dangled from its rows of disgustingly sharp teeth. Scars marred the tough skin of its nose. And there, just above its stony black eye, Hoku saw the tiny camera marking it as Strand's spy.

His heart beat faster. He wished it wouldn't, but his body rarely listened to him when it mattered. At least he hadn't gone into shock like last time. Aluna would be so proud.

Hoku looked down at the fish in his net. "Sorry, little warriors, but it's either you or me."

This plan had seemed logical enough in his head — stab the fish and their blood would distract Great White long enough for Hoku and Zorro to sneak into Seahorse Alpha. But now that he was sitting here, ready to make the first cut, it didn't feel so solid. He should have stolen one of Mags's poison needles. Or six. And brought Aluna to shove them into the shark's flesh.

Zorro squeaked, apparently hoping the fish were his next meal. That's the last thing Hoku needed— to have Zorro gnawing on a fish when Great White swooped in.

"Zorro, you will not eat these fish. Got it?"

The animal's eyes glowed green, maybe a little reluctantly.

"Then here we go," Hoku said. He watched Great White drift around the curve of the glowfield and out of view, then he stabbed one of the fish with the point of his spear.

The goldenrod squirmed wildly. A tiny dark cloud puffed up from the wound. Hoku pulled his hand back to avoid touching it. The other fish smelled of blood now, too, but they couldn't get out of the net.

Hoku wedged the net into the rocks where he was hiding, hoping Great White would struggle to get at them, then swam as fast as he could for the other side of the glowfield. He needed to get out of sight before the shark turned and came for the fish. If he didn't, Great White might decide that larger moving prey— him and Zorro—was the better snack.

He made it around the curve of the jelly field, his heart beating so loudly they could have heard it in the

Above World, and started to cut a hole in the web's tendrils. Bringing the spear instead of a knife suddenly seemed like a brilliant idea, since he could stay almost a meter away from the glowfield as he worked. Getting stung by the jellies would mean that he'd be stuck there, alive but motionless for weeks, while the hungry jellies slowly digested him. It'd be a fate far worse than what Great White had to offer.

Zorro clutched Hoku's ear. Hoku glanced over and saw Great White zoom toward the hidden net of fish. *Barnacles,* that shark was fast! Hoku returned to the glowfield and sawed tendrils with frantic purpose.

"Zorro, is Great White still eating the fish?"

The water around him glowed red. *No.* He swallowed thickly. *Next time, hide the fish deeper in the rocks,* he told himself.

"Zorro, is Great White headed this way?"

Green.

Hoku spun slowly, trying not to kick his feet or move his arms more than necessary. If Great White hadn't seen him yet, then —

Oh, Great White had seen him. Great White was, in fact, swimming right for him.

Hoku looked down at the spear in his hand. Kampii hunters used weapons just like it to kill sharks. It felt heavy and useless, and not nearly big enough. If only he had —

A bigger weapon.

Of course! That's exactly what he needed, and he knew just where to get it.

"Zorro, trust me," he whispered. The raccoon's eyes glowed green. Hoku knew he was programmed to say yes to things like that, but it made him feel better all the same.

Great White cut through the water, fast as a bird diving through the sky.

"Not yet," Hoku muttered.

He stared at the meat hanging from Great White's teeth. He stared at its widening maw. And when the shark rolled to its side to better snap him in half with its hideously powerful jaws, Hoku dodged.

Great White might have been fast and sleek, but it was also heavy. The shark started to change its angle to follow him, but its body carried it forward. Not far, because Great White was an agile monstrosity, but far enough.

Enough to carry it into the glowfield of paralyzing jellies.

The shark jerked, and for a horrible flash, Hoku thought Great White might be immune to the jellies' power. He bolted backward, windmilling his arms and kicking his legs, and hitting himself in the shin with the spear still stupidly clutched in his hand.

Great White thrashed its tail and bashed its head

against the jellies, trying to break free. The jellies only stung it again, over and over. Eventually, the shark's struggling slowed and stopped, until the massive beast hung still.

Sharks never stopped moving. Never, ever. And here was the biggest shark Hoku had ever seen practically frozen in place. He could only imagine how surprised Great White itself must be.

For a moment, Hoku thought about killing it. The shark could be stuck there for weeks or months before the jellies managed to absorb enough of its flesh to end its life. Great White would starve to death first, and that was certainly not a pleasant way to go.

But the shark was Karl Strand's creature. Strand might not know if it was stuck in the glowfield, but he probably had some way of knowing when it died, so he could send another. Letting the shark live might give Hoku more time inside Seahorse Alpha.

And besides, he had no idea how to actually kill the shark and not paralyze himself in the process. Imagine how stupid he'd feel if he defeated the creature and then killed himself by accident afterward.

"Come on, let's go to the other side," he said, eager to leave Great White's quivering bulk behind him. "Zorro, warn me if you see more sharks." They'd only faced one the last time they were here, but they hadn't stayed long enough to see if there were more. He didn't want any surprises.

Hoku found a weaker section of the glowfield where the jellies had grown slightly apart from one another, and he set to work. After an hour, his arms burning and his stomach begging for food, he'd carved a hole big enough to swim through.

After all these months, he'd finally made it to Seahorse Alpha.

If Zorro hadn't figured out the air-lock mechanism, Hoku might still be treading water in the tiny entrance room he'd discovered. The little guy had found an access panel and plugged in his tail. Within seconds, the room started draining and the pressure dropped slowly to Above World levels.

"Good thing I still have legs," Hoku said. "I don't think this place was built for tails."

When the last of the ocean had churned through the floor, a buzzer sounded and the light over the door turned from red to green. Hoku threw all his weight on the door's handle and it swung open with a long sigh.

Chunky desks ringed the circular room, each with a battered video screen mounted to the curved wall above it. Pictures, faded and wrinkled, clung to most surfaces like barnacles, too stubborn to let go. A drinking vessel sat on one desk, a bright-red spot amid the stark white of the floor and ceiling and chairs.

Hoku walked slowly around the room's circumference. His fingertips traced the edge of a decaying wooden frame holding the picture of a young woman with sun-bright hair. The inside of the red drinking vessel was stained brown with the memory of some dark liquid. Hoku picked it up and sniffed, but smelled only the same stale air that permeated the rest of the room. He threaded his fingers through the handle and lifted it to his mouth, as if he were taking a sip.

People had lived and worked here. Not phantoms, not faceless ancients, but real people just like him.

He righted a fallen chair and sat at a desk by the room's lone window. Had Sarah Jennings sat here? Or her assistant, the one she'd trusted with the water safe? Grandma Nani said he'd been Hoku's ancestor. Hoku wiped the dust and dirt from the desk's surface. It smeared across his palm and forearm in dark streaks. Had his ancestor done the same thing hundreds of years ago before he sat down and got to work?

Work. He was here to do that, too. His ancestor had helped build the first Kampii colony. Now, across the centuries, Hoku needed to save it.

"Zorro, look for an interface," he said. The raccoon's eyes glowed green. He hopped onto a desk and began to sniff for a place to plug in his tail.

Hoku stood and searched the room for anything that looked like it might be connected to the main computer system. When he found buttons, he pressed them. When he found switches, he flipped them back and forth until their lights blinked. He found the power switch under one large monitor, but when the screens lit up, he was surprised: instead of one big image, there were dozens and dozens of tiny ones. They each had a label displayed in blurry type, and he instantly recognized several of them:

SKYFEATHER'S LANDING
TALON'S PEAK
COILED DEEP
EQUIAN SETTLEMENT #1: MIRAGE

He even saw screens for Silverfin and Nautilus, two distant Kampii colonies he'd only heard of once before. Most of the screens were dark, but a few flickered with life: the inside of the communications room at Coiled Deep, and the back of an Equian's head in Mirage.

And then, on the monitor labeled EQUIAN SETTLEMENT #6, a familiar face zoomed in so close that Hoku could count its shaggy nose hairs.

"Took you long enough," Rollin said with a grunt. "Now, what are we working on today?"

CHAPTER 19

ALUNA SWAM TOWARD Daphine's surface colony, but when she neared the shallows of the reef, she stopped. Sharks filled the water. Before, they'd been milling around, lazily looking for easy meals. Now the ocean roiled with fins and sleek gray bodies and the flash of jagged teeth.

A feeding frenzy.

Not all the sharks were big, but many were vicious, trying to get a piece of whatever had died—and willing to kill in the process. To them, Aluna's beautiful Kampii tail looked like food.

She circled around the frenzy, keeping her short, sturdy spear tight against her body to minimize its drag in the water. The knife strapped to her waist had been freshly sharpened, and a harpoon—liberated from the training dome in the City of Shifting Tides—dangled from a bandolier across her back, along with a canister of bolts and hooks.

"This is Aluna," she called. "Can anyone hear me?"

Her brother Anadar's voice answered immediately. "Aluna! Get out of the water! We're trying to kill the most vicious ones, but it's only drawing more into the mix."

She surfaced to get a better view. Most of the Kampii lay clustered together on the reef like a pile of terrified seals. Unfortunately, the water covering the reef was still half a meter deep, giving most of the sharks plenty of room to navigate. Even Great White could leap onto the reef to grab a Kampii morsel, then wiggle its way back into the depths.

Anadar had arranged the colony's few warriors—and anyone strong enough to wield a weapon—in a circle around the rest of the Kampii. They seemed to be doing a good job keeping the sharks away, but blood stained the water around them and the current wasn't carrying it away. The sharks would keep coming, long after Anadar's warriors grew tired.

She couldn't see her brother well from this distance, but she recognized the way he held his weapons and the way he moved. He'd trained her, after all. Her own style owed as much to him as it did to High Senator Electra and the cappo'ra fighters in Coiled Deep.

The warriors couldn't hold out forever, so the sharks needed to stop attacking. They needed another target. Something to distract them long enough for the Kampii to escape. Aluna dove underwater. The sharks on the outskirts of the action were slower, older, weaker, or just opportunists waiting for leftovers. Well, she could capitalize on an opportunity when she saw one, too.

A lazy dark-gray shark drifted by her tail. It wasn't a big animal, not much of a threat to her, which made it a perfect choice. She spun, just like in the dolphin form she used to practice with Anadar, and stabbed it in the gills with her spear. She pulled the weapon out quickly, before the animal could jerk and rip it out of her hands.

Blood puffed up from the wound. Almost instantly, the other sharks smelled it. When they arrived, Aluna was ready. She got another one in the gills, then missed her mark on the third and watched her spear tip slide across the shark's flank, digging a shallow groove. The shark came for her. She unsheathed her knife with her left hand and punched at the animal's face. Her blade caught it in the nose. The shark twisted away in surprise.

Oh, she had their attention now. More and more sharks came, called by the blood. The first few sharks she had wounded were now fighting for their lives or trying to escape.

While she was aiming for another, a shark rammed into her from behind and scraped its tough body along her side. She sheathed her knife with fumbling hands and grabbed her ribs. The sudden pain made her nauseous.

But her sealskin shirt had stopped the shark from reaching her skin. She still wasn't bleeding, and that's all that mattered.

Aluna straightened her tail, turning her body into an arrow, and sank down through the water, quiet as a crab. Above her, blood billowed in the waves. More sharks came, leaving the surface colony for fresher, easier-to-catch prey.

She swam slowly in a wide arc around the new frenzy. She touched her side and winced. Kampii healed fast, but broken ribs still took time. *Please don't be broken.*

When she got close to the reef colony, she called out. Anadar and Daphine came to help her the rest of the way. She let them take her arms and tried to smile.

"You are so foolish," Anadar said. "What were you thinking?" His brown eyes seemed so familiar, and so strange, as if a lifetime had passed since the last time Aluna had seen him.

"She was trying to save our fins," Daphine said. "And she succeeded, at least for a little while."

Aluna relaxed and let them pull her through the water.

"Where'd you learn to fight like that?" Anadar asked. "Must have had a good teacher."

Aluna grinned. "Wish he'd spent more time teaching me how to actually fight things than making me do silly forms and exercises over and over again."

Anadar's face grew serious. She should have known not to insult his lessons. But when his words came, they were soft and kind. "Anyone who sees you fight will think I'm the best teacher in the world."

Aluna closed her eyes and leaned into Anadar. She felt tears forming, but she didn't know why. Her ribs hurt, true, but this pain felt deeper, confusing, unexplainable.

"We haven't got long before the sharks find us again," Daphine said. "I'm going to take everyone to the beach. We'll be easy prey for the land animals, but we're not faring much better out here. And the sooner our people learn to drag themselves on land, the better."

"No," Aluna said, opening her eyes. "I've got another idea. The people at the surface colony aren't the only ones that need help." She paused. "So do the Deepfell."

Aluna swam beside Daphine just under the water's surface, her ribs wrapped tightly in seal-hide strips. Behind them, the Kampii without breathing shells swam as best they could, surfacing like dolphins every few minutes for more air.

Hopefully the Deepfell would agree to an alliance, and Aluna wasn't leading them all to their deaths. If Prince Eekikee was alive, she'd have a chance. The Deepfell's hidden, air-filled cave would be the perfect place for the Kampii from the surface colony to stay until they found a more permanent home. It'd be cramped with all the Deepfell wounded, but safe.

"This is the first time we've swum together since you got your tail," Daphine said. "I used to dream about this day when you were young. Raising our three brothers . . . well, let's just say that I was thrilled when you came along. My own dear little sister."

Aluna was shocked into silence. As stupid as it was, she'd never thought about how hard Daphine's life had been, or wondered what her sister dreamed of. Aluna's life had centered entirely on her own problems with their father, her own feelings of inadequacy, her own far-flung wishes.

Daphine seemed happy to continue. "We never got

to talk about regular things. I always imagined you'd tell me about the boys or girls you were interested in. I don't suppose you've had a chance to meet anyone in the Above World? That boy with the dark hair . . . Dash. He's handsome. Of course, he's good with a sword, too, and that's probably more important to you."

Aluna felt her heart stop beating and then, far too slowly, start up again. "Dash . . . is a good friend. It's . . . good to have such a good friend."

"Direct hit!" Daphine said, laughing. "Maybe I'll make a decent big sister after all."

"Well, what about you?" Aluna grumbled. "Still fending off pods of slobbering Kampii? I remember when old Iokepa asked you to marry him and bear his children. Tides' teeth, he was older than our father!"

Daphine's smile quirked down at the corners. "My options have dwindled a bit. You might be surprised to learn that some Kampii aren't interested in women with a scope instead of an eye."

Aluna stopped swimming and stared at her sister.

Who was still, objectively, the most beautiful, smart, funny, and accomplished woman in the entire City of Shifting Tides.

"Then those Kampii are idiots, and you're better off without them," Aluna said coldly. "All the Upgraders have tech, and they don't seem to have any trouble finding one another attractive."

Daphine sighed. "Maybe I'll lure one of the Upgraders down here, then, just like in the old stories."

"Make sure he's waterproof," Aluna said. "Rust isn't good for relationships."

Daphine laughed again, a sound that always made Aluna's heart soar. She had successfully made her sister laugh *and* avoided answering any questions about Dash. She was turning out to be a pretty good little sister, too.

"What does your scope *do,* anyway?" Aluna asked. "It can't just be for looks."

Daphine's scope whirred. "That's what I tell people," she said. Her mouth twisted mischievously. "But, oh, Aluna, the things I see now!" Daphine swept her gaze up, down, and around. "The temperature of the water, of the fish, of you. There are twenty-six bluefins in that school over there, and I didn't have to count. I can see all the different colors of sunlight. I can see how fast your heart is beating and when it speeds up and slows down. I can tell when people are lying."

Aluna sputtered. "When they're lying? You're joking."

"No, I'm not," Daphine said smugly. "I didn't know how to do most of this at first. I kept the scope to teach the Elders a lesson, and as a reminder to our father that we can't stay hidden. But now I'm keeping it because I love it."

"That skill must make the Elders very nervous," Aluna said.

"And that's why they don't know—"

Daphine stopped suddenly, but her scope continued to twist and focus. She whispered, "Over there, in the kelp. A Deepfell."

Aluna followed Daphine's gaze and saw a slick gray form shadowed in the dark fronds. It was definitely one of Eekikee's shark people.

"Deepfell!" she called. "Your people are in grave danger. I am Aluna, an ally of Prince Eekikee's. We need to speak with him at once."

Nothing happened for several long moments. Aluna's tail twitched. Was the Deepfell still out there? Did it even understand what she was asking?

"His heart is beating fast," Daphine said. "He's not sure what to do."

Then, slick as an eel, the Deepfell emerged from the kelp. Its smooth, hairless head and wide black eyes no longer seemed strange to Aluna, not after everything she'd seen in the Above World.

The Deepfell spoke carefully around its mouth full of sharp teeth.

"Ffffoooollow."

CHAPTER 20

ALUNA FELT A BOND with Prince Eekikee. When she'd first gone to the Above World, she'd found him on the beach, the lone survivor of an Upgrader attack on his people. He'd been suffocating, but her own breathing shell had saved his life. He'd saved hers not long after that by bringing her, Hoku, and Dash down to the cave when the Upgraders were chasing them.

Later, Aluna, Eekikee, and Daphine had all witnessed Fathom's cruelty. They each knew, on a large scale and on a very personal one, how horrible living in a world ruled by Karl Strand would be. Despite the history of fighting between their people, Fathom had forged them into allies.

They trusted each other, and now that trust was the only chance they had of saving both their people.

The scout Aluna and Daphine had met in the ocean had taken them directly to Eekikee. The prince had accepted Aluna's warning about the Kampii attack without question and ordered his Deepfell to bring the Kampii waiting at the water's surface down to the safety of the cave.

Now Aluna sat on the sand and waited for a Deepfell scout to lead her brothers' hunting party into their trap. Daphine fidgeted on her right, and Eekikee sat motionless on her left. The Deepfell prince wore a thin circlet of gold around his bald gray head, the only thing besides the scar on his throat that marked him as any different from the rest of his people.

Anadar had arranged his small band of surface-colony warriors in a semicircle behind their group. The warriors would be ready to act, but wouldn't be seen as an immediate threat. Aluna had wanted them in the water where they could move and fight more freely, but Anadar overruled her. Without breathing necklaces, Kampii from the surface colony could be drowned too easily. Behind the row of hunters, the remaining Kampii from the surface colony spoke quietly with their new Deepfell hosts.

"It's been too long," Aluna said. "Maybe they caught the scout."

"Akkaia is best," Prince Eekikee said. "We waaait."

Daphine's scope whirred as she focused on the water. Aluna wondered what hidden mysteries her sister could see that were invisible to the rest of them.

Eventually, Deepfell brought large shells filled with dead fish, and they ate. Aluna did her best to answer Prince Eekikee's questions about Scorch and Strand's army, and she was pleased to see her brother Anadar starting to relax slightly in the Deepfell's presence. She didn't need Anadar to like Eekikee, but it helped. After seeing what the Equians and the Serpenti had done to each other in the desert, she was even more determined to build this alliance. Beginning to see one's enemies as people, not demons, was the first step toward peace.

Aluna was about to regale everyone with a highly dramatized retelling of her humiliating defeat by Scorch during the Thunder Trials when distant words buzzed in her ears, then fell silent. Every Kampii in the cave looked up at once.

"They're close," Daphine said. "Everyone back to your positions!"

Aluna dropped the fish head she'd been about to crunch and dragged herself back to the water's edge. She checked her wrist sheaths and found her talon weapons, Spirit and Spite, ready for action. She hadn't been wearing them since she returned to the ocean—trying to spin them underwater would be futile—and she hoped she had no cause to unleash them now. Without Vachir to grant her height, she'd probably hook one of them around her own neck instead of her opponent's.

"Daphine will do the talking," Aluna said. "They'll listen to her. Everyone does."

Daphine rolled her one eye and rewarded Aluna with a grim smile. "If that were true, we wouldn't be here right now."

"Quit bickering," Anadar called from his place by the warriors. "Don't make me get our father."

There it was again, the warmth that started in Aluna's gut and radiated outward, like the sun. She was about to toss a retort back at her brother when her ears erupted with chatter. "There, behind that rock!" "No, the kelp—I saw it hide in the kelp!" "It's headed for that tunnel!"

The Kampii in the cave fell silent. The Deepfell picked up on the change and followed their example.

This waiting was even harder than before. Seconds felt like hours. Aluna studied the waves. Her breathing shell pulsed at her neck, its glow reflected in the rippling cave pool.

And then the Deepfell scout shot out of the water with a gasp and landed hard on the sand, her gills puffing frantically. Aluna and Eekikee grabbed her arms and pulled her up the shore until she was safely behind them.

A moment later, Aluna's brother Ehu's familiar face broke the surface. His eyes widened and he brought his spear forward in a flash. "Stop," he called to his hunting party. "It's a trap!"

"You're safe. No one will attack," Daphine said quickly. "You know me. I'm your sister, but I'm also the Voice of the Coral Kampii. Please come here so we can talk."

Pilipo's head popped out of the water, but neither he nor Ehu came any closer to the shore.

"You're working with them, Daphine? And Anadar and Aluna?" Pilipo said. "What treachery is this?"

"We're allies," Daphine said. "Prince Eekikee and his people have granted Kampii without breathing necklaces sanctuary in this cave. In return, the Kampii will not hunt his people."

Pilipo and Ehu bobbed in the water. Aluna saw at least two dozen more hunters waiting just beneath the waves. She tried to still her body, despite how badly it wanted to prepare itself for battle. A clenched fist, a subtle shifting into an aggressive stance . . . Her brothers would notice these tiny changes and make changes of their own. Before long, the whole encounter might escalate to heated words and the first ill-advised throw of a spear.

Pilipo and Ehu murmured to each other, so low that their voices didn't carry to Aluna's special Kampii ears.

Daphine, who was no stranger to tense negotiations and who was no doubt using her scope to read their moods, kept talking. "We, the people of the surface colony, do not want breathing devices at this cost, brothers. The Deepfell are people, not animals, and deserve to be treated as such. To slaughter them for parts . . . would make us no better than the Humans who originally brought destruction to our world."

"Come into the water and we'll talk," Pilipo said. "Just you, Daphine, and the gray demon."

Daphine looked at Aluna. Aluna felt her heart break just a little to know that she still wasn't important in her brothers' eyes. But she nodded anyway. This meeting was too important to let her pride interfere.

"Fine," Daphine said to Pilipo, Ehu, and the rest of the Kampii hunters. "We agree to—"

"Nooo," Prince Eekikee said.

Aluna looked at him, aghast. He hadn't changed his stance, and his smooth gray face and bulbous black eyes remained calm. What was he doing?

Eekikee pointed a webbed hand at Aluna. "Aluuuuna, too," he said. "Or no taaalk."

Aluna felt her mouth drop open. "It's okay," she said to Eekikee. "They're my brothers. They still think of me as a youngling."

"It's not okay," Daphine said. She nodded to Eekikee. "Thank you for showing me that. You heard Prince Eekikee," she called to Pilipo and Ehu. "Aluna comes, too, or you can turn around and leave now, before anyone gets hurt."

Aluna shook her head. Even after all these years, Daphine still managed to surprise her.

Pilipo waved his hand. "If you feel some strange need to bring Aluna, then fine. It makes no difference to us."

"We'll meet you halfway," Daphine said. "Your hunters will stay back, and so will ours."

"This is ridiculous," Ehu said. "All the hunters are Kampii! If we fought together we could make easy work of these beasts and Peleke would have all the breathing—Oof!"

Pilipo had punched him in the stomach. Aluna just wished he'd done it sooner. How the same parents had spawned both Ehu and Daphine would forever be a mystery to her.

Daphine, Aluna, and Prince Eekikee dragged themselves to the water and eased back into its embrace. They swam slowly to the center of the watery portion of the cave to meet Pilipo and Ehu.

If Aluna couldn't convince her brothers to join their alliance, then the day might end in blood. Which side would Daphine and Anadar choose? No matter how strong their alliance with Eekikee was, they might choose family. Aluna wouldn't blame them if they did. This was a situation with no easy answers, no clear-cut right and wrong sides. Everyone was doing what they thought they needed to do in order to survive.

But if Aluna had learned anything during those long months in the desert with the Equians, it was that her word actually meant something. She could never harm her brothers or sister, but if she had to, she'd die defending the Deepfell.

CHAPTER 21

DASH WHISPERED TO VACHIR and she reared onto her back legs with a scream of fury. He swung his blade down, slicing a wild dog across its flank. The animal shook off the wound, spraying blood, and growled. Vachir twisted and dropped her front hooves on the creature, snapping its spine. A clean, merciful kill.

"Thank you, friend," Dash said, patting Vachir's neck. Sweat dripped from his face and soaked into his shirt. He called, "Who needs help?"

"Last one's mine," Odd shouted. Dash saw him grab a leaping beast out of the air and slam it to the ground. The creature yelped and lay still.

Dash calmed his breathing while he surveyed the field of battle. Mags was tending to Pocket. The boy had acquired a small bite when the pack of dogs first attacked. Squirrel seemed untouched, just as she remained after almost every fight. He needed to watch her more closely and learn from her. Fewer wounds would make him a better warrior. He had been spending far too much time under Mags's healing eye.

Odd grunted and wiped a hand down his tunic, smearing the splatters of red into ragged lines that only served to make his appearance more unwelcoming. Perhaps that was his goal. The rest of their kludge did not paint an intimidating picture. The dogs had expected an easy meal.

Dash counted five dead animals—two killed by his hand. The first had been a large beast the size of a newborn foal and the color of sunlit sand. They were refugees from the old Human cities, Mags had said. Not unlike their kludge.

Odd sauntered over, his breathing ragged, and clamped a bloody hand on Dash's shoulder. "Good work. We each got two."

"I try not to keep track," Dash lied. Death counts were bragging rights to Odd. But these dogs were not evil; they were merely fellow creatures trying to survive. To Dash, they were two more weights tied to his soul. Someday the memory of those he had killed would grow so heavy that they would drag him under the sand and out of the sun forever.

"Clean yourselves up," Odd told everyone. "We're moving on before every living thing in this wooded nightmare smells the gore and comes looking for trouble."

Dash nodded and got to work. He jumped from Vachir's back and began running his good hand—the one still made of flesh—over her sweaty back and legs, assessing her for damage. She stood quietly while he performed this routine, although he felt her muscles bunch and twitch under his palm. Vachir had all of Aluna's impatience, all of her wildness. Never had two souls been more perfectly matched.

He thought of Aluna and smiled. He would not have had to kill any dogs if she had been here, all flash and stormfire and ferocious skill. Vachir bent her neck and huffed in his face. He trailed a hand down her forelock and rested it on her nose. At least they could miss Aluna together.

"No injuries," he informed Vachir, and started on his sword. Leaves were plentiful here, in the outskirts of the forest. He used a large, unbroken one to wipe the blood and fur from his blade. Sharpening would have to wait until later, when the kludge had found a safer camp.

Squirrel watched him work. The girl had grown even quieter since Zeelo's death and had taken to wearing the old woman's sharp metal teeth on a chain around her neck. Squirrel was the only one who had not welcomed Dash back to camp after the Silvae had taken the others. She did not fully trust him, nor should she. He was lying to everyone.

As they trudged through the underbrush in the growing dark, Odd ambled over and walked next to Dash and Vachir, as he often did.

"You did good," Odd said by way of greeting. "Taught those pups a lesson."

Dash was frequently unsure of how to respond to such statements. He understood Odd's intent—to offer a compliment, to bond—but the sentiments were so unlike those Dash himself felt. He could not bring himself to partake, even though it would aid his cover. Perhaps silence would be seen as agreement, and they could both preserve honor.

Odd grunted. Dash had taken to cataloging the many meanings of the sound, as it seemed to change with its context. After dinner, such a guttural utterance might mean Odd was full. In the morning, the grunting usually accompanied the creaking of Odd's bones as he stood. During battle or when Odd was practicing with his sword, the noise meant effort fully engaged. Truly, a person such as Odd needed no actual words; his grunts were as meaningful as a language.

Tonight, the grunt meant that Odd wanted to say something, but had not yet determined how. And so Dash walked and waited and honored the silence between them.

Eventually, the kludge found a suitable clearing and made camp. Dash slapped a mosquito on his neck—perhaps the tenth that had bitten him in the last hour—and built the fire as he had begun doing every night. He enjoyed the simple gathering and arranging of the wood, the first tendrils of smoke, so hesitant as they swirled upward. He loved watching the fire gain confidence and begin to assert itself against the night.

And in his head, he imagined hearing the songs and hoofbeats of his people as the word-weavers took their turns calling to the sun.

Odd sat next to him as their food sizzled over the flames and clapped Dash on the back again. The maneuver was one of Odd's favorites.

"Take the twin swords," Odd said. "You said no last time, and I respect that. But you've been with us weeks now, even came back when you lost your friend and your pretty spoils. No member of this kludge doesn't get what they deserve."

Dash cringed. What he deserved was to be killed as a traitor.

"I don't even like the swords," Odd continued. "One's too cold, one's too hot. You have to clean them, keep the tech working, make sure you don't mix up the fuel they need. Bah!" He tossed a twig into the fire.

"Too much work for me, and no one else here knows the hilt from the . . . from whatever the pointy part is called."

The swords of fire and ice. Dash had seen them sheathed on Odd's hip during three fights now, and he wondered why the man had swung with his fists when two such weapons waited at his side, begging for their taste of battle.

Dash looked at the faces around the fire. Pocket was having a long, in-depth conversation with Squirrel, wherein the girl was not required to say anything for long stretches of time. Occasionally Mags tossed in a comment or a correction, a wise teacher letting her pupils learn for themselves.

These were decent people, and he was lying to them. To steal from them as well would compound his guilt past bearing.

"I am sorry," Dash said quietly, "but I cannot accept the honor."

"Sure you can!" Odd said. His bright-red hair had faded over the last few weeks and picked up a few leaves and twigs, but it still whipped around like a horse's tail when he talked.

The big man jostled himself closer to Dash and lowered his voice, an uncharacteristic and unsettling move. "You probably guessed this, but I'll never have runts of my own. Not meant for spawning, you see. Or for keeping things alive instead of making them dead. But you know what it's like, wanting to see a wee fleshy thing with your nose, and that rush of warmth knowing that someday it'll get your eyes, too."

No, Dash most definitely did *not* know what that was like.

"What I'm trying to say is, that it does me some good to see those in the kludge taken care of," Odd said. His voice had reached such a hush that Dash could barely make out his words. "Take the swords for me, if you can't see fit to take them for more reasonable reasons. Maybe your honor's got room for that."

Odd meant it. Dash could see it in his furrowed brow and in the slight twitching of his wide, flat nose.

Dash stood. One moment he was comfortable on the ground, his legs crossed, his tired body at ease, and the next he was up, stiff-necked and tense. The kludge fell silent. Even Pocket, who, before that moment, had not stopped talking even long enough to eat.

"I must tell you something," Dash said.

"You have words that need speaking, then get them out," Mags said. "We got no secrets here."

"Yes, we do," Dash said. "We do have secrets. *I* have secrets."

Mags's hand slid into her pocket of needles. "You're about to tell us you work for Strand, then you may want to rethink."

They were all tense now. Squirrel bouncing on her metal feet, already meters away from the fire, Pocket reaching for something hidden inside his leg. Only Odd had stayed where he was. Then again, Odd himself was a weapon.

But Dash could not continue like this. Not when Odd was treating him . . . acting like Dash was his . . .

No. The lies had to stop. By the sun's light, he would not lead good people unknowingly to their deaths, no matter how honorable his cause. Not even for Aluna. He only hoped that if he ever saw her again, she would understand and forgive him.

"I am not an Upgrader, and I do not work for Karl Strand," Dash said quietly. "I have come here to stop him and to end the war before it begins."

CHAPTER 22

THE SCENE AROUND THE FIRE might have been a brush painting on the side of a tent, everyone still and unmoving, forever poised on the edge of action.

Dash knew exactly where Vachir stood, had calculated how many steps he would need to take in order to vault onto her back and flee from this place. He would not fight the kludge. He would not inflict any more harm upon them, emotional or physical. He would escape or he would die.

Mags was the first to speak, her voice slow and careful. "Well, now. This is interesting. Us taking you to Karl Strand, not knowing you intend to betray him. Wouldn't look good for us, you putting him in chains while we stand by, dumb as anything."

"You would likely be killed as traitors," Dash said. Truth felt like sunlight, making his words light and easy. After so many weeks of trying to hide, he had no desire to return to the darkness. "Your association with me would condemn you instantly."

"You were planning to let us die!" Pocket said.

"No," Dash answered quickly. "I do not want you to die. I do not wish you any harm at all. But I will not let Karl Strand rule our world. Not while I still breathe."

Odd grunted. This one did not sound good. "Best sit down, boy, and start at the start."

Vachir sauntered up behind him, offering silent support. Dash reached back and patted her neck, then lowered himself down to his spot by the fire. "First, I must tell you that I am not an Upgrader. I am an Equian of two herds, Shining Moon and the newly born Flame Heart."

"An Equian!" Pocket said. "But you're not a horse. You don't even have a tail!"

Mags shushed him. "What we look like isn't all that we are. You should know that by now, Pocket, or we've done a broken job of teaching you."

Pocket stared at his hands in his lap.

"Here is what I am," Dash said. "A person with the heart of a horse, the blood of the desert, and a desire not to see the world I love fall into the hands of the twisted man trying to control it."

Dash did as Odd suggested and started at the beginning — even before his own part of the story, when he met Aluna and Hoku. He began with Karl Strand and Sarah Jennings being in love hundreds of years ago and losing their only child, a boy named Tomias, to a terrible sickness. He told them how Strand became obsessed with living forever and somehow found a way to survive centuries.

He chose his words carefully and spoke slowly, watching their reactions. Mags narrowed her eyes, Squirrel crept carefully back toward the fire in order to hear. Pocket seemed rapt, his jaw slack, his knees tight against his chest.

Dash told them about Aluna and Hoku and Calli, about HydroTek and Mirage and the Thunder Trials. He kept his voice even and soft, unaggressive, even when he got to the part where they donned disguises and decided to infiltrate Odd's kludge.

"I knew it!" Pocket exclaimed. "I knew they weren't really prisoners! The one with the tail fought good as Odd, only she pretended she couldn't."

Odd raised an eyebrow. "And what manner of magic made you keep your tongue, boy?"

"Hawk — I mean, Hoku — was so nice," Pocket

said. "I didn't see what it hurt, helping keep his secret."

"Stupid child," Mags said. "A nest of vipers slithers into camp, and you want to pet them and feed them treats!"

"No, no, it wasn't like that," Pocket said miserably.

"Do not blame the boy," Dash said. "No one can resist Hoku."

"I could resist him," Squirrel grumbled. It was the first thing the girl had said all evening, and she fingered the sharp teeth hanging from her neck while she said it.

Dash smiled. "We do not all have your strength." He had wanted to call her *friend,* but stopped himself; he did not deserve that honor. And now, he had only one truth remaining until he was free of lies.

"The Upgrader kludge who came through the forest before us . . . they held two of my family as prisoners," Dash said. "Although I wish to stop Karl Strand, you should know that my immediate goals are selfish. I want, more than anything, to save my fathers."

A heavy silence descended on the kludge. Night had come with its blanket of darkness, and the flames of the fire had shrunk to wisps. Dash had stopped worrying about being attacked—none of their body signals indicated that an attack was imminent. But he expected and perhaps even desired exile. He knew what it felt like, and it seemed an appropriate punishment for his crimes.

"You lied to us," Odd said quietly.

Dash hung his head. "Yes."

"You said you weren't an Upgrader," Odd said.

"I am not," Dash agreed.

"You know what *kludge* means?" Odd asked. "You know what it means to us?"

Dash considered his response. "A *kludge* is your herd."

"It's our family," Mags said. "Made up of bits and pieces, just like we are. An ugly mess most times, but stronger together than we are apart."

"Don't always work well, just like our tech," Odd said. "Aren't always the best mix, the shiniest people, but we come together and we do what we can to survive."

"Like you," Pocket said softly. "You've got a metal arm and no horse legs and friends with wings."

"Flame Heart herd," Dash said, his thoughts swirling through his head faster than he could make sense of them. "Flame Heart has Equians and Aviars and Kampii and Serpenti. It has me and Vachir."

"Sounds like a kludge to me," Odd said. "Not always pretty, these people and things we pull together"—he tapped his goggled eyes—"but somehow we work."

"You've fought with us and for us," Mags said. "You got your reasons, same as the rest of us, but it's your actions we judge you on."

Odd's heavy hand descended on Dash's shoulder. Dash welcomed both its weight and its meaning. Odd said, "We're part of your kludge now, too, and you're part of ours. No ceremonies, no songs. Don't care who your parents were or who did your raising. Don't care what blood chugs through your body or which parts are made of machine. Not what we're about."

Dash found himself trembling under the gaze of the people around the fire. The people who should be hating him and planning his punishment, but who were, instead, welcoming him closer. Telling him he belonged.

"Family's a good reason to go after Karl Strand," Mags said. "No higher cause for fighting than that."

He didn't trust his voice, not right now, but he spoke anyway. "Will you help, then? Even after everything I have done, will you take me to the army so I can find Strand?"

"I'll do what I can to help you," Odd said. "Can't speak for the others, but that's me. That's what I'm going to do."

"I'm going, too," Pocket said. "I want to rescue Dash's family."

"Squirrel?" Mags asked. "I won't abandon you if

this isn't your wish. You decide what you want, and I'll go with you. We'll meet up with the others when they're done doing what they have to do."

Squirrel's mouth pressed thin. "Kludge stays together," she said. Then her face brightened in the firelight. "At least now I know why Dash smells so funny."

Dash once again found himself stunned. "I can never thank you enough. For myself and for my fathers, and for Aluna, Hoku, and Calli, too. I am truly humbled by you all."

"Thanks. Bah!" Odd said. "Not how we work." He grunted and pushed himself to his feet with great effort. "Now, you stay there and build up that fire. I'm going to get your new swords."

CHAPTER 23

*C*ALLI BEAT HER WINGS against the wind. The air was already cold and thin—she should have found another layer to wear over her shirt, or something to wrap around her legs—but she had to keep climbing. Strand's army had Skyfeather's Landing surrounded. The ground crawled with warriors, their weapons and tech gleaming. Rhinebras and huge, armored insects pulled carts burdened with weapons. Higher up, mechanical dragonfliers swooped and swarmed around the mountainside looking for Aviars trying to escape.

But they weren't looking for a lone Aviar trying to find her way *in*. A few hundred Upgraders weren't nearly enough to keep Calli from seeing her mother.

She tried to remember her mother going off on one of her angry tirades, or embarrassing Calli in front of the senators, or lecturing her yet again on responsibilities of leadership. Instead, Calli could only remember her mother's face the last time she'd seen her . . . when Calli had asked to leave home and join Aluna and Hoku on their quest. Her mother's eyes had been filled, maybe for the first time, with pride for her only daughter. *Pride.*

Calli blinked and headed into another cloud. When she was young, her teachers recited an ancient legend about a Human whose father built him wings of feathers and wax. The Human flew so high that the sun melted the wax and he fell to his death.

It was a silly story, because that's not at all what would happen. Everybody knew it wasn't the sun you had to worry about—it was the ice.

Like most Aviars, Calli played Icewing when she was young. They waited until none of the adults were watching, then everyone flew up, up, up as far and as fast as they could. The person who made it the highest won.

The real trick was knowing when to turn back. If you let too much ice form on your wings, they grew heavy and stopped working. Then you found yourself plummeting down toward the mountain, frantically shaking the frozen water from your wings and begging the wind to catch you and slow your descent.

But after that, you always knew how high you could go.

Calli had never won Icewing. She'd never even come in second or third. There were always stronger girls playing, or braver ones. Girls like Aluna. Calli had never seen the point in taking the risk when she had no chance of winning. She'd even told herself she was just being responsible. Smart. Maybe, deep down, she even thought she was smarter than all those girls who tried and failed.

Calli laughed through a shiver and rubbed her arms. But she'd been the stupid one after all. She'd been trapped inside the limits she'd set for herself. She'd built a cage and then dutifully stayed inside it. Unlike her friends, she had no idea how high she could go.

When she reached a good altitude, high enough to be safe from Strand's army, she drifted, counting troops and beasts and whatever else she thought her mother and the other tacticians might find useful. Was that a catapult or a trebuchet? Why were certain groups clustered together, while others were spread out? If only she'd paid attention in her warfare classes instead of doodling equations in the margins of her books.

The Upgraders had the mountain surrounded; that much was clear. But where were the platoons of Aviars fighting back? Where were the countermeasures? The army swarmed in far larger numbers than Calli had anticipated, but her mother was not one to play a defensive game.

Calli felt the pit of worry in her stomach grow two sizes bigger. She circled again, identifying a few Upgraders who were clearly commanding forces and some structures that were either strategy tents or medical buildings. Either way, they'd probably make good targets.

Her stomach clenched again. She couldn't help but think of Pocket and Squirrel from Odd's kludge. Everything had been easier when she'd hated the Upgraders without reservation. Knowing that there were real people on the other side—some *nice* people, even—made the prospect of war almost too horrible to contemplate.

She soared, letting the wind lift her up and over the scooped-out basin of Skyfeather's Landing. The Palace of Wings jutted up from the middle of the city, a lone, defiant spire, and Calli's chest puffed proudly. Even under siege, her home was beautiful.

The Aviars, though . . . they were everywhere, scattered like feathers in the wind. Calli sensed no pattern to their movement, no plan behind their defense. They fought in small clusters and rushed toward the areas of most need. It looked like triage, not strategy. Where were the senators? They should have been commanding their forces, directing the flow of battle, not just reacting to it.

A thought pierced Calli's mind: if her mother was alive, she would never allow this to be happening. Her mother—and maybe High Senator Electra—could be dead.

Calli began her descent, forcing herself to spiral slowly instead of diving, despite the painful racing of her heart. Her body needed time to adjust to the changes in oxygen levels in the air, and she needed to keep an eye out for enemy scouts. Five more minutes of drifting wouldn't make any difference.

Yet . . . she couldn't keep the logic in her head. It kept slipping away every time she thought of her mother's face. Her mother could be dead, and here she was, being overly cautious again. Would Aluna take her time if Hoku were in danger?

Calli pulled her wings in close and let herself fall.

The sky streamed by, a smear of clouds and a howl of wind. Skyfeather's Landing grew from a tiny, toy-size abstraction to a larger-than-life city filled with panic and feathers and hoarse battle cries. A few Aviars called out to her, "The nest grows warm at your return!" Calli gave the traditional response without even thinking: "And warm grows my heart!"

Home. She was home.

She opened her wings and gasped as they caught the air, her body suddenly torn about which way it wanted to go. Her descent slowed and she regained control of her direction. By the time she reached the base of the palace, her speed was perfect, her landing requiring only the slightest bend of her knees.

If her mother was still alive, this is where she'd be: in the war room at the bottom level of the palace. Previous presidents used the war room at the top of the spire, since the vantage was good for strategy and it put them in the center of Skyfeather's Landing. But the Aviar's previous leaders all had two wings, not one. Instead of accommodating tradition, her mother had simply bent it to her will.

There was only one guard outside the palace entrance, a girl not much older than Calli with dark skin and fierce wings painted green at the tips. The girl nodded. "Warm at your return, Vice President Calliope."

The words startled her. Calli hadn't been called that in months . . . or was it years? It felt like forever. As quickly as she could, Calli relaxed her face and nodded in return. "My thanks for your service, Senator."

Those words, too, felt strange. Since when had being around Aviars become something alien to her?

She entered the darkened hallway and paused as her eyes adjusted. Mosaics and frescoes covered the walls in bright colors. Most depicted the Aviars' greatest battles, since artists seemed to be in love with sprays of blood and pointy spears, but there were a few honoring achievements in science. They'd always been Calli's favorites.

She paused by the faded figure of Architect Stephanie, a young woman with a bright grin and brown hair that curled around her face. She'd been the first to harness waterfalls for their power. Not only had her discovery given the Aviars the means to free themselves from SkyTek, it had brought untold beauty to the city. The largest waterfall in Skyfeather's Landing was named Steph's Smile, after her. It was the sort of legacy that Calli had one day hoped to create for herself.

She walked quickly down the corridor and tried to wrap herself in resolve. When she'd convinced her mother to let her go off with Aluna and Hoku, she'd been worried that she might die far from home. It had never occurred to her that her mother would be the one who . . .

Calli ran, her wings bouncing uselessly against her

back, and muttered prayers to the sky and the sun and the waves and anything else she could think of. She shifted through the palace's halls, not even thinking about direction, just letting her feet carry her along the path she followed hundreds of times as a child.

She burst into the war room to find it stuffy and stale, packed with dank wings and women hunched over battle maps. "My mother," Calli said. "Where is she?"

The Aviars looked up, startled, as if she'd woken them from a collective dream. She recognized some of the senators, but saw none of her mother's closest advisers except Senator Niobe.

Niobe rushed forward as if she were going to hug Calli, but stopped herself. She stood a meter away, respectful, and adopted a formal tone. "Vice President Calliope, you're safe! We've all been so worried."

"My mother," Calli repeated. "Is she alive?"

Niobe frowned. "Yes."

Calli breathed deep, surprised to find tears suddenly pooling in her eyes.

"She lives, but . . ." Niobe's composure broke and she reached out to touch Calli's arm. "We don't know for how long."

Calli didn't trust herself to speak. She couldn't break down here, in front of her mother's warriors.

It would make them both look weak. She wiped the unspent tears from her eyes and straightened her shoulders.

"Where is High Senator Electra?" Calli asked. "I have to talk to her right away." Her voice threatened to crumble, but held.

"Of course. She's with your mother in her chambers," Niobe said. Calli started to walk toward the back of the room, but Niobe gripped her arm and whispered, "Electra . . . she's not herself. We're trying to give her time, but we can't give her any more. We've probably waited too long as it is. I'm doing what I can, but I don't have a head for this." Niobe released Calli's arm and put her palm against her forehead. "So many dead, Calli. I was never meant to lead. I never wanted this."

Calli pulled Niobe's hand away from her face. "I know, Niobe. You're doing what you have to do. It's not your fault."

If she said anything more, Niobe would crack. She could see that in the way the woman's eyes grew large and wild, the way her pupils darted left and right, the way her hands shook. She knew exactly how Niobe felt.

Calli took a step back and lifted her chin. "Thank you, Senator," she said briskly, and loud enough for the whole room to hear. "You may return to your duties."

Her tone seemed to shock Niobe out of the panic

she'd been succumbing to. The Aviar rustled her wings into place behind her back and stiffened her spine. She said, "Yes, Vice President," her voice crisp, precise. Calli knew Niobe would be able to hold herself together a little longer.

While Niobe rejoined the other Aviars, Calli marched across the room toward her mother's chambers. She paused only a moment outside the door before sucking in a huge breath and plunging inside.

CHAPTER 24

Her MOTHER'S ROOM STANK of sweat and medicine. Calli put a hand over her nose and mouth but it did little to temper the stench. Heavy cloth had been hung over the tall windows, casting the large suite in darkness.

"Get out," a shadow by the bed snarled.

Calli squinted. "Electra? Is that you?"

The shadow paused. "Calliope?"

She nodded, which was a stupid thing to do in the darkness, but she wasn't exactly thinking properly and her eyes were already threatening to fill up with even more stupid tears. "Is my mom . . ."

Electra slumped. "Iolanthe—your mother—is alive, but not awake. She hasn't opened her eyes for days, and she hasn't spoken in almost two weeks."

Calli walked slowly toward the bed, stepping over discarded bandages and soiled clothes. The room felt thick with futility. Her mother seemed impossibly small in the huge bed, her body curled into one corner, her remaining wing hanging out of the covers and lying slumped on the floor. She could just make out her mother's features pressed into her pillow: her small nose, thin lips, scarred cheek. Her mother's hair, normally spiked and fierce, lay matted and defeated against her head.

"What happened?" she asked quietly.

"Infection," Electra said. "The Upgraders sent someone to talk under a flag of truce. I wanted to send him back in pieces, but your mother . . . but Iolanthe wanted to hear what he had to say."

"He attacked her?" Calli asked. She touched the scar across her own ribs where Weaver Sokhor's men had stabbed her. "With poison?"

Electra slammed her fist into the wall and Calli jumped. Electra's knuckles came away bloody, but the woman only dropped her hand as if nothing had happened. "No poison, just a dirty blade."

"Where is he?" Calli said. "I want to talk to him. Maybe I can figure out where—"

"He's dead," Electra said. Her tone told Calli everything she needed to know about the man's death: that it had been immediate, and that it had been at Electra's hands.

Calli sat on the edge of the bed and stroked her mother's hair. It was thick with sweat and grime. "Where are the healers—the medics? They should be in here cleaning the room." *And cleaning my mother.*

"Useless," Electra said. "I sent them away. I sent them all away."

"Niobe needs help," Calli said. "The battle—it isn't going well."

Electra leaned over the bed and tucked the blanket under Iolanthe's chin. "She needs me. I'm not leaving her side."

Calli sat back, shocked. She knew how Electra felt about her mother—the whole city did. But of all the people in Skyfeather's Landing, she never expected Electra to be the one to fall apart. Not even for something as unspeakably horrible as this.

She felt heat rise to her cheeks, felt the first stirrings of anger course through her veins. Iolanthe was her mother. Calli was the one who should be sitting by her bed and wallowing in misery and self-pity. But now she couldn't, not when Skyfeather's Landing needed a leader and Electra refused to fly up and take her rightful place.

"Get up," Calliope said, her teeth clenched. She'd never spoken to Electra like that, not ever. Her body trembled. "Get up now."

Electra ignored her. "Go, child. Get something to eat and take a nap. I'm sure the others will want to hear of your exploits."

Calli raised her chin and stood. "I told you to get up, High Senator, and that was an order."

Oh, now she had Electra's attention. The woman turned, red-hot rage flashing in her eyes. "What did you say?"

"You're a disgrace," Calli said. "Half the world is at war, fighting for its very freedom, and here you are, living in filth, forgetting your duty, letting your own people die. Niobe thinks all the deaths are her fault, but they're not. They're *yours.*"

Electra was up in heartbeat, her nose a centimeter away from Calli's, her breath rank.

"Who are you to talk to me that way, little girl?" Electra said, her jaw clenched.

Calli wanted to cringe, to cower, to crawl under the bed and hide. Maybe even to whimper or cry. Her hands shook, so she gripped the hem of her shirt and silently begged them to stop. "I'm the vice president," she said, trying to disguise her fear with anger. "I'm my mother's heir."

Electra's lip curled up, ugly and threatening. "Well, then it's your job to fix this place, not mine."

"Skyfeather's Landing is crumbling around you,

and you won't lift a feather to help?" Calli said. This could not be happening. Her mother couldn't be lying there one breath away from death, and Electra could not be this grief-worn shell of the woman she once was.

"I know my duty," Electra said. She pulled away from Calli and resumed her seat by the bed. "Now go do yours."

And just like that, Electra was gone, spiraling back down into the pit of despair where she now lived.

Calli swallowed, uncertain of what to do. More yelling? Gentle pleading? A hug? All her options seemed to carry the same dismal chance of success. She longed to leave the room, to run away from Electra and her mother, and return to adventuring with Aluna and Hoku and Dash. She never felt alone when she was with them. She never felt so without hope.

She stood there, uncertain, feeling more and more awkward with each passing moment. If there was a right answer to her current problem, it eluded her. Her mother had to face moments like these all the time. So did Aluna. Right or wrong, they made a decision and acted. They led.

"I'm going," she said finally. "I'll do whatever I can to save our home from the Upgraders and keep our people from enslavement. If I come back to this room, then I expect to find those curtains down, the floor scrubbed, the linens changed, my mother wearing fresh clothes, and every ounce of dirt erased from this place."

Electra snorted quietly, but didn't even turn her head.

Calli continued. "And if I don't come back to this room, then you, Electra, my mother's most trusted friend, will be the one who tells the president that her only daughter is dead."

Electra stood, but Calli didn't wait for her to speak. She turned and left as fast as she could. She didn't have time for more tears—not for her mother, not for Electra, and not for herself.

She joined Niobe at the strategy table. "Niobe, I want every senator who is not engaged in maneuvers to meet me in the audience chamber within the hour. And I'll also need three volunteers—preferably scientists or techs—to meet me in the comm room right now."

It only took Niobe a moment to recover from her surprise. She nodded. "It will be done."

Calli pulled her aside. "Send medics into my mother's room every hour. Electra will undoubtedly toss them out, but keep sending them. If she doesn't relent by dawn, start sending in warriors as well."

She gripped Niobe's arm, just under the scar on

her shoulder. "You've done well," Calli said. "I know it doesn't seem like it, but you have. And from now on, you don't have to do it alone."

Niobe nodded and sighed. Calli could see some of the tension ease in the woman's body.

Niobe turned back to the Aviars in the room. She began rattling off names and issuing orders. "You heard the acting president, get moving!"

Acting president.

Calli had never wanted to lead her people, not in any way except through scientific discovery. But sometimes life wasn't about what you wanted; it was about what needed to be done.

Her legs trembled. Her wings rustled against her back. People were going to die because of her, because of orders she gave them. The thought made her want to vomit. She didn't know strategy and tactics, or even all the parts of an army and what they did. She didn't understand supply lines or know how much fresh water they had on hand. She had no idea how long the city could withstand a siege.

But Calli had paid attention during all those long conversations with Dantai khan-son. They'd talked about leadership, about what it meant to make life-and-death decisions, and about the best way to serve one's people. She was grateful for his tutelage.

She would surround herself with smart people

who knew everything that she didn't. She would ask them for advice and she would listen to their answers. She would take responsibility for lives that were lost so that no one else had to. Her primary job was to help everyone else do theirs, and to ensure that Skyfeather's Landing and its Aviars survived this battle and knocked Karl Strand's army back to whatever hole they'd come from.

Electra was right: Calli had a duty to lead her people. It was time for her to stretch her wings and finally see how high she could fly.

CHAPTER 25

HOKU SLURPED the last of their clams and let Zorro lick the remaining goo out of the shell. Data streamed across the largest monitor in the room: complex diagrams, maps, logs, and file names so technical that he couldn't even begin to figure them out.

Almost a full week in Seahorse Alpha and he had yet to find a way to save the Kampii. The most obvious sources of energy were the sun, wind, and waves, all available in great supply. But sun and wind catchers would be too obvious floating on the ocean's surface, and the Kampii didn't have the materials to build them. Harnessing the power of the currents seemed like the smartest, most sustainable choice, but he didn't have a *turbine* — the ancient tech that took flowing water and turned it into power.

He'd even looked into diverting the power from Seahorse Alpha itself, but there was precious little to spare. What had been a thriving research outpost hundreds of years ago was now barely operational. Hoku was lucky its generators found enough power to run the computer and comm system in even one building.

Rollin had been no help, with her constant wisecracks from the Shining Moon comm screen and suggestions like "Be smarter" and "Maybe if you bash it with a hammer, you noodly basic." Now she was off arguing with the Equians about their preparations for war. He hoped it took a long time.

"Zorro, show me the turbine again."

A complex device forged from metal rotated on the screen, a hundred different labels and formulas popping up as it spun. Working with metal required fire, so even if he could figure out how to shape something similar, it wouldn't be a good choice for the long run. If the Kampii couldn't fix the tech when it broke, they'd be no better off than they were now.

Hoku rubbed his eyes. He needed a break. Maybe his subconscious would figure out a solution if he worked on something else for a while. Something like finding Karl Strand. He reached over and scratched Zorro behind the ears. "Zorro, show me everything you can find that mentions Strand."

Zorro's eyes glowed green. The screen flickered

and a list appeared on the monitor. Hoku groaned as the names of thousands of files slid down the screen. And the first few items weren't even about Karl Strand at all, but something called DNA.

He sighed. "Zorro, pick a random file containing the words *Karl Strand* and enable audio playback." Zorro's eyes glowed. Soon a sleek voice began reading a report titled "Effects of Seawater on Human Digestive Processes."

Hoku flopped onto the smooth plastic floor and tucked his hands under his head for a pillow. The computer droned on about "sodium chloride" and test subjects. He studied the room again, begging his brain to take mountains of overwhelming data and distill it into the answers he needed.

From the floor, he could see the undersides of the workstations that ringed the room. They looked as smooth as the surfaces, except for a few long scratches starting at the edge and going back to the wall. Only . . . the scratches weren't random. They were spaced evenly under each station in pairs.

Hoku crawled over to the nearest work space for a closer look. The marks weren't scratches, they were grooves. And there. In the middle. A button.

He pressed it. With a soft hiss, the smooth white drawer slid out.

"Barnacles!"

Hoku scrambled to his feet and examined the drawer's contents. Sheets of yellowed paper, some with doodles of fish in the margins, a piece of desiccated food in a shiny wrapper, a photograph of a handsome Human man somewhere in the Above World.

"Zorro, stop playback," he said. The computer voice cut off in mid-sentence.

Hoku hopped from one workstation to the next, pressing buttons and hearing the exhalation of a dozen new places to explore. All these secrets just waiting to be found, and he'd almost missed them!

One drawer slid open revealing row after row of what looked like tiny sets of goggles. He stopped to examine them. They weren't goggles at all, but little cases clearly meant to hold eye lenses of some kind. The first ten he opened were empty, but the last two . . . the last two still held their prizes.

Hoku brought the case closer to his face and studied the lenses up close. The first set was orange and glittery, like scales. At certain angles, he could just make out a reflective matrix of dots. The second set was clear with ghostly blue swirls.

Upgrades.

But what did they do? He closed the lid on the orange pair and turned the case over in his hands. There, on the back, almost too small to see, was a strange pattern of dots and lines.

"Zorro, come here and scan this code."

His faithful little buddy unplugged his tail from the computer interface and bounded over, leaping the distance between workstations and scrabbling against the plastic with his black claws. Zorro paused in front of the lens case. His eyes emitted a slender green beam that the animal dragged over the strange code.

Zorro edged backward and plugged his tail into the nearest workstation interface. Words appeared on the monitor.

CONDUIT 5000.1: DATASTREAMERS™— OPTICAL NEURAL INTERFACE DEVICE

Screen after screen of legal and medical disclaimers followed. Hoku saw the words, but didn't actually read any of them.

Optical neural interface. He wasn't entirely sure what that meant, but he wanted it. *Needed* it. Wasn't sure how he had ever survived so long without it.

He picked up the case containing the blue lenses. "Zorro, scan."

This time the words confused him.

VISIONWORLD RECREATIONAL OVERLAYS 7101A-6: OTHERLANDS LENS SUPRA™

A similar jumble of jargon followed, but Hoku understood even less of it. Clearly the swirly blue lenses did something wonderful; he just couldn't figure out what. He snapped the lid closed and placed the lenses back in the drawer.

"Zorro, show me instructions for inserting the Datastreamers," Hoku said. *Datastreamers.* It sounded even better when he said it out loud.

A series of diagrams appeared on the screen. Apparently he was supposed to wash his hands in clean water first. Except he had no clean water, so seawater would have to do. Maybe the instructions were written by Humans who couldn't handle salt in their eyes.

He dragged a chair over and sat. The instructions didn't look difficult. The worst part would be touching the lens to his eye. Eyes were too mushy. Too much like the gooey insides of oysters. He didn't look forward to poking his finger into one.

But the idea taunted him: *Datastreamers.* Streaming data. All for him. Imagine what he could do! Surely he'd be able to save the Kampii and find Karl Strand when data was literally streaming to his brain.

The instructions were as easy to follow as they seemed, and soon an orange lens was perched on the tip of his newly cleaned finger. He stole one more glance at the diagram on the screen. Using his other hand, he kept both his inner and outer eyelids open and gently touched the lens to his eyeball.

He blinked instinctively, but the lens was in and stuck to his eye. It burned, like grit stuck inside his inner lid, but he forced himself not to rub it. The instructions told him to keep blinking, to let the lens naturally find its way to the curve of his eye. So he blinked, and blinked, and cursed a few times, and blinked some more.

Was this how an oyster felt when some stupid bit of dirt found its way into its shell? No wonder the oyster wrapped up the grit in a pearl coating! Hoku wished he could do that now. He gritted his teeth and put his palm over his eye to stop himself from rubbing. Or digging. Or scratching. The ancient Humans were tough if they did things like this all the time. Eventually, the blinking felt less and less like he was dragging his eyes over a sandbank. And then, miraculously, the irritation disappeared entirely. His eye felt puffy and red, but it didn't hurt.

"Zorro, do you need to wear both lenses for them to work?"

Zorro's nose twitched while he searched the information about the lenses. When the raccoon's eyes glowed green, as Hoku had secretly known they would, he sighed and prepared the other lens.

The second one went more smoothly. Or maybe

Hoku was just expecting the pain and suffering this time and was mentally prepared. But within a few flashes, the second lens found its rightful place on his eye.

Hoku's head tingled. He thought he heard a click and a whir, but no. Those noises were inside his head—little feedback impulses telling him the lenses were messing with his brain.

His insides lurched and the room spun sideways. He tried to right himself and landed with a thud on the floor. Except it was the ceiling. Or was it a wall?

Stupid, stupid, stupid! The lenses were old tech intended for Humans, not for Kampii. Did his eyes and his brain even work the same? What if the lenses made him blind? Here he was, out in the middle of nowhere by himself.

Not by himself.

"Zorro!" he croaked.

A thud, and then tiny licks covered his face. Licks that smelled like clams. His vision blurred into gray and white streaks. He reached out his hand and grasped Zorro's fur, focusing on the soft tufts caught between his fingers. "Good boy. You're the best raccoon ever. Do I tell you that enough? Because you are."

Slowly, his vision began to clear . . . but not entirely. Tiny words now hovered in the air. Words describing what he was seeing. LOCATION: SEAHORSE ALPHA.

A string of coordinates followed. Hoku pushed himself up, now fairly certain he understood what direction that was. Words continued to scroll by, indicating chairs and workstations and even an arrow pointing at Zorro with ZORRO™ - WILD BUDDIES PROGRAMMABLE PETS, SERIAL NUMBER SF01081962.

It was too much. There were words everywhere, constantly moving, and he couldn't even begin to process them all. He didn't need to see Zorro's name every time he looked at the little guy.

And just like that, the words hovering around Zorro disappeared. He'd made them go away just by thinking about it!

He changed the color of the text to green, then to white, then only some of the data to blue. He turned off most of the location alerts. Did he really need to know the type of chair he was sitting on? No, he did not.

Hoku looked at the closest computer monitor and the word PASSWORD? floated in front of him. He remembered the password from a few days ago, when Zorro had helped him access the system. The prompt changed to CONNECTED, which blinked twice, then disappeared.

Connected. To Seahorse Alpha. He now had a direct link to every last bit of data Sarah Jennings and the other Human ancients had ever known.

CHAPTER 26

HOKU SHOULD HAVE let his eyes rest and adjust to the new implants. The instructions recommended six to twelve hours of nonuse and relaxation. But that was time he and the Kampii didn't have.

"Hey, basic! You there?" Rollin's voice called from the comm screen.

Hoku started to roll his chair over to the monitor, then stopped. He told his eyes to connect to the comm system and bring up the Shining Moon feed, and there it was: Rollin floating in midair, looking sun worn and crotchety as ever. She'd cut her hair short and done something to her wild eyebrows. If he'd met her now, he might have assumed she was male.

"Rollin," he said, telling his new computer eyes to transmit his voice back to her.

But Rollin only squinted. "Where are you? Shark finally get you? Or maybe that raccoon? Told you the little thief was up to no good, but did you listen? No. Basic knows best."

Of course! He was too far away from the input devices—the camera and the microphone. His Datastreamers could tap into the feed and redirect it to his lenses, but they had no way of transmitting his voice or a picture of his face back to Rollin. He'd need a mobile input device for that.

He stayed in his chair and pushed himself over to the comm wall.

"There you are! What took you so—" One of Rollin's eyebrows arched, her mouth cracked into a toothy grin. "Ooh, not so basic anymore, are you, boy?"

Hoku tried to smile, but moving his face hurt his eyes. He settled for a tiny grimace.

"Not good," Rollin said. "Bad tech?"

"The tech is fine, but it hurts and I can't seem to take it out," Hoku said. "The lenses are stuck behind my second eyelids."

Rollin's shaggy brow furrowed. "Second eyelids?"

"That's what I said," Hoku grumbled. "What went wrong?"

Rollin scratched her cheek. "Well, off the top of my

brain, I'm thinking that most of us only have one set of eyelids. Second pair must be a fish thing."

"You only have one . . . ?" Hoku repeated.

She nodded. "Only *need* one."

Hoku sighed. "I used tech that wasn't intended for Kampii eyes. Barnacles! Does that make me the dumbest Upgrader ever?"

"Saw someone try to cut off his own head once, when he found a better one," Rollin said. "Hard to beat that on the idiot scale."

"Will it ever stop hurting?" Hoku asked. He dropped his head into his hands and closed his eyes. Glowing words flickered through his vision anyway. There was no escape from the Datastreamers unless he consciously closed every feed.

"We got good medteks among our folk," Rollin said gently. "When this war business is over, we'll get you righted."

The fact that she was being so nice only made Hoku feel worse. She was *never* nice—not even back when Calli got poisoned. He must be doomed.

"Oh, back to feeling sorry for yourself," Rollin grumbled. "Your default setting is 'Poor me.' 'I give up.' 'I stuck something in my eye and can't get it out.' Well, we have more to worry about than a silly mistake made by some wrangly basic!"

Hoku opened his eyes and forced a smile.

"Good," Rollin said. "Any sign of Strand's hideout? Figures, that coward holing up someplace in the darkness, not showing his face. Just like him. Now we have armies—big armies full of Equians and Serpenti—and nowhere to send them."

"No word from Dash, and I haven't found anything in the Seahorse Alpha data yet," Hoku said. "I'm hoping the Datastreamers will make it easier to search. No offense, boy." He paused to scruffle Zorro's head. "I did find something interesting, though. A letter from Sarah Jennings—she's the founder of the Coral Kampii—to Karl Strand. They used to be a family, if you can believe that."

He used his eye tech to pull up the letter from storage. It floated in front of him, invisible to Rollin, and he read it aloud.

"My dearest Karl,

We're both grieving. I'm running away from the world, from my memories of Tomias and of our life together. That's not fair to you, but it's what I need. I have to put my energy into building something new. Into hope. It's not brave, but it's honest, and it's the best I can do right now.

But you, Karl, you need help. Your friends have been calling and e-mailing me about your wild experiments. Don't be angry; they're just worried about you. You've declared war on death, but it's not a battle you can win. Don't let your brilliant mind and your good heart be casualties of your grief. None of this will bring Tomias — or me — back. Our hearts were broken when we lost our son, but they still work. I still love you.

Your Sarah"

Rollin whistled. "Isn't that a pretty bunch of words. Did Strand respond?"

"Yes," Hoku said, "although I'm sure Sarah Jennings wasn't too happy with what he had to say." He pulled up Strand's letter even though he remembered every harsh word of it. "He wrote, 'I have no time for cowards.'"

"Pain makes us ugly sometimes," Rollin said, and he was surprised to hear no hint of judgment in her voice. "Losing his little one must have been bad, but losing his partner at the same time? Explains a lot. No wonder the man buried himself in obsession."

Hoku's mouth fell open. "You're defending Karl Strand, after everything he's done? After everything he wants to do?" He shook his head. "I don't care what happened to him. There's no excuse for his actions."

"Maybe no excuse," Rollin said, "but maybe understanding." She mumbled to herself, "Yes, maybe a little understanding."

She looked away then, fiddled with something offscreen. Hoku wondered what she wasn't saying. Did it have something to do with Karl Strand, or her own mysterious past?

"You're never going to tell me what happened, are you?" he said. "You could have come with us when we infiltrated the Upgrader kludge. You could be down here with me now. Why not?"

Rollin shook her head, still looking at her lap. "Sometimes it's easier to forgive others than to forgive yourself."

He wanted to hug her. Instead he said, "Oh, 'Poor me,' is that it? 'I give up'? Well, we don't have time for that right now. Get your brain back from wherever it went, and start helping me."

Rollin looked up, shocked, and he worried that he'd gone too far. But her hurt expression disappeared quickly, replaced by her familiar grumpiness. "Quit your yammering, then, and tell me what you want to do next."

Hoku was ready for that question. His brain had been working, even if his eyes weren't.

"First, I need to know everything there is to know about turbines and wave traps, and how I might be able to build one big enough for Kampii but simple enough for their tech. I've been looking at the most advanced turbines, but the ancients had to start somewhere, right? They didn't always have bendable metals and everything they needed. If they could do it, we can do it, too."

Rollin whistled. "Tough."

"Then I'm going to build a mobile comm device using these Datastreamers and whatever spare parts Zorro and I can find here," Hoku continued. "Can you work on a comm scanner? Try to tap into every communication feed you can find? Maybe we'll get lucky and Karl Strand himself will tell us where he is."

Rollin slapped her forehead with her palm. "Comm scanner. Who's the gobbly Gizmo now? I should have come up with that."

"Well, when you figure it out, tell me how to do it," Hoku said. "I have a feeling we'll need every last bit of information we can get."

Another one of Seahorse Alpha's comm screens flickered on, as if it had heard Hoku's conversation. The image resolved into two Aviars: Calli and an older woman that Calli was yelling at. Hoku's heart tripled its pace.

"No, even if you have to relieve yourself, you find someone else to watch the monitor," Calli told the woman. She hadn't yet looked into the monitor herself.

Hoku studied her. She looked thin and tired, her eyes puffy and rimmed with red.

He whispered to Rollin, "I've got to go—Skyfeather's Landing is calling. Here is the frequency they're using, but . . . don't tune in for a few minutes, okay?" He pulled up the data on Calli's feed and repeated the numbers to Rollin.

"Give the girl a big yo for me," Rollin said, and she was gone.

"Hoku?"

He turned to find Calli's face centered in the Aviar feed.

"Calli! I'm so glad you made it home okay," he said. He reached out to touch the screen, but let his hand drop when he realized how stupid that was. Calli sometimes smiled when he did silly things, but she didn't now.

"I'm home, yes," Calli said. "And I'm glad you've made it to Seahorse Alpha. What's the status of the Kampii and Deepfell armies? Have you made any progress with an alliance? Is Aluna there?"

Calli's questions struck his chest like daggers. Hoku searched her face, looking for a hesitant smile, the hint of color in her cheeks, a sparkle in her eyes just for him. He didn't find any of it.

"Aluna isn't here," he said. His voice cracked, and

he scowled. "There are problems here. Big problems. She's trying to forge an alliance between the Kampii and the Deepfell, only the Kampii from the city want to kill the Deepfell instead and steal their breathing devices. It's a mess."

"What about Karl Strand?" Calli asked, as if she hadn't heard him. Or hadn't cared. "If the Equians killed him already, maybe I can get his army here to surrender."

Hoku shook his head. "We haven't found him. The armies are amassing, but they aren't in contact with each other yet, and no one knows where Strand is."

He heard someone enter the room on Calli's end. She looked over, her face grim, and listened to whoever had come in. "Have the wounded been recovered?" Calli asked. The other person answered, but Hoku couldn't hear what she was saying. "Pull back," Calli said. "Regroup inside the bowl. Have the archers dip their arrows in acid and aim for the catapult."

Hoku felt dizzy. He looked around the room, at the piles of clamshells and fish bones scattered around the desktops. Days and days here, and he hadn't helped a single person yet, while Calli was dealing with a war.

Calli's face appeared close in his monitor. "I've got to go, but I'll leave someone on this commbox at all times. Let me know the moment you learn something."

He nodded, suddenly too ashamed to speak.

"Stay safe," Calli said, and walked out of range of the camera.

Hoku was left staring at a strange Aviar he'd never seen before. She had dark skin and thin lips marred by a vertical scar on one side. She sat down in front of her monitor and nodded. "My name is Senator Melaine. If you have any messages or information for the acting president, you can give them to me."

Acting president. He shook his head. "Nothing right now. But I . . . I have things to do."

Senator Melaine nodded and rustled her wings. "Then I will wait."

Hoku rolled away from the monitor and told his Datastreamers to shut off the microphone. But not for long; he had work to do.

Calli hadn't even noticed his eyes.

CHAPTER 27

FOR THE TENTH TIME, Dash touched the hilts of the swords belted to his waist. Despite Odd's insistence that he name them Hot and Cold, Dash had finally settled on Blaze and Shatter.

He had been practicing with them every chance he could get, and they were starting to feel like extensions of his body. Vachir had hated them at first, but now even she was used to the flames and the searing cold that the swords produced. Eventually, if Dash kept working, wielding Blaze and Shatter would feel as easy and effortless as playing with toys. His old sword instructor used to say that was the true sign that you had mastered a weapon.

After that night around the fire, the night Dash had finally told the truth, it had become just as easy and effortless to pretend he was part of Odd's kludge. Because he *was* a part of it now, as strange as that seemed. And once they had made their decision, they were done. He had not witnessed a single moment of doubt from anyone, not Odd or Mags or Pocket or Squirrel.

Squirrel bounded up to his side. "You're in love with those things," she said, pointing to his swords. "Maybe you should try to be in love with people instead. At least they can love you back."

Dash laughed and turned his head so she would not see the color rise to his face. Squirrel only meant to tease him, he was sure. It had become one of her favorite pastimes during the last week. But sometimes her jibes hit too close to his heart.

"And you?" he asked her. "Are you quick to give your heart to others?" She was not, as he knew well, but he enjoyed invoking her outrage. Aluna would like her very much. Vachir already did.

"Never giving my heart to anyone," Squirrel said resolutely. "They'll just stomp on it, and then I'll have to bash in their head. Messy-messy."

"That would indeed be sad," Dash said. "But someday a person may surprise you. People are good at that."

She blinked up at him, suddenly appearing as young as her age. He worried the girl was forming an unfortunate attachment to him, which he might need to address. But so far, she had not crossed any boundaries or gone too far in her jests.

"Don't think I'd mind being surprised like that," Squirrel said. "Someday, I mean. After we've got your folks back. Then maybe I'll go looking for a surprise."

"Oh, you cannot look for a surprise," Dash said. "In fact, it usually finds you at the moment you are looking the least." He thought about the SkyTek dome, about how a tiny creature had stolen his last apple and a minute later he was on the ground with a broken wrist and Aluna threatening to break even more.

As they drew closer to Strand's army, they joined a steady stream of other kludges and lone Upgraders traveling the same way. Odd and Mags made friendly conversation with those that seemed open to it and asked if they had seen two Equian prisoners. So far, no one had.

The threat of attack from other kludges had diminished with the looming promise of war. No one wanted to start a skirmish and end up facing the army as punishment. Odd's kludge had, possibly for the first time in its existence, the comfort of safety.

Unfortunately, no one they had met so far knew the whereabouts of Strand himself. Odd had been right—apparently only Strand's trusted lieutenants had that information.

Which made it even more critical that Dash discover Strand's hideout and find a way to transmit its location to Aluna, Hoku, and Calli in the HydroTek dome. His chest tightened at the thought of the three of them together, laughing, sharing meals, sharing stories.

Vachir walked next to him. He patted her on the withers. The two of them were doing well enough, but that did not stop him from missing the others. No one made him laugh like Hoku. No one made him believe in the inherent goodness of people like Calli. And there was simply no one in the world like Aluna.

"There you go again," Squirrel said. "Dreaming about your swords."

Dash smiled. "You know me so well."

The thick forest had long ago given way to the rocky skirt of the mountain and smaller, tougher trees. The path they now walked was well-worn, perhaps an Upgrader thoroughfare of some sort. It was strange to think of the Upgraders developing trade routes, but they had. Unlike the LegendaryTek splinters, theirs was a world of travel and exploration, not isolation and defense. It was the harder path, and he admired them for it.

Odd returned from a conversation with another kludge and spoke with Mags. Dash watched their faces, the way they carried their bodies, the intensity of their voices. Mags glanced back once, but quickly turned to Odd when she saw Dash watching her.

So this was about him, then.

He touched the hilts of his blades, taking comfort in the smooth leather strips in which he had wrapped them to improve his grip. The last few days of safety had been a welcome change after so much uncertainty. He should have known it would not last.

"Please, excuse me," he said to Squirrel. "I must speak with Odd and Mags."

Squirrel followed his gaze. The girl was quick and could read situations better than almost anyone he knew. "Yeah, you do," she said. "Luck."

He nodded and whispered to Vachir. She whinnied and nudged him forward with her head.

"There's good news and not-so-good news," Mags said.

Odd snorted. "Crap news," he said. "And worse-than-crap news."

"I am ready for both," Dash said.

His fathers might be dead. The idea had formed in his heart the moment he learned they had left Shining Moon. The seed had grown when he heard about their abduction by Upgraders. And now that seed had flowered into a vast tree of fear and doubt, its branches spread throughout his entire body.

"On the good side," Odd said, "that ugly brute

Grid says he saw—with his own shiny eyes—one of Strand's head warriors use a bit of tech to talk to someone else, someone nowhere nearby, far as he could tell."

"A portable commbox? That is good news!" Dash said. "We must find that warrior immediately. With that device, we could coordinate the movement of our own allied forces, assuming the Kampii, Equians, Aviars, and Serpenti are now using the devices they already have."

"Get hold of yourself," Mags said. "We aren't walking up to Strand's army and demanding they give us their tech, and I don't care how good you're getting with those swords. Can't put us back together when the army cuts us to a gadzillion glittery shreds of flesh, can you?"

"Of course not," Dash said quickly. "I only meant that the communication device is the key, and that we need to gain access to it."

Odd scratched his mostly bald scalp, making his bundle of red hair twitch. "Well, then, here's the problem, boy," he said. "That wasn't the only tidbit old Grid had for us. Traded a nice cutting knife to learn that he and his kludge also saw two of your horse folk handed off from one batch of their captors to another."

"My fathers," Dash said. The words came out of

his mouth like whispers, so fragile he was afraid they might disappear.

Mags put a hand on his arm, and even with his heart racing and his mind reeling, he took note of it. Mags rarely touched anyone outside of tending to their wounds.

"They're alive," she said quietly. "Grid said one was limping, but hey, they have four legs, right? Could be worse. Thought it would be."

"I did as well," he said. He winced, though, thinking of his fathers wounded, being forced to march. They were brave enough, but not stupid or foolish. He could only hope that they managed to fight the fear and hopelessness a little longer. "We must find them and the comm device at once," he said. "Every moment could mean the difference between their survival and us winning this war. Which direction do we go?"

"The horse folk were taken north," Odd said.

Mags's hand tightened on his arm. "And the comm device is west."

The hope rising in his chest sank back down into nothing. "This cannot be," he said. Had he so angered the sun that she now thought to toy with him, to give him an impossible choice so she might enjoy the entertainment of watching him suffer?

On a larger scale, the comm device was more important. The allied splinters needed to know where to find Karl Strand, not just his army. They could fight for years and never see an end to the war . . . unless they removed Strand himself. He was the serpent's head, and they needed to cut it off.

"There's a wee bit more," Mags said. "If you've got ears for it right now."

"It's bad, boy," Odd said. "Make no mistake."

Dash closed this eyes and breathed deep. He did not want to know whatever news Odd and Mags thought was *worse* than what they'd already told him. But ignorance was only the illusion of a shield, not a shield itself. It could not protect him.

"Tell me," Dash said.

Odd nodded, started to speak, then changed his mind. He nudged Mags in the shoulder. She scowled at him, but took the hint.

"The horse folk, the two that raised you, they were given to one of Strand's generals," she said. "As a prize."

Dash swallowed. "Do you know the name of this general?"

Mags nodded. "They call her Scorch."

His fathers were not warriors. Erke and Gan would not bear up well against torture, and the experience would not harden their resolve. If Scorch found out they were related to him or in any way connected to Aluna, she would exact revenge. Erke and Gan would suffer, and no matter how hard they fought it, they would break.

Dash knew this. And yet, he knew something else just as true: Erke and Gan would be disappointed in him if he chose to save them instead of helping so many others. They did not raise him to be that boy, or that man.

There were so many things they did not know. Perhaps the Upgrader they sought had no comm device after all, and perhaps Erke and Gan were already dead. Right now, all he could do was act on the information he had and follow his heart. In this case, it was telling him not to rescue his parents, but to honor them.

But perhaps, just perhaps, he could do both.

CHAPTER 28

DASH HELD HIS ARM STILL while Mags sliced a thin line through his flesh with a scalpel. He felt no pain. The skin covering his mechanical wrist and hand contained only a few vital nerves, and Mags had skillfully avoided them. She pulled his skin back to reveal the blood-slicked metal underneath.

Mags whistled. "Good work, this. Where'd you get it?"

"The HydroTek dome," Dash said. "The Meks there have access to entire laboratories of ancient tech and are fully programmed for its use." He thought of Liu the crab-girl and tried not to blush.

Mags used a tiny pincer to pick up the small device she was inserting into his arm. "Easy to hide the homer in all this tech," she said. "They'll never find it unless they tear your arm apart." She looked up quickly. "Which they'll have no cause to do, I'm sure."

He nodded, his mouth dry.

"You don't have to do this, you know," Mags said quietly. "There's other ways we could manage."

"If you think of any, I would enjoy hearing them," Dash said with a smile. "Karl Strand is the key. We can fight his army forever, but until we remove him from power, this will never be over. I do not know any other way to find him."

Mags poked something in his arm and he flinched. "Nerve," she said. "Almost done." She pulled out her pincers and reached for her stitching needle.

"Where is your homing beacon?" Dash asked.

She tapped a spot behind her ear, somewhere in the dense cloud of her hair. "Had to have someone else put it in, but it was worth it," she said. "No one ever looks there."

"Odd truly cares for you all," he said. "These devices must have required a steep trade."

"Kludge comes first," Mags said, as if no other explanation were needed. "And that includes you now, too. I just hope the homer signal screams loud enough to reach our receiver. Rumors say Strand is holed up in the mountain somewhere. You go in too far, and we won't be able to find you."

"Then give my last position to the others. It will be better than nothing," he said. His plan had many risks and only a small chance of success. He liked to think that Aluna would approve.

Odd ambled over just as Mags was using skin glue to hide the last traces of the incision in his arm.

"Squirrel spotted our target over the next ridge," he said. "Girl says he's got the weirdest upgrades she's ever seen. Not just horns like Pocket, but *horns.*" He held his hands out half a meter from either side of his head. "Face like an animal, she says, but I don't know about that. Seen many a punched-ugly face in my years, and never seen one yet that surprised me."

Odd pulled a thick rope from his waistband and waited.

Dash stood, touched fingers to his heart, and bowed to Mags. "Thank you."

She nodded and shooed him with her hand. "Just don't get yourself killed now that I've spent so much time on you."

"I will try not to invalidate your work," he said. Although, truthfully, the homing beacon would continue to function even if he was killed. It was one of the benefits of his plan that he had chosen not to mention to the others.

Dash put his arms behind his back and stood quietly while Odd tied them together with his rope.

"I wish I had thought to take one of the fake restraints we used on Aluna and Calli when we first joined you," Dash said. "If they see how we have weakened the rope, they may suspect something."

"Most folk are lazy. Won't even check," Odd said. "You want me to keep your swords? Won't use them or anything. Won't mess with your changes or nothing. Just to keep them safe till you get back."

"Yes, thank you," Dash said. He had forgotten about the swords. Of course they would be taken from him, and better for Odd to have them than for someone in Strand's army to wield them against an ally. "My retractable blade is hidden in its sheath at my waist. I will not be entirely unarmed . . . unless they are less lazy than you say."

"Lazy," Odd repeated. "The whole lot of them."

Pocket ran up to them, his face scrunched with worry. "Squirrel says they're getting ready to move and we have to go in now." He rubbed his hands on his pants. "I'm not sure I can do this. Maybe someone else should try."

Odd put a meaty hand on the boy's shoulder, and Dash felt a small pang of regret. He had experienced the weight of Odd's affection perhaps for the last time.

"You can do it and you will do it," Odd said.

"Didn't earn your name for nothing," Mags added.

The boy's name wasn't Pocket, but *Pickpocket.*

Dash had been surprised to learn that the boy was named for more than the secret compartments hidden in his limbs. Surprised, and pleased. Pocket had a crucial role to play in their upcoming maneuvers.

"One last piece before we go," Dash said. "Odd?"

"You ready?" Odd asked. "This might hurt a touch."

Dash lifted his chin, held his breath, and nodded. He watched Odd pull back his massive arm and squeeze his hand into a fist. A fist that seemed the size of Dash's entire head.

The blow fell, and Dash found himself on the ground with no real memory of how he had gotten there. His cheek ached and burned and felt as if it were already swelling to twice its normal size. A trickle of warmth dripped down his brow and he wondered for a moment if his entire skull had been crushed, and if he would ever be able to stand up again.

He was vaguely aware of Vachir whinnying, of her hoof scraping the ground not far from his head and her hot breath huffing in his face.

Then Odd reached down, grabbed him by the arm, and yanked him back to his feet as if he weighed no more than a feather.

"Well hit," Mags said. Dash tried not to wince as her fingers probed his face. "Looks a mess, but there's nothing broken. The cut will bleed good and long."

Dash stood there, swaying slightly, and said nothing. The world felt muted, as if his friends spoke in the distance. Only the thunderous throbbing in his head seemed real.

"Thank you," he finally managed. "I appreciate your restraint."

Odd slapped him on the arm. Dash groaned as the reverberation made his skull pound even more. "Hitting is the one thing I'm good at," Odd said. "Don't get to do it nearly enough. Even the little love taps like that one make me smile."

Love tap?

"Get yourself ready, now," Mags said. "Best be moving."

Dash nodded. He could feel blood drip down from his brow and spot his cheek. At least Aluna, Hoku, and Calli were not here to see his face. Then again, Aluna would probably have attacked Odd with her talons, even though he was only doing as Dash asked. He never minded when Aluna came to his defense. It was . . . refreshing . . . after a lifetime of fighting for himself almost every day.

Vachir bent a knee so Dash could hop on her back more easily. He had wanted her to run off and hide until this was all over. A horse of her caliber would be a tempting prize to bring into Strand's army. But Vachir disagreed, and Dash did not argue. She was her own person and he would not deny her a role in this if she wished it.

"Don't know how many eyes they have out here," Odd said. "Best play our parts now." He thumped Vachir on her rump, and she whinnied angrily. "Sorry," Odd grumbled. "Still not used to a four-feet with a brain."

Odd, Mags, and Pocket wore grim expressions as they flanked Dash and Vachir. Dash lowered his head and let his body slump in the saddle, doing his best to be a wounded, defeated traitor.

They walked through the outskirts of what appeared to be a major stronghold for Strand's army. Men and women gathered in organized clusters, cooking food in huge pots over their campfires, sharing stories, and even trading tech. Dash saw more bizarre enhancements than he had even thought possible. He had a hard time looking away from the man with slitted eyes and fangs who had grafted spotted animal fur to his torso and legs. He had made himself into a Human cat.

Some Upgraders looked up as their small group passed, but most continued with their gossip and their tasks. They saw only a plain, dirt-covered prisoner being brought to justice. He was nothing to them.

Odd handled the first army official who approached them. She identified herself as "Winder's left-hand woman, second only to Winder's right-hand man and to Winder himself."

"Got a special prisoner," Odd said. "Need to see Winder. . . . Unless there's someone more important than him around?"

"More important than Winder?" The woman barked a laugh. "No one of that particular description, unless you talking about one of the old man's own children, Fathom or Scorch!"

"Well, can we talk to one of them, then?" Mags asked. "Or send us direct to Strand, if you want."

"Oh, sure, if you want your limbs ripped off and your face melted for fun," the woman answered. "Because that's going to happen, or worse, if you waste the Sea Master's or Sand Master's time with a silly little nothing like this." She poked Dash in the leg with a finger sharp as a dagger.

"They'll want this boy, I promise you," Odd said. "We're willing to bet our lives on it."

The woman looked Odd up and down, then sighed. "Follow me. I'll take you to Winder and we'll let him decide what's to be done with you. Don't be surprised if he slices you into pieces on the spot, though."

She trudged through the camp and people scattered to get out of her way. The five of them followed. And somewhere out there, watching, was Squirrel.

The groups of soldiers grew thicker and better

equipped as they neared Winder. What appeared as a ragtag army on its outskirts had become an organized, clearly experienced force at its core. Dash imagined his fellow Equians with their swords and spears and bows lining up to fight this heavily armored, heavily weaponized army. Despite their ferocity and skill, his people would be killed in great numbers.

"There he is," the woman said. "There's Winder."

Squirrel had been right; Winder was no ordinary Upgrader. From his waist up, the man was covered in brown hair splotched with white, like the hide of a horse. His head, so massive it dominated his three-meter frame, had a long snout ending in wide nostrils. Some of the Equian herds raised cows, and Winder reminded Dash of a bull.

"Minotaur," Mags whispered. "One of the splinters Strand made up for himself."

CHAPTER 29

DASH TRIED TO TURN HIS HEAD to escape the pungent odor emanating from Winder's mouth, but the minotaur gripped Dash's chin in one of his huge, hide-covered hands and held it in place. He could feel Vachir trembling underneath him, but thankfully she stayed still and did nothing.

"This runt doesn't look dangerous enough to scare an itsy-bitsy bird," Winder said, "and you think the mighty Karl Strand cares if he lives or dies?"

"He does, and so does Sand Master Scorch," Mags said calmly. "They will both care very much."

Winder pulled away from Dash and crossed his arms over his chest. "And I suppose you want to take him to Strand all by yourself and take the reward,"

Winder said. "Greedy Gizmos. No eye for the big picture. No head for strategy. For tactics!"

"Don't want the reward," Odd said. "Just doing our part for the war. For Strand. Helping him bring about a better world, and all that talk."

"Oh?" Winder said. "And so you want me to march up to Strand with this little nothing and risk my reputation on your say-so?" The last few words came out as a growl.

"Talk to the Sand Master," Mags said quickly. "Tell her who you've got. Tell her his name—Dash from Flame Heart herd. Friend of Aluna. And say you got Aluna's horse, too. You say it just like that, and she'll know right away."

Winder appeared to be thinking. Dash heard the *thump-thump-thump* of his massive fingers along the metal bracer on his other arm. Finally, Winder reached into one of his belt pouches and pulled out a small device no bigger than the leaf of a tree. He motioned to some soldiers milling around their area. The men and women immediately stood and encircled their group.

"If Sand Master Scorch doesn't know the boy, then you'll all die at my feet," Winder said. "You still want me to call?" He held the device up, his finger poised above its surface.

"Call," Odd said. "We're speaking true."

Winder punched a button on the device. Dash

glanced over at Pocket and was pleased to see the boy entirely focused on what Winder was doing. He had stayed quiet until now, hopefully too small and inconsequential to be of interest to Winder, but his part of the plan was quickly approaching.

Winder held the device half a meter from his face and spoke into it, just as Dash had spoken into the comm screens he'd found in Coiled Deep. Someone spoke on the other end, possibly Scorch, but Dash could not discern her words.

"Flame Heart," Winder repeated. "And there's a horse. And some mention of a person named Aluna."

The minotaur's eyes widened and his head snapped back.

"Yes, Sand Master," he said. "At once. By the gate. As you wish."

The tension crushing Dash's chest eased its grip slightly. One step closer to Scorch. One step closer to his fathers.

Winder turned off his device and stowed it back in its pouch. He pointed to his soldiers. "You six, pack my tent and things. I'll be making a delivery. One of you tell Tank that he's in charge until I get back."

Once the soldiers started to move and not all eyes were focused on Winder, Odd and Mags made their move.

"See? What did I tell you?" Odd said, landing a

heavy hand on Winder's shoulder. It almost looked small resting on the huge creature's arm. The minotaur barely seemed to notice.

Mags moved to his other side. "Need help transporting the prisoner, do you? We can hunt and cook, better than what you're eating now, I'd wager." She pulled a grilled squirrel torso from her long coat and held it up under Winder's huge nose.

Meanwhile, Pocket snuck around, sly as a desert fox, and slipped his hand into the mess of bags and pouches affixed to Winder's waist. The boy yanked his hand back so fast that Dash worried he'd been hurt or discovered. Dash caught just a glint of something small and shiny slip from Pocket's hand into one of the hidden compartments in his calf. And then Pocket was back, hanging by Mags and doing his best to look innocent and invisible. *A good little thief,* Dash thought.

Winder shoved Odd and Mags out of his way and stomped toward Dash and Vachir.

"Hood! Rope!" Winder called. A soldier rushed forward and threw a rope around Vachir's neck. Another came carrying a sack of black cloth. Dash felt a knot form in his stomach. The soldier yanked Dash to the side, almost pulling him off Vachir, and shoved the hood over his head. The world plunged into blackness.

The kludge was gone. He could not see them, he

could not hear them. His world became filled with the chaos of clanking soldiers and orders barked too close to his ears. His only comfort was Vachir, calm beneath him despite the storm everywhere else.

Vachir jumped forward, and Dash cursed under his breath. They had yanked the rope around her neck too harshly. Now it was his turn to stay still and let the game play out. The time for weighing options and making choices was gone. They were now prisoners, truly cut off from their friends and powerless against their enemies.

Dash thought he heard Odd's voice calling over the crowd and twisted in his saddle. Something hard slammed into his face. His head felt loose, as if it had become unfastened from his neck.

"Eyes front," a gruff voice said.

He tried to calm himself. When he trained falcons, the hood was often the most important part of the process. It acclimated the birds to Equian touch and kept them still and at ease. But as soon as the hood was removed, the falcon was alert, ready. As fierce as it ever was before.

If he wanted to survive this ordeal—not just in body, but also in mind—then he must find a way to be like a falcon.

They traveled for hours, stopping only once so Winder and the soldiers could drink and relieve themselves. No one gave him or Vachir water or food, or checked their wounds. He wanted to talk to Vachir, to offer words of comfort, but he was not that foolish. Instead, he bent forward and pressed his cheek against her neck. Vachir whinnied softly.

When Dash had first proposed this plan to the kludge, they had been against it. Squirrel had wanted to sneak into Strand's secret lair somehow and keep the group together. But Dash had fought hard for this—it meant less risk for the others, a better opportunity for getting crucial information to Aluna and Hoku, and the chance that he might see his fathers one last time.

Erke and Gan had already been given to Scorch. If he was lucky, she would imprison him and Vachir in the same place.

If. If. If. There were too many variables, too much left to chance. Scorch might kill him the moment she saw him. Because of the hood, he would never even see the blow falling.

The air grew colder. They were walking up, into the mountains. The soldiers in their group grunted more often, and occasionally one of them commented on a part of the landscape. Dash listened closely to everything they said.

Eventually, Winder called, "Halt." Hands pulled Dash off Vachir and dragged him forward.

A familiar rhythmic thudding broke through the silence. Hoofbeats! He wanted to drop and put his ear to the ground, but a soldier held him in place. Instead, he closed his eyes and counted. Four horses, approaching fast but beginning to slow. They pulled something behind them, a vehicle with two large wheels that crushed the earth as they rolled.

The horses slowed, their harnesses jangling, the wheels of the transport sliding to a stop. Someone jumped down and walked toward them, boots crunching the earth with each step.

"Sand Master Scorch, I've brought the boy and the horse, as you commanded," Winder said, far more humbly than Dash had thought him capable of being. Scorch strode forward as if Winder had said nothing.

Dash tensed as she stalked closer and closer. His hands were tied behind his back and he was essentially blind and surrounded by enemies. Even if he could reach his sword, they would cut him down before he managed to extend the blade. And then they would kill Vachir.

Scorch stopped in front of Dash. He could feel her there, a predator waiting to pounce. He tried to step backward, but a soldier held him firmly in place. Scorch leaned closer until he could feel her hot breath through the cloth over his ear.

"Are you in there, little failed Equian?" Scorch whispered. "If it's really you, then I've got a nice present for you."

Scorch ripped off his hood. The sun blinded him. He squinted and blinked, trying to recover his eyesight. When the white glare finally began to subside, he found Scorch had moved to the side, giving him an unobstructed view of her vehicle.

A chariot. He had seen books depicting the ancient carts. But instead of harnessed horses, Scorch's chariot was being pulled by four Equians.

"Erke! Gan!" Dash cried. His voice cracked.

His fathers were tied to the chariot as if they were animals. He saw cloths tied around their mouths and tight ropes binding their Human hands behind their backs. Their horse flanks were wet with sweat and bled from Scorch's lashings.

Erke looked up at Dash's outburst and his eyes widened. Gan made a strangled noise through his gag.

Dash felt his heart swell. Tears formed in his eyes and slid down his bruised cheek. It had been almost three years since he had seen them. Even now, with all of them prisoners facing death at Scorch's hand, he felt nothing but relief at seeing them again.

No matter what happened after this, regardless of how each of them went to their endless night, they would know that he tried.

"Pretty horses, don't you think?" Scorch asked. He had almost forgotten she was there. "Not as obedient as real horses at first, but they've been broken nicely.

Of course, now I'll need to get rid of one to make room for Aluna's four-legged piece of meat."

Dash looked at his captor. Her brown hair was still short, and she wore it just like the old Karl Strand from the picture. Her black-rimmed glasses remained the same as well, although up close, he saw that they contained no glass or material of any kind. They were merely frames intended to make her look like her father.

She loved her father, or at least desired his praise, Dash thought. Could he use that? Then again, perhaps she did not know he was related to two of her Equian prisoners.

"No Equian should be treated like that," Dash said. "If you release them, and Vachir, I will do anything you wish."

Scorch laughed, reminding him that she was neither stupid nor merciful. "You'll do anything I wish no matter what I do to your fathers."

He cringed.

"Oh, they talked," Scorch said. "Not at first. Equians are stubborn, I'll give them that." She reached out a hand and pressed a fingertip into the damaged flesh on Dash's face. "But everyone breaks in the end."

Dash gasped from the pain. "I will make you a bargain," he said. "I will give you—"

Scorch's fist smashed into his face and his vision exploded in black sparks. He fell to his knees.

"Take him to the chariot," Scorch said. "Tie the horse behind it."

Strong arms dragged him over the ground. His head throbbed. He could not find the strength to pull his legs under his body and stand. The soldiers threw him into the chariot and he stayed where he fell, crumpled against the curved plastic shell. Scorch stepped in and picked up her reins.

The chariot roared into motion, each bump and rock under the wheels making Dash groan. He touched his arm, where Odd's homing beacon silently signaled his position to the kludge. He was helping his friends. He was helping the world. No matter what happened next, that thought would be *his* beacon.

Scorch cracked her driving whip. The chariot circled around and headed back up the path, Vachir galloping behind it on a short lead. Dash managed to keep his head, looking at her, until Scorch drove the chariot into a wide tunnel carved into the side of the mountain. As they thundered down the passage, he watched soldiers block the entrance with a massive boulder.

The world plunged into darkness again. Dash closed his eyes and made one last wish: that the homing beacon gave the others what they needed to defeat Strand . . . even if he was not alive to see it.

CHAPTER 30

ALUNA SHOULD HAVE BEEN GRATEFUL. The encounter between the Deepfell, the surface colony, and the Kampii hunting party had not ended in anyone's death. But the discussion hadn't resolved anything, either; it had only bought them time. In order to forge a real alliance, they needed approval from the Kampii council of Elders.

And before they could win over the council, they needed to win over its most intimidating Elder of all: her father.

Now Aluna found herself in her family's nest, trying hard not to slip back into the person she was before she'd left for the Above World. She'd felt small then. Unimportant and invisible, except when she was causing her father embarrassment. It didn't help that everything about the nest looked the same. The lichens on the walls glowed in colorful but fading patterns. Their resting sticks stuck out of the coral floor in the same weary circle around the carved coral dais where Daphine was busy hooking nets of oysters, mussels, kelp, and fish.

Only Anadar was missing. He'd stayed behind with Eekikee to get the surface colony Kampii settled in their temporary cave home. Aluna missed his presence greatly—he was almost as big as Ehu and Pilipo and had a knack for calming everyone down when tempers swirled too fast.

Aluna wrapped her tail around her old resting stick, amazed at how different it felt to anchor oneself with a tail instead of legs. A tiny surge of confidence swished through her body. As the youngest, it wasn't her place to talk first. Kampii younglings were supposed to sit quietly and listen. Then again, most young Kampii hadn't walked in the Above World.

"Let's get started," Aluna said, pleased that her voice sounded strong and clear. "We've come here to discuss an alliance with the Deepfell and our participation in the war against Karl Strand."

That was all it took. Her brothers' voices filled her ears, angry and loud.

"The Deepfell have killed our people for

generations," Pilipo said. "Any truce would insult our ancestors."

Ehu interrupted. "We need their breathing devices. What matters more than that? We all know Peleke can't invent his way out of a clamshell. If we don't take what we need, then we all die."

"Tides' teeth, you're both idiots!" Daphine said, which shocked both brothers into silence. "One of you is looking backward, and the other is only looking forward a year or two. We need a long-term solution so we're not having the same argument every season!"

Ehu swished his tail. "You think that scope reminds us of the danger of the Above World, Daphine, but it just tells me that we're smart to stay hidden and take care of our own."

"Except that *our own* are all going to *die*," Daphine countered.

As her siblings rehashed the same arguments they'd made in the Deepfell cave, Aluna watched her father. Elder Kapono swayed in the water's currents, his eyes sharp, his arms relaxed at his sides. Only his clenched jaw and twitching neck muscles betrayed his concentration. She hated that the future of the entire Kampii colony rested on her father's willingness to open his mind, look at the facts, and listen to his people.

He reminded Aluna a little of the Shining Moon

khan, and of Calli's mother, and even a little of Tayan. But Aluna and Hoku had gotten through to all of them eventually. President Iolanthe had imprisoned them at first, seemingly without regret, and then let them go. Likewise, Khan Arasen had been against Aluna, Calli, and Hoku joining the Shining Moon herd, yet he had walked out on the field of battle and defied the High Khan and Scorch on their behalf. And Tayan . . . Tayan had ultimately risked her life and her honor by forming herd Flame Heart.

But Aluna had grown up fighting with her father. After his wife had died, he'd rebuilt his emotional defenses with inflexible, impenetrable walls. Nothing could get in. Not new ideas, not new love, and not acceptance for the daughter who seemed to willfully disrespect him.

Those defenses had kept her father safe all these years, but they'd kept him the same, too. Aluna kept beating on those walls, kept trying to find a way in. Not just for the safety of the Kampii and the Above World, but for herself. She'd never given up on anything in her entire life. She simply couldn't face the idea that this battle—in some ways, the most important—was one she could fight forever and still never win.

"Enough!" Elder Kapono yelled.

Aluna froze, wondering how her father had managed to see her thoughts. But no, he was talking to Daphine, Ehu, and Pilipo.

"Do you not see?" Kapono asked. "If you, members of the same family — our Voice and our best hunters — can't agree on this, then what hope has our beloved city of resolving this issue?"

"But, Father —"

"Aluna, no," he said. "I have listened to your stories, and I do not doubt what you have said. But you have been infected by the Above World and its problems, and you can no longer see with clarity the issues that belong to the Kampii alone. You and Daphine are no longer fit to speak or act for the City of Shifting Tides."

"Exactly! It's —"

"Pilipo, silence!" Kapono snapped. "Did I raise none of you to respect me?" Pilipo shrank back, looking more the awkward youngling than the powerful hunter he had become. "We cannot afford to fight among ourselves," her father said. "Indeed . . . we cannot afford to fight at all." He looked at Aluna, a strange, sad smile tugging at his mouth. "Did you know that our women once hunted alongside our men? I often wonder if you had been born in that far-gone age, if perhaps we might have been civil to each other."

"They fought?" Aluna said. "With spears?"

"And knives and harpoons and their own

well-trained hands," her father said. "But we don't make enough babies, and too many of them die. Or their mothers die. Or the sharks find them as younglings. We have had to be more careful, and we have tried to protect our women. Without women, our entire people will dwindle into nothing."

Aluna thought of the Serpenti and how they were doomed. She had no idea that the Kampii were facing the same fate.

"Is that why you sealed off Seahorse Alpha?" Aluna said.

Kapono nodded. "We truly felt that was what Sarah Jennings and our ancestors wanted. In part. But we also did not want our young growing enamored of other places or other people. We did not want them to yearn for the Above World or go off and die in the name of adventure."

Aluna looked at Daphine and watched her sister's scope spin and focus. Daphine sighed and looked at Aluna. "It's all true."

"Of course it's true," Kapono said, not realizing what his daughter had just done. "Losing a dozen Kampii would be a tragedy. Losing hundreds would mean the end of a viable population. It would doom us completely."

"I had no idea that things were so bad," Aluna said.

"The Elders are to blame for that, myself included,"

Kapono answered. "We thought to protect you all from the truth, but also, we wanted to protect our pride. We didn't want to admit that our city was failing."

Pilipo stood straighter. "We can't go to war, and we need breathing necklaces to replace the ones that are failing. We have no choice but to take them from the Deepfell."

"No!" Daphine said. "Our need does not justify the slaughter of another people."

"Daphine is right," their father said. Then, shocking all of them, he smiled. "Perhaps Daphine is *always* right." She reached over and squeezed his hand. "Here is what I will tell the council: We cannot go to war . . . not even with the Deepfell. We will abide by the treaty the surface colony has created and put an end to our fighting."

Aluna felt her mouth drift open.

"But the necklaces," Ehu said. "More will fail!"

"Then Peleke will have to find another way," Kapono answered. "And until then, the alliance will give our people a safe place to live."

"So we won't help defeat Karl Strand," Aluna said. "After everything that's happened, we still won't help."

"No," Kapono said. "Even if we had the numbers we needed, I would not allow it. The ocean is our home and always will be, even if we must find a new place to hide our city. The Kampii colonies of Silverfin and Nautilus are also options, though we would lose many people on such a long journey. But no matter what befalls us, Kampii were not meant to meddle in the affairs of the Above World."

Aluna was about to speak again, to lob another useless attack at her father's towering mental wall, when Hoku's voice burst in her ears.

"Aluna? Are you home?"

She was about to reply when Hoku swam through the archway, his familiar pale legs kicking in the current and Zorro clinging to his shoulder. Had it really been more than a week since she'd seen him? Aluna wanted to poke his freckled nose and ruffle his shaggy reddish-brown hair. And then she saw his eyes. His *orange* eyes.

"What did you do?" she whispered.

He lifted up the force shield still wrapped around his arm. "Oh, this? I'm using the power source to run the audio pickup and the camera for my portable comm system," he said as if all the words made perfect sense. "I had to dig the camera out of a decomposing Great White. That part was not fun. I made Zorro do most of the squicky stuff."

Your eyes, she wanted to say. *What did you do to your perfect Hoku eyes?*

"Hoku, did you interrupt us for a reason?" Kapono asked. "I sincerely hope your answer is yes."

Hoku started, apparently noticing Aluna's family

for the first time. Her father had always terrified him. Actually, her brothers did, too. She started to answer on Hoku's behalf, to save him from having to do it.

But this Hoku, the one with the strange, glittery eyes, recovered from his surprise quickly. "Of course I have a reason," Hoku said, his tone direct and easy. In fact, he didn't seem scared at all. "I've made contact with the Equians, the Serpenti, the Aviars, and—"

"Dash?" she asked quietly.

"No, with Pocket from Odd's kludge," he said. "He said Dash and Vachir are together, but they don't know where. As soon as Pocket calls back, I'll have a better idea. And then, if we're very lucky, we'll know something else, too. We'll know the location of Karl Strand's lair."

CHAPTER 31

Hoku HANDED THE TINY PROJECTOR to Elder Peleke. Peleke's face contorted, as if he were being asked to stick his hand inside a squid. Finally the wrinkles around his eyes began to relax and the old man took Hoku's offering.

"This box contains the answers we need?" Elder Maylea asked.

"Yes," Hoku said. "The schematics for our breathing necklaces and some ideas for generating energy from the currents so we can recharge the necklaces ourselves. The Aviars use a similar device for trapping wind energy in Skyfeather's Landing, and they helped me and Rollin modify the design. We'll have complete control of our own tech, including recharging everyone's breathing shells."

A few months ago, standing in front of the council of Elders would have turned him into a stammering, blubbering mess of jellyfish goo. But compared to President Iolanthe of the Aviars and High Khan Onggur of the Equians, the Kampii Elders just seemed . . . smaller.

Peleke pressed the control button on the tiny projector and started glancing at the schematics. "These diagrams are gibberish," he said. "They make no sense."

"Yes, they do," Hoku said. "If I have time before I leave, I'll explain what I can. I've tried to label everything important and have removed the more complicated formulas."

Peleke sneered. "No sand-sider youngling will explain anything to me!"

Hoku shrugged and turned to Aluna's father, Elder Kapono. "Elder Peleke has two apprentices who I can work with instead. I've already spoken with them and they're excited to get started."

"Excellent!" Kapono said. "I will inform them that they report to you now."

Hoku kept his gaze on Kapono but couldn't help watching Peleke out of the corner of his eye. The Elder sputtered and turned red as fire coral. The old man tried to speak, but the words seemed to stumble off his tongue. In that moment, Hoku felt as light as one of Calli's feathers.

After the council meeting, he spent two hours with Peleke's apprentices, Loni and Udale, showing them how to read the tech diagrams and answering their endless stream of questions. His mood fluctuated from joy at sharing his knowledge to despair when he realized how little they knew.

But he'd started with even less and had managed to learn. Loni had a mind quick as a dolphin, and Udale's slower but more analytic approach made them an excellent team. When Hoku left them, they'd already started arguing about the best methods for creating the pieces they'd need for the simplified turbine. He promised to check on them again as soon as he could.

Hoku swam toward his own nest, but changed his mind and headed for Aluna's instead. The worst thing about his new eyes — aside from the occasional stabbing sensations — had been his mother's reaction. When she'd seen him, she had recoiled, turning her body to protect the baby in her belly from the apparent monster who'd just entered the nest. Hoku's father had been more understanding and had brokered an uneasy peace between them. But his mother . . . The wariness hadn't left her eyes. Hoku had no doubt that she still loved him, but now she feared him a little, too. The thought made him sick.

He lifted a hand and scruffled Zorro behind his good ear. The little guy clung to his shoulder and kept his eyes squinted as they swam. *Are you happy?* Hoku asked. Zorro's slitted eyes pulsed green and *Yes, yes, yes!* appeared in Hoku's vision. He grinned.

By far the best side effect of his Datastreamers was his new relationship with Zorro. Just as he'd connected to the computers at Seahorse Alpha, he'd managed to bind his tech to Zorro's. Now the two of them could talk and share data without even using words. It felt like Zorro was now a cute, fuzzy extension of his own brain.

Aluna wasn't in her nest, so he swam to the training dome. She'd been living there lately, relearning all her weapon forms now that she had a tail. She looked up when he neared, but didn't stop her spear strike against her invisible opponent. "Have you heard from the kludge?" she asked. "Are Dash and Vachir alive?"

"No word from Pocket yet," he answered. They'd had this exchange two dozen times in the last day. "But Rollin is going to call soon, and I asked her to find Nathif."

Aluna performed a long series of moves involving spinning and somersaults and more spear thrusts than

Hoku could count. She almost impaled her own tail with one of them, but adjusted, tried the move again, and performed it flawlessly. Kampii women weren't allowed to be hunters, but not even her father dared trying to stop her from practicing now.

Hoku watched Aluna's next set, too, marveling at how sharklike her movements were; how crisp and sharp, even in the thick water surrounding her torso and tail. She was utterly beautiful. He told Zorro to record her, though he wasn't quite sure why. Maybe with everything happening, he wanted to be sure to capture this one moment forever.

When his Datastreamers buzzed, he almost didn't answer, not wanting to miss even one of Aluna's twists or attacks. But Zorro nibbled his finger, and he relented. Instead of Rollin's familiar face, Nathif's sleek cheekbones and slitted snake eyes appeared before him.

"Hoku, are you there? Rollin says you wanted to talk to me," Nathif said. His lips curled up at the corners. "I am not surprised that you miss me, of course. I frequently have that effect on people."

Hoku grinned and rolled his eyes before activating the device on his force shield. "I'm here," he said, "and although I do occasionally miss your bizarre sense of humor, Aluna is the one who wants to talk to you."

He waved, trying to catch Aluna's attention. She stopped mid-spin and swam toward him immediately.

Hoku sent the comm feed to Zorro and asked him to project it for Aluna. Nathif's face appeared in the water, wobbling slightly in the current. Hoku issued a few commands to the comm device, increasing its range and the direction of the camera to encompass Aluna.

And then he watched and listened, his heart slowly constricting in his chest as Aluna told Nathif about Dash.

All traces of mischief melted from Nathif's face. The pupils of his snake eyes widened. His nose flared. The muscles in his neck tightened. And when Aluna finished the story, Nathif's voice came over the comm device, soft as sand.

"We do not know if he lives?"

"We do not," Aluna said, her own voice strained. "But Vachir is with him, and I will act as if they're both alive until I have proof of anything else."

Nathif lowered his head for a moment. When he raised it again, he had recovered himself slightly. "Thank you for telling me."

Aluna reached out and touched the hovering image, sending ripples through Nathif's face.

The second after Nathif signed off and Zorro's eyes

fell dim, Hoku looked at Aluna. She treaded water, staring at the place where Nathif had been, her fingers splayed as if she were fighting the urge to ball them into fists.

Hoku touched her arm and she crumbled, a mighty fortress of sand that only needed one small lap of water for permission to collapse. He pulled her into his arms and held her while she sobbed in great choking gasps, her strong body racked with the weight of so much worry.

Hoku said nothing. There were no words better than wrapping his arms around her back and resting his cheek against her short, wild hair.

His comm device buzzed, indicating an incoming message. Aluna jerked away and wiped the tears from her eyes, a habit from the Above World that was completely unnecessary underwater.

"Who is it?" she said.

He accessed the message's location. "Pocket," he said, and asked Zorro to once again display the video. He couldn't help smiling just a little as Pocket's face and horns popped into view.

"Hoku, Aluna," Pocket said. "Why is the picture all blurry and dim?"

"We're underwater," Hoku answered. "The camera was built for this, so it pulls in as much light as it can, but the picture will never be as clear as it is when there's no refraction—"

"Save the science lesson for later," Aluna snapped. "Have you found them, Pocket? Have you found Dash and Vachir?"

"Still have Dash's signal, though it went all fizzly for a while," Pocket said. "Far as we can tell, he's been in one place for more than half a day now. Don't know about the horse. Mags figures Dash is . . . where he's gonna stay for a while."

Or maybe he's not moving because he's dead, Hoku thought, but he didn't dare say that out loud.

"Did Squirrel follow them?" Hoku asked.

Pocket nodded. "She did good. Stayed hidden all the way into the mountains, so now we know where the opening to the tunnel starts."

"Do you have coordinates for that? If Squirrel noted the time when Dash passed into the tunnel, then I can search the homing beacon's data and find his location at exactly that time," Hoku said.

"Just what I was thinking," Aluna grumbled, but she looked a little awed, too.

"Squirrel said the sun was just starting to slide behind the sea," Pocket said.

Hoku grunted and accessed a data set of scientifically calculated sunset times, then cross-referenced it with Squirrel's location and the data from the homing beacon. "I've got it!" he said. "I've got the entrance point!"

"Can you figure my coordinates, too?" Pocket asked. "We're staying here. Any folk come by who want to go in after Dash and Vachir, they should come talk to us. Send us a message on this frequency, and as long as we're still breathing, we'll find them. Odd says he's got some swords that belong to Dash, and he wants to give them back himself."

Hoku saw Aluna's face start to contort again, and he moved the camera away from her. "Yes, I've just accessed your location and will transmit it to our allies along with the other information. Pocket, you did really well. Aluna and I thank you."

Pocket shrugged. "Nothing to thank. Kludge watches out for its own."

When they hung up, Aluna grabbed his arm. She'd fended off the tears this time, and her eyes held their familiar ferocity.

"How far inland is the tunnel?" she asked.

Hoku pulled up a map and had Zorro project it. He overlaid the new coordinates, putting big red dots to indicate Pocket's location, the entrance to Strand's secret tunnel, and Dash's final position inside the mountain.

Aluna groaned. "That's too far. It's going to take us

weeks to get there. Not to mention the mountainside will be swarming with Upgraders." She looked down at her shimmering, fluid tail and scowled. "I never should have swallowed the Ocean Seed."

Hoku stared at the map, a thought itching at the back of his mind. The map looked familiar, but why? He accessed the data from Seahorse Alpha and started throwing other dots on the map: Seahorse Alpha, the City of Shifting Tides, the HydroTek dome, the house that Karl Strand and Sarah Jennings used to live in . . .

"Stop!" Aluna said. "What is that dot? The one you just put up?"

He tossed up a label: 465 EAST RIVER AVENUE, ARCADIA, CA. The words were meaningless to him. How did the ancients find anything by using strings of nonsensical words?

"Wait, this map isn't right," Hoku said. "This is from ancient times, when the sea level was much lower. Hold on a flash." He asked the computer at Seahorse Alpha to estimate how much land the ocean had eaten over the centuries, and he watched, fascinated, as the map changed. Huge areas marked as cities fell quickly to the water, until everything along the shore that was not a mountain had been subsumed.

"The dot is underwater now," Aluna said. "The place where Karl Strand and Sarah Jennings used to live got swallowed up by the ocean."

"Dash is close to where they lived, but inside the mountain," Hoku said.

Aluna shook her head. "It can't be a coincidence. Karl Strand would not have *accidentally* built his lair near his ancient home."

"We've got to go there," Hoku said. "We can swim and be there in a few days, if we swim hard. Maybe there's some way into the lair from his home."

Aluna pulled him into a hug, but this time, she wasn't crying. When she released him, she looked like herself again—the Aluna he hadn't seen since the desert, before her defeat in the Thunder Trials.

She smiled and said, "It's time to meet Karl Strand."

CHAPTER 32

*C*ALLI STARED AT THE BATTLE MAP and tried to find answers amid chaos. But war was nothing like science. She couldn't learn formulas, conduct experiments, or rely on matter and energy to act the way she predicted. There was no simple and elegant solution.

No, strategy and tactics had consequences that dripped with blood and heartache. Even when she sent a dozen loyal soldiers to their deaths, she had no way of knowing if she'd made the right choice. Every lost life felt wrong.

And Dash and Vachir. She couldn't stop thinking about them. Hoku's message had been brief, and the woman who'd delivered it had clearly not recognized its importance: "Dash and Vachir captured by Scorch. Should have Strand's location soon."

Senator Niobe joined her. "Are you feeling unwell, President?"

"What?" Calli said, rubbing her eyes. "No, I'm fine."

Her eyes burned from exhaustion and her wings drooped behind her, almost dragging on the floor. If she'd had five minutes to herself, she would have curled up on one of the war tables and closed her eyes. Sleep never came—not once for more than an hour since she'd arrived home—but even the pretense of sleep would be welcome.

"Did we hear from President Minerva yet?" Calli asked.

Niobe nodded. "Zarek, the president's consort, answered their comm this morning. He said our refugees will be welcome at Talon's Peak. Minerva will send a squadron of her warriors to meet us halfway. We need only tell her when."

"Good," Calli said. "Make arrangements for the sick and wounded to begin the journey as soon as possible."

"Including your mother?" Niobe asked gently.

"Yes," Calli said.

Niobe frowned. "High Senator Electra won't like that."

"And I should care what she thinks?" Calli asked. "Iolanthe is my mother, Skyfeather's Landing is my responsibility, and this is my call."

Niobe stiffened. "Yes, President Calliope."

Calli regretted her tone—Niobe had been nothing but supportive during all of this—but she didn't have the energy to apologize. "And tell Hypatia to report to me. We're losing too many along the eastern rim."

"As you wish," Niobe said. She turned to leave and almost collided with a young Aviar rushing into the war room.

"President Calliope!" the girl gasped. "The comm room. Hoku. It's urgent."

Calli strode past the girl, remembering at the last second to turn her body so her wings didn't smack the girl in the face. "Follow and tell me everything," she said.

The girl—who might have been a year or two older than Calli—scrambled to catch up.

"Hoku said they have a location for Dash, and they think he might be close to Strand's base of operations," she said.

"Are Dash and Vachir alive?"

The girl blushed. "I . . . I didn't think to ask."

Calli bit back her response. She had forgotten that Dash and Vachir meant nothing to her people. They were not leaders of splinter groups, not powerful warriors, not great scientists. She could never explain *why* they were so important, could only keep repeating that they were.

"Wait outside until I'm done." Calli swept into the room and sat on the lone chair in front of the comm wall. Hoku was on the screen, gnawing on his lip, his image blurry from the water.

And his eyes . . . there was something wrong with his eyes.

"Calli!" Hoku said, his expression shifting from nervous to excited as soon as he saw her. "I don't have long. I'm going to transmit a series of coordinates to your computer."

She watched the data come in and was relieved when her brain parsed it without effort. This is where she belonged, amid beautiful strings of numbers, not studying battle formations.

"The tunnel entrance leads down to Strand?" she asked.

"It leads to Dash, and hopefully Vachir is still with him," he said. "We think Strand might be there, too. See this other point I've marked? It's underwater now, but Strand used to live there back when he was an ancient Human."

"That's too perfect to be a coincidence," Calli said.

"Aluna and I agree," Hoku said. "The Serpenti and Equians are headed toward the mountain tunnel. Rollin even convinced some Upgraders to join our side. The bulk of our allies are going to engage Strand's forces near the mountain while a small team tries to sneak into the tunnel. I told them you'd send Aviars, too."

"What? Why did you say that?" She felt heat rise to her cheeks and anger fly to the surface of her brain. She didn't try to stop it. There he was, safe underwater, while her people were dying all around her. "We're losing the war here, Hoku. We're outnumbered and our people are being slaughtered! I can't spare warriors for an assault on Strand. We're doing everything we can just to save Skyfeather's Landing!"

Hoku pulled back, away from the camera, apparently trying to distance himself from her assault. The action only fueled her rage. She yelled, "And why are your eyes orange?"

"Calli, I—"

"No, wait." She held up her hand to the camera and bowed her head. *Breathe,* she told herself. *You're tired. You're worried. You're angry . . . but none of those things are Hoku's fault.* When she lifted her head again, she felt reasonably confident that logic once again ruled her thought processes.

"I'm sorry, Hoku, I really am," Calli said. "We just don't have any warriors to spare."

Hoku pulled the camera closer. "Not even for Dash and Vachir?"

Calli winced. Hoku must have known she would. "I'd risk my life for them," she said. "But everything is different now. It's not about my life anymore, or what I want. Thousands of lives depend on me. My people need me, and I have to do what's right for them, not for myself."

She watched Hoku struggle to find the right words to say. He hadn't yet learned that *right* and *wrong* were illusions.

"I'm sorry things are going so badly for you," he said finally. "I wish we could help, but the mountains are no place for Deepfell and Kampii, even if we had extra hunters to spare."

"And it's no place for Equians either." She sighed. "No, I've known all along that this is our fight, and ours alone. No one can help us." She ran a hand through her hair and it snagged on a tangle. "If my mother were well, she would say that she preferred it this way. That the Aviars didn't need help from anyone."

"She'd have been wrong."

Calli spun in her chair and stood as High Senator Electra stalked into the room. The woman had dark patches under her eyes and dry, cracking lips. The feathers on her wings stuck out at odd angles, in desperate need of grooming. But Electra was wearing armor and her bloodshot eyes finally held something more than grief.

Calli could only think of one reason why Electra might leave Iolanthe's bedside.

"My mother . . . is she dead?"

"No," Electra said quickly. "She continues to fight."

"Then why are you here?" Calli felt her anger begin to rise again. "Go, escape back into your pain and leave the work to those of us brave enough to face the world."

Electra looked sheepish, an expression so out of place that Calli's growing anger dissipated with surprise.

"I deserved that, and I deserved what you said to me in your mother's room," Electra said. "You called me a disgrace."

"I shouldn't have—"

"Yes, you should have." Electra took a long, slow breath. "If Iolanthe had woken and seen what I had become . . . What she would have thought . . . What she would have said! I cannot bear to think of it."

Calli pictured her mother's snarled lip and hard eyes. She'd leveled that look of disappointment at Calli her entire childhood. High Senator Electra wanted Iolanthe's love and respect more than she wanted air or sky or wind. Such a look would have destroyed her.

Still, Calli couldn't forgive Electra that easily. She wanted to ask, "How could you abandon us? It's *my* mother on that sickbed. How could you abandon *me*?" But she knew, even as the questions crowded her mind, that they were childish.

Instead she asked, "What did you mean? That my mother would have been wrong for wanting the Aviars to take care of themselves?"

"We fought the Battle of the SkyTek Dome to win our independence, but this is a different war," Electra said. She seemed relieved to talk about war, suddenly comfortable again, in the same way that Calli was her best self when talking about tech. "The scope of this battle is bigger, the stakes higher. We are fighting for our survival, and the survival of our entire way of life."

"But we're losing," Calli said. "I'm doing everything I can, reading books on strategy, studying old skirmishes, asking everyone for advice . . . and we're still going to lose."

Electra stepped closer and put a hand on Calli's shoulder. "Yes, we are going to lose Skyfeather's Landing. But we are not going to lose the war."

Calli narrowed her eyes. "We will not give up our home."

"We will," Electra said. She paused, considering her words, then continued. "You are the acting president, and I will honor your decisions as if the president herself had made them. But you should not have had this burden so young, and that is my fault. Let me make it right. Let me lead our people so that the weight of their deaths is mine to bear, not yours."

It took all of Calli's willpower not to scream, "Yes,

take it, it's yours!" But she was still the leader of her people, and she would not dismiss that responsibility lightly.

"What do you have planned?" Calli asked.

Electra shifted into full-on commander mode. "We send the sick, wounded, and noncombatants to Talon's Peak, as you already ordered. Then we leave a small force here to keep the Upgraders occupied while our main force escapes high above the mountain and joins the Equians and Serpenti at the front."

Abandon Skyfeather's Landing.

"What of the troops we leave behind?" Calli asked.

"The Upgraders will figure out what happened sooner or later, and then our holding squadron will escape to join either the war front or the refugees."

Someone coughed.

Calli turned and saw Hoku staring back at her from the comm screen. She had completely forgotten he was there.

"Aerial scouts could really help us find Strand's tunnel on the mountain," he said. "The Equians and Serpenti can't fly and don't have dragonfliers, like the Upgraders do."

"Yes," Electra said. "Our contribution to the war effort would far outweigh our simple numbers. We might be the force that means the difference between winning and losing. Whereas here . . ."

"We've already lost," Calli said. She tapped a finger on her lip and ran through the scenarios in her head. There was still no "right" answer that gave them everything they wanted. But at least Electra's plan offered hope.

Calli stood taller and threw her wings back. "High Senator Electra, I hereby cede the presidency back to my mother, Iolanthe, and put you in charge of all Aviar forces. I only have one condition."

"Name it," Electra said.

Calli glanced at Hoku. Despite his strange orange eyes, his smile washed over her like a spring breeze. "That you help me find the tunnel that leads to Karl Strand's lair so I can go rescue my friends."

Electra raised a crisp hand to her forehead and saluted. "It will be my extreme pleasure."

CHAPTER 33

WHILE HIGH SENATOR ELECTRA and Senator Niobe led the first flocks of Aviars up and over the Upgrader army, Calli said good-bye to her room. The colors were all light blues and whites, meant to mimic the sky that every Aviar longed for. Well, *almost* every Aviar.

Calli dragged her fingers over the curve of an equation written in thick black pencil on the painted surface of the wall. Formulas covered every stylized swoop of wind, every puffy cloud—some repeated a dozen times, until her younger self had memorized the symbols, and some half-finished, old puzzles never solved.

Books crowded her shelves and fought for space on every reasonably flat surface, including her wide, sturdy desk. Even now it was burdened with texts on electricity and aerodynamics, with notebooks and spare equipment. All shrouded in dust. She'd grown up in this room. No, that wasn't right. She'd only lived and learned in this room, but she'd grown up out in the world.

Her pack bulged with a few of the books she couldn't bear to part with — the oldest, the rarest, and the most sentimental. One was a crudely illustrated adventure story her mother had made for her when she was six. By any standard, it was ugly and poorly told, but Calli didn't care. Now her mother was on her way to Talon's Peak, carried by four warriors not at all happy to be flying away from the war instead of toward it, and Calli had only the slenderest feather of hope that she'd ever see her again.

If only she'd been able to talk to her mother one last time. Iolanthe would be proud of her for trying to rescue her friends. But, oh, how Calli yearned to hear the words.

She'd thought about leaving an explosive for the Upgraders to find. Maybe something in the microscope on her desk, or in the telescope fixed to the window near the room's highest perch. But what would that accomplish? Another senseless death, maybe to someone like Pocket or Squirrel. Her things, no matter how precious, were not worth a life. Not even the life of an enemy.

Calli checked in one last time with Senator Hypatia, the brave warrior who'd volunteered to lead the holding force and keep the Upgraders occupied while the rest of the colony escaped. She had no words of comfort or inspiration, only thanks.

And then Calli was flying up, up, up with the last squad of warriors. Up into the cold air and over the enemy army slowly strangling their home.

On their way to the front, they stopped at strategic mountaintop roosts where they could store their treasures from Skyfeather's Landing out of the reach of anyone without wings. The roosts were marked from above, easy to spot if you knew which symbols to look for. Calli packed her books into a crevice safe from water in the last one.

The women were silent as they flew, both to conserve energy and because they were preparing themselves for battle. They soared over a large force of Upgraders — reinforcements for the battle at Skyfeather's Landing — and Calli had to resist the urge to drop rocks on them. Instead, she offered another silent thanks to the brave women who had stayed behind.

Later, more of Strand's army started to appear below them, a slow line of ants crossing over mountain paths and swarming into larger and larger units of death. Calli and her sisters flew higher, looking for scouts from the earlier Aviar squad, and soon found Senator Niobe.

"We're glad you made it," Niobe said. "High Senator Electra has set up camp on the far side of the mountain peak and has already been in contact with the Equians and Serpenti, who are coming from the southeast." She twisted her face. "The Upgrader named Pocket has spoken to her, too."

Calli beat her wings harder in order to keep pace with Niobe. It had already been a long day, and she'd been fighting the wind since the last resting stop.

"Are the other armies already here?" Calli asked.

"No," Niobe said. "The Equians and Serpenti are fighting their way in, but making good headway. Strand's armies are falling back to the mountain on that side. And we think Strand sent another army toward Skyfeather's Landing, which has weakened his forces here."

"He did. We saw them," Calli said. She surveyed the distant ground and could make out wispy armies through the clouds. "Karl Strand's army is weak here. It's a good time for us to strike."

Niobe grinned. "Electra thinks so, too. I'll tell her you approve."

"I'll tell her myself," Calli said.

Niobe shook her head, opened her wings wide, and hovered upright in the air. "The rest of the squadron will meet Electra, but I'm taking you straight to the infiltration team. You need to be ready when we attack tomorrow morning."

Calli beat her wings slowly, keeping her place in the current. "So soon?"

Niobe raised one slender eyebrow. "Isn't that what you wanted?"

"Yes," Calli said immediately. "The sooner we go after Dash and Vachir, the better our chance of rescuing them. I only thought we'd have more time to plan." And more time to steel herself, too. Already she could feel fear coating the tips of her wings like ice. Too much, and she'd be frozen with it.

"Maybe this will help," Niobe said. She unhooked a retractable spear from her belt and handed it to Calli.

Calli took it, rolling the scarred metal tube over in her hands. She recognized the weapon, of course—every Aviar in Skyfeather's Landing knew President Iolanthe's bright-gold and green markings. The spear's name was Seeker.

"Electra wanted you to have it," Niobe said. "She said your mother would, too."

Calli pressed the release switch and the spear shot out to its full two-meter length. "It's so light," Calli said, giving it a test spin.

"Don't let that fool you," Niobe said. "I've been whacked with that spear in more training drills than I'll ever admit. Strong as your mother, I'd say."

Strong as my mother used to be, Calli thought, but outwardly she smiled. Many months ago, her mother had given her beloved talon weapons, Spirit and Spite, to Aluna. Calli hadn't wanted them; at the time, she had rejected everything that the weapons stood for. But Calli was her mother's only daughter and the gesture still stung. Electra must have known all along.

Niobe whistled and another scout took over leading the squad. Calli watched them fly by in a flurry of wings and armor. Old and young, battle worn and green . . . they'd all be warriors by sunset tomorrow.

"Come," Niobe said. "I'll take you to your team."

Calli followed Niobe, trying to catch the same updrafts, and beat her wings in the same rhythm. *Her team. A team that would walk into the very home of Karl Strand himself.* Niobe got too far ahead and Calli focused on her flying.

Below them, Strand's army grew like weeds among the rocky skirt of the mountain, their tiny fires blooming like lonely flowers. As Niobe led her past kilometers of camped armies, Calli felt her chest tighten. Hope made her feel light on the wind; right now, she was surprised her wings could keep her in the air.

Niobe pointed to an Aviar symbol painted on the rocks beneath them. It was more subtle than the others, no doubt to keep it secret from the Upgraders' dragonfliers. Calli and Niobe flew past it, to an area more protected by the mountain, and dove.

Calli had never plummeted from so high. The wind screamed past, buffeting her face and trying to toss her like a toy. She kept her eyes slitted and her chin tucked to her chest. Her hair whipped around, lashing her cheek and forehead. She wanted to yell her fear and defiance into the raucous whoosh of air surrounding her.

She opened her wings against crushing pressure and trembled with relief when they caught the wind and she started to slow.

"Well done," Niobe said. "That was no easy descent."

They landed on a wide, flat rock. Niobe checked her compass and pointed. "That way, no more than two kilometers. You saw the mark on our way down?"

"Yes," Calli said. "Thank you."

Niobe grabbed her into a hug. Calli breathed in the woman's scent, relished the softness of Niobe's hair against her cheek.

"Tell High Senator Electra that I'll do my best," Calli said. "Tell her . . . tell her to take care of my mother for me if I don't make it back."

Niobe frowned. "You two can take care of the president together, after all of this is over."

"Of course," Calli said, forcing a smile. "But please tell her anyway."

Niobe put a callused hand on Calli's cheek, and Calli leaned into the warmth. "You are your mother's daughter. Do not forget."

Then her hand was gone. Niobe sprang into the air, her wings snapping open with military precision. Calli watched, marveling at the beauty of her flight and wondering if she'd ever see another Aviar again.

She picked her way over the rocks in the direction of the meeting spot. She hadn't gone more than half a kilometer before the Upgrader girl Squirrel hopped onto the rock next to her.

"This way," Squirrel said. Calli tried to follow but her legs weren't springs, and they weren't particularly used to rough terrains, either. "Hurry," the girl admonished, and Calli did her best to comply.

The team was already assembled when Calli and Squirrel arrived. She stared at the familiar faces of Odd, Mags, and Pocket and introduced herself as if they'd just met. She'd been "cargo" the last time, and the formality felt right. Odd seemed a little more banged up than when she'd last seen him, but Mags, Pocket, and Squirrel seemed largely unchanged.

"What, no kiss?" another voice said.

Calli turned and found Nathif slithering out from a makeshift tent, his long tail undulating over the hard-packed dirt. A sly grin twisted on his face.

"Nathif!" Calli said, and tackled him with a hug.

"It's not a kiss, but it will do," Nathif said after he'd righted himself again.

"I didn't expect to see you here," Calli said. "How did you get through the army?"

"A lone snake may go where an army of hooved horse beasts may not," Nathif said. "Oh, and Tayan says hello. She said it rather haughtily, of course, but you probably assumed that."

"Tayan is with the army, then?"

Nathif laughed. "No. Despite her exalted status as Flame Heart Khan, she will never be fit for battle with her heart injury. I wanted to be the one to tell her, but alas, they let someone else do it."

Calli looked around camp. "Did anyone else come? I expected to see Rollin here, too."

"Rollin said her presence would harm us more than help us." Nathif shrugged. "It is just as well. Her expertise is needed with the comm devices."

"Very well. Everyone, gather around," Calli said. "The Aviars will attack tomorrow morning at dawn, and we need to be ready to infiltrate the secret tunnel."

She looked at each of them, spending long enough to make eye contact for a moment before moving on to the next person. She'd seen her mother do this in almost every important meeting in the war room.

"If Dash and Vachir are still alive, we're their only hope. We're not going to let them down."

CHAPTER 34

HOKU TAPPED THE COMM DEVICE on his arm. Tapping it didn't do anything useful, but it made him feel better. Zorro, perched on his shoulder, seemed to agree.

"Still nothing," he said. "It can't connect with the satellite or any nearby computer systems. Almost two days! We have no idea what's happening with anyone else."

Aluna swam next to him, taking one powerful kick of her tail for every dozen of his ineffectual leg spasms. Daphine, Anadar, and Prince Eekikee flanked them, looking similarly sleek and effortless in the water.

Just below them, the bones of a vast ancient city slumbered in the sand. They'd been swimming through its broken towers and ruined buildings for hours, using the ruins to hide their presence. Hoku tried to estimate how many Humans had lived in the city, but got lost in the numbers. No matter how many times he did the math, the answer seemed impossibly large.

He caught Aluna stealing glances, her gaze lingering on the faint structures of the citywreck. A year ago, exploring this old place would have been their grandest adventure. But its mysteries had survived centuries, and they'd have to wait a little longer.

"We're nearing Karl Strand's house," Hoku said. He'd loaded some maps into his Datastreamers just in case he lost his connection with Seahorse Alpha. Now he pulled one up and overlaid it onto the landmarks around them. "Another kilometer or two, I'd guess."

"Oh, we're definitely getting close," Aluna said. She pulled to a stop and motioned for the others to do the same. Eekikee released a piercing shriek, and the Deepfell forces following behind them in a dark wave slowed.

"Up there," she said, pointing to the surface. "I see five great whites. They probably have cameras in their heads."

"And over there. Deepfell," Anadar said.

"Not Deepfell," Eekikee corrected. "Slaaaaves."

Hoku stared at what appeared to be a kelp forest

growing in the middle of the citywreck. But it wasn't kelp. It was the sleek bodies of Deepfell arrayed in lines.

"It's not a large force," Anadar said, "but it's bigger than ours." He cursed and adjusted the borrowed breathing shell at his throat. "I wish the Elders had given us hunters. Even a few, and we'd have a far better chance."

"I don't like our odds," Aluna said. "We could be fighting them for days, and the casualties . . ." She looked at Eekikee. "We can't ask you to lose so many."

Hoku added the sharks and Deepfell slaves to his maps, then told Zorro to project the image into the water in three dimensions. Aluna, Daphine, and Anadar were used to his tech by now, but Prince Eekikee jumped. As soon as Hoku started explaining the image, Eekikee's mouth hung open and he swam in closer to touch it for himself.

"Strand might have more troops we can't see, but this gives us a good idea," Hoku said. He rotated the map with his mind and highlighted Strand's ancestral house.

"Strand's forces surround the house," Aluna said. "At least we know we're right about it being important."

Anadar pointed. "Look. Something's moving."

Hoku peered into the murky distance, expecting another platoon of Deepfell slaves or a few more great whites, but the creature was something else entirely. He told his Datastreamers to magnify the image, correct for light refraction, and add it to the map at the correct scale. Everyone gasped, including Hoku himself.

It was an octopus. A giant octopus, its fleshy head inside a helmet of thick bars, its eight tentacles limber and metallic.

Prince Eekikee emitted a string of low-pitched noises, and Anadar cursed again.

"I could probe it," Hoku said. "If it's got a computer, maybe I can access it and turn the creature off or take control or something." He pictured himself riding the octopus into battle, his foes scattering like fish before him.

"Will the octopus sense you doing that?" Aluna asked. "We have the element of surprise now, while we're hidden in the citywreck. I don't want to lose it."

Hoku rubbed Zorro's head and thought. "It might," he said finally. "I haven't had much experience with different systems. And besides, we don't even know if it's entirely mechanical, of if there are people controlling it like a vehicle."

"It's your call, Aluna and Eekikee," Daphine said. "We're part of your army."

Eekikee continued to stare in horror at the image of the octopus. "No fiiiight thing is gooood."

Aluna nodded. "I agree with the prince. See what you can do, Hoku. Just . . . be careful."

Hoku calmed his breathing and closed his eyes. It was easier to read the output from the Datastreamers when he couldn't see his friends staring at him, silently asking him to be brilliant. His left hand was still threaded through Zorro's fur, and he left it there, drawing comfort from the raccoon's tiny body and unwavering adoration.

He used his Datastreamers to search for computer signals. Maybe the octopus was being controlled from somewhere else, and he could take over the command signals. Text streamed in front of his eyes. Yes, the octopus was using a network of some sort. Hoku poked at it, looking for a way in.

"What's he doing?" he heard Anadar whisper. Because Hoku's Kampii tech brought the sound directly to his ears, Anadar might as well have been shouting.

"Shhh," Aluna said.

Hoku heard a smack, like a wet fish flopping on a rock, and Anadar said, "Ow."

Hoku found a security hole, and in a flash, he was inside the octopus. His Datastreamers had just started sending their invisible tendrils into the tasty new computer system when the octopus launched some sort of defense program. The glowing text streaming across his eyelids fell dark, replaced by only one phrase pulsing in the center of his vision:

WHY, HELLO THERE. THIS IS FATHOM. REMEMBER ME?

Hoku sputtered and snapped his eyes open, but the words still hung there. He told his Datastreamers to remove the words, to stop its attempts to connect with the octopus, and then, when he sensed Fathom was probing for him, to cut off all transmissions and lock itself down.

"What? What is it?" Aluna asked. She took his arm, gently, and he shuddered.

"Fathom," he said. "That thing is Fathom."

If his reaction was bad, it was nothing to Daphine's. Aluna's sister hugged her arms and seemed to cave in on herself. Aluna and Anadar swam to her side instantly.

"How could it be Fathom?" Aluna asked him. "We took him apart, limb by disgusting limb."

"But we kept his brain, his consciousness," Hoku said. He put his hand to his head and pressed his temple. He didn't need another headache now, not when he needed to think clearly and stay ahead of Fathom. "That's why they attacked HydroTek. They stole his brain so they could transfer it to the octopus."

"Karl Strand loves his children," Aluna said. "He wants them to live forever."

Eekikee squeaked and pointed. Hoku squinted through the throbbing in his head. In the distance, the octopus and the slave armies were moving.

"Fathom noticed you, didn't he," Aluna said.

Hoku grimaced. "He seemed delighted by our presence."

Eekikee began screeching to the pods of Deepfell waiting behind them.

"Daphine, you need to go back to the colony," Anadar said. "You're not a warrior, and you're not up for this. You'll get yourself killed."

Daphine shook him off. The scope over her left eye whirred. "I'm not going back," she said. Her voice trembled, but there was steel under it. "I'm going to make sure he stays dead this time."

"We can't all stay and fight," Aluna said. "Some of us need to sneak past Fathom and make it to Karl Strand. He's the goal. As much as we want to defeat Fathom in this battle, we can't lose sight of the war."

Water whooshed as the pods of Deepfell began swimming into their formations.

"Aluna and I will go for Strand," Hoku said. "We've been fighting him for so long; we have the best chance against him." He patted the satchel at his side, reassuring himself that the water safe was still inside. "Besides, I think I might be a liability in a fight against Fathom now. He knows too much about my tech."

"Yes, Aluna and Hoku will go," Daphine said. "And Anadar. You'll need his skill, too. I can stay with Eekikee."

"No," Anadar said. "That's not going to happen, and don't even try to convince me. I won't leave you, Daphine."

Hoku watched Aluna's face to see if she was angry, but she looked relieved. She'd always said that Daphine was the sticky jellyfish goo of the family, the only thing holding them all together. Apparently Anadar agreed.

Eekikee finished talking with his pod leaders and swam over to them. "We lead aaaarmy there," he said, pointing. "You goooo there." He pointed in the other direction. "Go now."

While Aluna hugged Anadar, Hoku found himself pulled into Daphine's arms. "Stay safe, little fish," she said.

He smiled and said, "Show Fathom what little fish can do."

The look in her one remaining eye turned fierce. "You can count on it."

Aluna wanted to make good time, so she made Hoku hold on to her shoulders, as if he were drafting off a dolphin. He kept his head down and his feet out of her way and told Zorro to do the same. Even with his weight and drag in the water, Aluna was swift as a seal.

Hoku wanted to turn his head and watch the battle unfold behind him. Would Fathom the octopus cut down the Deepfell with lasers? Did he possess some secret death weapon? His heart ached for the prince and his brave army, for Anadar, and especially for Daphine.

"Am I going the right way?" Aluna asked.

Hoku looked up. They were farther from Fathom now, so he turned his Datastreamers back on and accessed the map. "Down there," he said, indicating a squiggly line far below them that used to be a Human street. "We're almost directly over it now."

"No guards," Aluna said. "Strand must think he's hiding it this way."

"Hiding has worked for the Coral Kampii for centuries," he countered. "It's a time-honored tradition."

She snorted, and it was almost as if they were simply on another adventure, and not sneaking into the lair of the most dangerous man in the world.

CHAPTER 35

*C*ALLI CROUCHED LOW behind a rock, trying to keep her wings hidden. Orange and pink tinted the sky at the horizon, announcing dawn.

"Now?" asked Squirrel.

"Not yet," Calli said. She scanned the sky, looking for a sign from Electra that the Aviar's attack had begun.

Nathif coiled next to her, his body low to the ground. Pocket, Odd, and Mags waited beside him. Six people. Was that a good number for a secret assault? Calli wished her people were at least a little superstitious so she could take comfort in the number, even if that comfort was irrational.

"There," she said, pointing to the sky. "An Aviar. The battle has started."

The others squinted, but only Odd's goggle-covered eyes could make out the flying woman in the sky.

Below them, a band of ten Upgraders guarded the entrance to Strand's secret tunnel. Squirrel had followed Scorch's chariot and marked the location well. A towering rock blocked the entrance, but from up here, Calli could see the partially hidden rails it was sitting on. Pushing the rock out of the way looked impossible, but if they'd rigged it properly, it would actually be easy to move.

"Are you ready?" Calli asked Squirrel.

Squirrel, her dull-brown hair hanging around a face covered in layers of dirt, smiled with perfectly white teeth. Her green eyes glinted in the tentative light of dawn. "I'll be fast," she said. "Faster than all of them."

"You stay away from the tunnel," Mags said. "We'll find you when it's over."

Squirrel nodded solemnly. For a brief moment, Calli could see how young the girl was, how skinny and frightened. It was so easy to forget.

"Blue skies," Calli said, and Squirrel was off.

Calli watched Squirrel circle around and hop down the rocky mountain face as if she'd been born here. A moment later, the first Upgrader saw her and sounded the alarm.

Squirrel bolted down the path, screaming, "Secret tunnel! Secret tunnel!" Seven of the ten guards followed her, some pausing to shoot flames or harpoons from their arms or weapons.

"That is one brave girl," Nathif said with no hint of humor in his voice.

"Now let's do our part," Calli said. She gripped her mother's spear and silently hoped she'd remember how to use it.

"I'll bash them two, the closest Gizmos," Odd said, hefting his club. "Snake-boy can help."

Nathif's Serpenti body made him the largest person in their group, but he was no fighter. Not only was he bad at it, he was "ethically opposed to hurting others." In retrospect, perhaps he hadn't been the best choice for their tiny rescue team.

"Right. The rest of us will take the farthest one. The woman," Calli said. "Mags?"

Mags lifted her hand and waved a needle full of dark-purple liquid. "Give me an opening and she'll be snoring like a rhinebra in two beats of a drum."

Calli sucked in a huge breath and said, "Go!"

She scrambled down the rocky slope with the others, afraid that if she flew, her wingspan might alert the other guards and bring them back. Odd got down to the path first so he could suck the remaining three guards in, like iron filings drawn to a powerful magnet. They saw him and charged.

Calli's heart fluttered in her chest, her hands trembled. She'd hoped some sort of battle calm would overtake her and she'd be able to scan the fight, assess their situation, and call out orders. But once the first blow fell—Odd's huge club crashing into the arm shield of the first guard—all reason fled her brain.

She found herself yelling as she charged the third guard, her mother's spear out and extended and aimed at the woman's heart. The Upgrader batted it out of the way with her own weapon, a sword crackling with blue light.

Calli's hands buzzed with pain. Electricity! She wanted to drop her spear but she couldn't. Her arms were frozen. Calli watched the Upgrader lift her other arm until Calli was staring into the sparking barrel of a flamethrower.

Pocket smashed into the woman from the side, knocking her over. Flames gushed from her weapon. Calli managed to twist just in time, getting her wings out of the cone of fire.

The Upgrader backhanded Pocket, and the boy flew back in a graceful arc and smashed against the pebbly ground. Calli heard him groan. She started to race over, but Nathif got there first. He coiled his snake tail around Pocket and hovered over him, protecting the boy with his body.

Mags maneuvered behind the Upgrader woman, her needle raised and ready. Calli's hands and arms still tingled, but she kept her grip on Seeker and charged again, trying to give Mags the opening she needed.

Fire bloomed before her, hot and needy. Calli leaped to the side and felt it scorch her cheek and left wing. Black smoke billowed up around her eyes. She thrust her spear blindly. The point connected with something and she pushed, hard, trying to drive it further in. It sank in another centimeter and stopped.

Calli pulled back and swung the butt end of her spear around, aiming to whack the woman in the head. The Upgrader got her sword up to block, and Calli's body once again shook with electricity.

She couldn't move. The woman still had two deadly weapons, and now there was nothing stopping her from using them. Calli watched, comforted by the way the world had slowed down around her, letting her see everything that was happening even though she was unable to stop it. The Upgrader moved her flamethrower toward Calli's face.

It never made it. The Upgrader collapsed to the

ground, an empty needle protruding from her neck. Mags stood behind the Upgrader's body and felt for her pulse.

"Alive," Mags said, clearly disappointed.

Odd grunted and Calli turned to see him drop the second of his foes to the ground. One of them twitched and rolled, holding his side. The other lay still.

"Two broken ribs," Nathif said as he helped Pocket back to his feet. "I will wrap them to help with the pain."

Pocket nodded, his dark face an ashen gray.

"After we get inside," Calli said. Her teeth still vibrated from the electric shock. "Squirrel has probably lost the others by now. Nathif, help me with the rock."

As she suspected, the huge boulder moved easily on the hidden rails. With just Nathif's help, she managed to move something that would have taken a hundred people to move otherwise.

They ran inside and pulled the rock back in place behind them. The tunnel fell into darkness. Only Odd, with his strange goggles, could see more than a meter in front of him.

"I'll search for a control panel. There must be an artificial-light system in here," Calli said. "The rest of you, try to destroy the track that the rock is on. Make it as hard as possible for anyone else to get in here."

Calli ran her hands along the wall, grateful that the

feeling had returned to her fingers. Nothing on the left. She stumbled over to the other side and quickly found a smooth patch of stone. The panel sat in the center, but too high up to reach unless you were standing in a chariot.

Or unless you had wings.

A moment later, she pressed enough buttons to illuminate the tunnel in thin lines of light. Her team cheered.

Calli lowered herself back to the ground. "How is the rock?"

"We could do more damage from outside, but even so, I believe the stone to be stuck," Nathif said. "We have bent the rails, wedged smaller rocks under the big one, and basically wreaked havoc."

"Havoc is good," Calli said. "Pocket, are you doing okay? Odd, were you injured in the fight?"

"I'm good," Pocket said. He seemed to be breathing shallowly. "Not going to say much, though."

"Mags patched me up," Odd said.

"I always do," Mags added.

Calli nodded, suddenly overcome with emotion. She wasn't even sure which emotion it was, only that her battle mind was fading, leaving her mentally tired and a little fragile. She hopped into the air and spread her wings, grateful that the tunnel was wide enough to accommodate them. "Let's go," she said. "I'll take the lead and look for traps. Are we still tracking Dash's homing beacon?"

Pocket pulled out a device. "Yeah, still got him. He hasn't moved since I sent the coordinates last time."

No one said anything to that. No one wanted to think about—or admit—what it might mean.

"Keep the scanner out," Calli said. "That's our prize. Let's not lose sight of it, even for a minute."

She flew ahead slowly and occasionally circled back to give them time to keep up. Five. Her team was now five. Maybe that was the lucky number.

CHAPTER 36

ALUNA SWAM THROUGH the small hatch that led into Karl Strand's ancient house, although she could just as easily have swum through the large hole in the roof. Unlike the other skeletons in the underwater city, this one had been rebuilt over the centuries. Its walls had been patched and reconstructed, and a crude roof rested on its frame, complete except for the gaping hole near the back. This house meant something to Karl Strand. No matter what else was true about him and his plans for the future, he'd never forgotten the past.

"Creepy," Hoku said. "I can't believe Sarah Jennings used to live here."

"Big, too," Aluna added. "So much space for just two people and a youngling. Why are all the doorways so big? Great White could swim through here without a problem."

"There's not even that much stuff in it," Hoku said. "You'd think if he went to all the trouble to fix the walls that he'd have found some way to fix the furniture, too. It's almost empty."

Aluna picked up a piece of cold white stone resting on the floor, turned it over in her hand, and put it back. "It doesn't look like there's anything important in here. We need to find the passage into the mountain, if there is one."

Hoku's voice sounded in her ears. "Oh, there's definitely a passage."

She swam through the house until she found him in the back room. Unlike the others, this one had been reinforced with metal, even on the floor and ceiling. The entire back wall was a massive gate crisscrossed with thick metal bars, offering them a glimpse of a dark tunnel beyond.

"Can we open it?" Aluna wrapped her fingers around the metal and lifted. It didn't budge. "Heavy as a whale."

Hoku seemed lost in thought. His orange eyes glittered. Suddenly Zorro jumped off his shoulder, swam to the gate, and squeezed through the bars. The raccoon immediately swam over to some sort of control panel on the other side that Aluna hadn't even noticed.

"Is there a code?" She shook the bars again. "Maybe we can smash the tech and the gate will open."

Hoku said nothing. He just hovered there, letting the room's current move him gently back and forth.

Aluna heard a beep and saw Zorro project the image of an eye into the water, right in front of the control panel. The light on the panel switched from red to green, and the gate rose with a clank.

"What? How did you—"

"Retinal scanner," Hoku said, smiling. He was back from wherever he'd gone. "Luckily I brought Strand's extensive medical files with me. Thought I could sift through them and look for a physical weakness. I never thought I'd need them for this!"

"You really are brilliant," Aluna said.

Hoku used to blush when she called him that. He didn't now. "Let's go before Strand figures out what I've done. And . . . can I hitch a ride again? I want to try accessing his network, but if I try to do that and swim at the same time, it won't be pretty."

She nodded. "It's not pretty when *all* you're doing is swimming."

They darted under the gate as it rose. Hoku gripped Aluna's shoulders and she took off, adjusting her tail kick to avoid his gangly legs.

The tunnel started dark, but illuminated itself as they swam, thin lines of light glowing faintly in the water. The Kampii—and probably the Aviars, Equians, and Serpenti, too—would have decorated this passage with vibrant murals. Karl Strand had left them sleek and simple. Eventually the curved walls transitioned from metal to smooth stone.

"We're in the mountain," she said. "Can you pull up Dash's location?"

Hoku didn't respond, but a moment later Zorro projected a detailed map in front of her. It seemed to mimic their current location, as if detailed notes had been overlaid on what she would normally see. But far away, up the corridor and to the right somewhere, a green dot pulsed.

"Dash," she said, and hoped that Vachir was still with him. She could handle their imprisonment so much better when she pictured them together.

She swam hard. Hoku and Zorro ruined her sleekness, but she made up for their bulkiness with sheer power. One kick after the next, faster and faster.

And in her mind, she begged them to be alive. She begged the ocean spirits and the ancients, the Equians' sun god, and the Aviars' sky. If she'd remembered what the Serpenti cherished, she would have added their gods to her growing list. But mostly, she begged Vachir and Dash. *Hold on just a little longer,* she told them. *I'm coming. Just hold on.*

The tunnel curved down and then turned up

sharply, until Aluna felt like she was swimming straight for the surface. Just as she was about to stop and recite the ritual of ascent to let her body recalibrate for the change in pressure, the passage twisted back down and leveled off.

"You still back there?" she asked. Hoku used to talk when he was nervous. She hadn't realized how much his jabbering had calmed her nerves as well.

"Still no connection to a comm satellite," he said. "I'd feel better if I could contact the others. I think this tunnel is doing something to dampen the reach of my Datastreamers. I'm using Zorro's processor to boost my signal, but still nothing."

"So yes, you're still back there," Aluna mumbled.

He continued to ramble about his tech, and although most of the words slid off her mind like droplets of water, his voice echoing in her head helped to keep out other, darker thoughts.

Sometimes the pulsing green dot indicating Dash's location got farther away on Zorro's projection, and Aluna's chest tightened. All she could do was swim faster, concentrating on her technique with every ounce of her being to keep from panicking. But eventually, the tunnel would twist and turn and they'd be heading for him again. The fist around her chest would release its grip, and she'd be able to slow down a little and breathe.

When the current shifted, Aluna knew they were close to surfacing in an underground cave inside the mountain. She kicked toward the water's surface, her hands twitching for weapons.

"Wait!" Hoku said.

She slowed down, irritated, and watched him unfasten the force shield from his arm. He plucked the comm device from its center and handed the shield to Aluna.

"You might need this," he said. "I can still get messages from the others with the comm unit. I just won't be able to send any back. Unless . . ." He looked at Zorro and the animal's eyes glowed green. "Yes, yes, I can use Zorro if I need to, although I don't want to compromise his systems unless I have no other choice." He scratched the raccoon behind the ears. "What a good little universal communication system just waiting to be converted!"

Aluna secured the force shield to her left forearm. Such a small device with so much power. She'd have been killed sixteen times over in her battle with Scorch at the Thunder Trials if Hoku hadn't gotten her that shield at the last moment. She suspected it would save her again when they found Strand.

Hoku told Zorro to turn off the map projection, and they surfaced in the back of the cave in the shadow of a rocky overhang. Aluna searched for threats, but the cave was empty. Not even a lone Upgrader left to watch the water.

"He didn't think we'd find this place," Hoku said.

"We wouldn't have, without the old files from Seahorse Alpha," Aluna said. "Maybe Sarah Jennings never told him what she was storing there."

"Wait. Then why were Fathom and the Deepfell slave army out there?" Hoku asked.

Aluna groaned. "Tides' teeth. If they weren't guarding the entrance, then they were preparing to go to war."

"Against . . . us?"

She nodded. "If Daphine, Anadar, and Eekikee don't stop that army, I bet it will head straight for the City of Shifting Tides."

Aluna clung to the rock wall and imagined what Fathom might do to her people. To her family.

"Strand," Aluna said. "We need to stop him."

"Strand," Hoku agreed.

The cave had no sandy beach, like the Deepfell cave. Instead, a metal platform had been installed near the only doorway. They swam over and hauled themselves out of the water.

"I don't have a sheath for my tail," Aluna said. "Do you have any straps of hide or rope?"

Hoku dug into his satchel, pulled out an extra shirt, and began ripping it into strips. Aluna folded her delicate tail fin up and wrapped it around the bottom of her tail, where her calves used to be when she had legs. She used the cloth to tie it securely in place.

"It's not as good as protective leather, but it'll be good enough," she said. "At least now I can fight with it."

She hadn't brought walking sticks with her, either, so she dragged herself through the door using her hands.

"Stop!" Hoku yelled, but it was too late. Aluna looked down and saw a thin line of light hitting her arm. In the distance, an alarm sounded.

"Barnacles," she muttered. "Well, come on. They know we're here now."

The corridor outside the cave had been carved from mountain rock but filed smooth as plastic. They reached a fork in the passage and Hoku consulted his map. "Dash seems to be in the middle," he said. "I can't tell which path to take."

"We need to know. Have you tried breaking into the system, or whatever it is you do with your new tech eyes?" she asked.

"Zorro is trying all the passwords I have on file from the water safe, and extrapolating—guessing—at new ones. No success yet." Hoku looked back and forth between the hallways.

"Left," Aluna said.

Hoku looked confused. "Why left? Do you have a feeling about it? Is there some data I'm overlooking?" His orange eyes flickered, and she imagined him scanning tiny files, looking for answers.

"Left because we'll be dead if we just sit here trying to decide," she said. "Now, pull your head out of your tech and run!"

She dragged herself down the corridor, her arms straining. Hoku caught up to her easily.

"There are doors ahead," he said. "I'm trying to access them, to find somewhere for us to hide until they stop looking for us."

Huge metal doors appeared on both sides of the hall, each big enough for a whole family of Kampii to swim through at once. Footsteps sounded behind them. People called out to one another up ahead.

"Open a door," Aluna said. "Tides' teeth, open a door!"

"Got one!" Hoku said, rushing ahead. Huge metal doors sighed open and Aluna pulled herself faster. As soon as she was inside, Hoku punched a panel on the wall and the doors closed behind them.

CHAPTER 37

AN ALARM SOUNDED in the tunnel and Calli swore. "How do they know we're here?" The team had made good distance so far, but they still hadn't reached Dash.

"It is my fault," Nathif said. "I dazzle without even trying. Curse my unforgettable nature!"

"Not funny," Mags said. "Could mean they got Squirrel."

"I apologize," Nathif said quickly. "My tongue gets away from me sometimes."

Odd grunted, but Calli had no idea what he meant by it.

"Can you run any faster, Pocket?" Calli asked. If only she were a little stronger, then she could carry the boy herself.

"I've got him," Odd said, lumbering over.

"No, let me," Nathif countered. "If we are attacked, you need to be ready to . . . bash things. I, however, have no purpose in a fight."

Pocket didn't argue and Nathif hefted him up like a small sack of grain. They sped down the tunnel until the sound of stomping horse hooves made Calli pull everyone to a stop.

Mags sniffed the air. "Squirrel says the evil woman was riding a chariot pulled by horse folk. Smells like we're close."

"They do have a distinct odor," Nathif said, but almost to himself. Maybe he was trying to refrain from joking, but this was as close as he could get.

The horse smell became stronger as they approached a large, well-lit opening on the right of the tunnel. None of them were particularly stealthy now that Pocket was injured, so they had no choice but to creep forward, as inconspicuously as five strange people could.

Calli craned her neck and peered into what seemed to be a vast stable. Rhinebras, horses, and two giant insects stood in the closest stalls, their heads tied to the sturdy metal gates. A collection of saddles and two chariots sat nearby, ready for use.

There was no sign of Vachir.

Farther back, she saw the Equians. Two women

stood together, their heads almost touching, next to two men. One of the men had his eyes closed, possibly unconscious, while the other dabbed his face with a bloody cloth.

"Dash's fathers are in here," she whispered to the others.

"We can get them after we save Dash," Nathif said. "We cannot spare any time."

"No," Odd said, just as Calli opened her mouth to say the same thing. "Dash would want us to grab them first."

"Agreed. You don't know the boy like we do," Mags said to Nathif.

Nathif hung his head, almost buried it in Pocket's chest. The others didn't know of his history with Dash, how Dash had risked everything to save Nathif from Shining Moon and its torture.

"There are no guards," Calli said. "We'll save the Equians and leave the animals tied up. We might need them for our escape."

Odd grunted. "Good noggin work."

It sounded like a compliment, so Calli took it as one. She was still smiling when she tried to step into the room and ran straight into a force shield.

Pain ricocheted through her body. She tried to scream, but couldn't open her mouth. She tried to step back, away from the pain, but none of her muscles would obey her. She smelled something burning and wondered if it was her wings.

Gloved hands grabbed her shoulders and pulled. Calli came unstuck from the force shield and the scream inside her burst out, raw and powerful.

"Make sure she does not bite her tongue," Nathif said. "Test her eyes. Do they still dilate?"

"I'm no green basic," Mags retorted. Mags's head, with its halo of wavy black hair, filled Calli's vision. "I'll bet a black cat I've seen more electrocuting than you."

Calli felt Mags's hands on her face, gentle but insistent. Calli blinked, grateful that her body was once again taking orders. Mags patted her on the shoulder. "You'll be right as rocks, little bird. No more shocks for you today, though. Don't want those wings all fried up."

Calli nodded and let Mags help her to her feet.

"Controls are here," Pocket said. He stood by another of those glowing control panels, this one situated at Human height. "Don't know what to push."

"Nothing," Calli said. "Don't push anything. The wrong combination might shock you, or set off another alarm." She joined him and studied the panel. "I don't have the right equipment to override the security. Scorch has the passcode, and Hoku could probably access the computer system and get it. We'd need one of them in order to shut off the force wall."

"I vote for Scorch," Nathif said, his eyes dark. "Willing or unwilling."

"After we find Dash and Vachir, we'll look for her," Calli said. After one last look into the stable and a silent apology to Dash's parents, she led them farther down the tunnel. Nathif had picked up Pocket again, and the boy called off their distance to Dash's homing beacon.

"Two hundred meters."

"One hundred fifty."

"One hundred."

Rooms and new hallways beckoned them from both sides of the tunnel. Four times they had to sneak past an open door where Upgraders were repairing weapons, cooking meals, or working at desks piled with scientific equipment.

"So few Gizmos down here," Mags grumbled. "Not much of a secret base."

"Perhaps Strand does not trust many of his own people with his secrets," Nathif said. "Have you seen some of these Upgraders? Who can blame him."

"Still prettier than snakes," she countered.

"Keep moving. Stay quiet," Calli said, and was pleased to see both Mags and Nathif look momentarily ashamed.

There were no troops down here, no wounded, no

bustling war rooms filled with maps and screaming generals. The whole place felt . . . strange. Like an abandoned outpost or an ancient temple. Karl Strand was no typical warlord.

"Fifty meters," Pocket said.

Calli flew faster and the others kept up with her. She could hear Nathif breathing more heavily, and sweat dripped down Odd's brow, but no one uttered a word of complaint.

"There's the door," Pocket said. "It looks like Dash is inside!"

"I don't like how easy this has been," Calli said, and yet, she couldn't make herself slow down. Her mother would have been more cautious. Electra would have chided her for her recklessness. But . . . *Dash.*

"The door is closed," she said. "We'll have to pry it open or—"

As she spoke, the wide doors slid open with a hiss. Some doors at Skyfeather's Landing were pressure sensitive; this one probably was, too. Calli flew in and the others followed. As soon as Mags was inside, the doors slid closed behind them.

They were in either a laboratory or a torture chamber, or possibly both. Tables with restraints connected to hulking machines that beeped and flickered with lights. Drains dotted the floor at regular intervals. A familiar horse stood chained to the floor, her legs splayed for support, her head hanging so low that her black nose almost touched the floor.

Vachir. *Alive.* Calli wanted to weep with relief, not just for herself, but for Aluna.

"Dashiyn!" cried Nathif.

Calli followed his gaze. In the back of the room sat three small cages. Two stood empty, their floors smeared dark with old blood, but the third cage held a crumpled, unmoving body that she recognized immediately.

"Dash!" Nathif called again. He put Pocket on the ground, then burst forward . . . into another invisible force wall. Odd yanked him back immediately, and the damage was slight. Nathif groaned and put a hand to his head.

"Another force wall. It's blocking off the whole room," Calli said. "We're trapped!"

A small woman walked out from behind one of the massive machines. Her brown hair and glasses were unmistakable, but it was her cruel smile that Calli remembered most.

"Scorch," Calli said.

Scorch wasn't tall, but she carried herself like a great eagle, as if there were no predator in the world dangerous enough to be a threat to her.

"I can't tell you how pleased I was to find Aluna's

beast and this pathetic boy practically begging to be captured," Scorch said. "But you know me—I never settle. I want it all." She walked crisply to the other side of the force field. "Thank you for complying."

A trap, Calli thought. It was all a stupid trap, and she'd fallen for it completely.

Odd ran back to the door and tried to pry it open with his fingers. Calli let him try, but she knew it was hopeless. Those doors weighed tons. They were stuck in five meters of empty space between the door and the force shield, and Scorch could do whatever she wanted with them.

Vachir lifted her head and let out a strangled cry. Calli winced. How she longed to run over and throw her arms around Vachir, to break the chains around her hooves and neck.

But Dash . . . Dash didn't move at all. He lay on the floor of his tiny cell, and for the first time since they'd started this rescue mission, she realized that he might truly be dead.

"You've hurt them," Calli said, her heart a painful rock in the center of her chest. "If you've *killed* them . . ."

"You will suffer if you have," Nathif added, his voice anguished.

"Oh, the boy is not dead yet," Scorch said. She smiled and tilted her head. "At least, not since I last checked. I wanted to catch a few more flies with my honey. Now that you're here, well, I don't need the boy or the horse anymore, do I?" She laughed.

Scorch walked over and stood in front of Nathif. "I remember you. You cured that fool Onggur and turned those ridiculous Equians against me. I might have to kill you first . . . after a little fun."

Nathif's face drained of color and he balled his hands into fists. Calli could see him struggling to hold himself together. He'd been tortured before, by Dash's own herd. Even the mention of it seemed too much for him to handle.

"Leave the snake be," Mags said. "You want to tussle, tussle with your own." She motioned to Odd and Pocket and shoved her hands into her coat, no doubt selecting the perfect poison for the occasion.

Scorch ignored Mags and turned to Calli. "Ah, the girl I should have killed in the desert. Your entire race will be wiped out for what they did to my brother Tempest. Your precious mountain home is being sacked even now. When I see one of our people wearing feathers after this, I will wonder which one of your friends they killed." She spat at Calli. Her saliva sizzled against the force wall. "I see you've won a few of the weaker-minded Gizmos to your side. What did you promise them?"

Calli glowered, but kept quiet. Anything she said now would only make things worse.

Scorch stalked back to Mags, ran her gaze up and down the Upgrader's coat-clad body. "Actually, you look like a smart, resourceful sort of Gizmo."

Odd lumbered over and stood next to Mags. He grabbed Pocket to his side and gripped his club in his other hand.

Scorch nodded appreciatively. "Big. Strong. And the boy has hidden talents, too, I suspect. So the question is, are you loyal?"

Pocket started to answer, but Odd clamped his huge hand over the boy's mouth. Scorch smiled.

"We Upgraders need to look out for one another," Scorch said. "The Aviars have never liked us. They live in their high towers and they hunt us! All of the splinters think they're better than us. More deserving of respect. More worthy of life." She leaned in toward Mags. "Whatever this Aviar is paying you, I will triple it . . . and guarantee that you'll never go hungry or want for anything ever again."

Mags narrowed her eyes. "We'll be safe?"

Calli held her breath. Odd's kludge had wanted this from the beginning—a reward for turning her in to Karl Strand and the promise of an easier life. How had she not seen it? They'd been working with

Strand's Upgraders the whole time. No wonder it had been so easy to sneak down the tunnel!

"You'll all be safe, even the quick rabbit of a girl outside," Scorch said. "You have my word."

No. No! Calli screamed, but the words stayed trapped inside her, like birds in a cage.

Scorch smiled and pushed her glasses further up her nose. "All you have to do is kill the girl and the snake-boy. Right here. Right now."

CHAPTER 38

W HEN HE TURNED AROUND, Hoku's first thought was that they'd hidden in the trash room. Far overhead, stalactites hung from the natural cave ceiling, threatening to drop on their heads. Water trailed down the walls and dripped onto the towering piles of discarded items filling every centimeter of the vast cavern, except for the wide path leading from the door.

"What is all this stuff?" Aluna dragged herself to the nearest junk heap and lifted up a small cylinder made of glazed pottery.

Hoku told his Datastreamers to scan the item and cross-reference the image with the data he'd uploaded from Seahorse Alpha. The answer came back almost immediately.

"A vase," Hoku said. "The ancients used to stick flowers in it."

"Because . . . ?"

Data whirred in front of his eyes, telling him the object's height, the circumference of its opening, and its probable weight. None of that answered Aluna's question, so he took a guess: "So they could eat them later?"

Aluna snorted and put the vase back on the pile. "Let's move away from the door in case they check in here," she said, and began pulling herself down the path. "At least until the alarm stops."

Hoku followed, his eyes filling with words he only occasionally understood: rocking chair, bathtub, sectional sofa, floor lamp, bookcase, mirror, alarm clock, refrigerator. His Datastreamers highlighted each item as it displayed its name. He struggled to understand the words, but something in here could be useful. Microscope, clipboard, telescope, centrifuge.

"Everything here is from ancient times!" he blurted out. He swept his gaze across two more piles. Data bloomed in his eyes. "Nothing here is less than five hundred years old, I'd guess. In such a wet room—I'm surprised it's not all covered with mold."

A clang rang through the cave. Hoku looked up and saw an eight-legged Humanoid creature about ten meters away, atop a pile of furniture. A Dome Mek!

It seemed focused on cleaning the "dresser" in front of it. After wiping the whole thing with a cloth, the Mek lifted the large piece of furniture over its head, skittered to another pile, and gently placed the dresser amid a different collection of strange objects.

"That's some job it has," Hoku whispered.

"Is the Mek dangerous?" Aluna asked. "It doesn't seem to see us."

Hoku scanned the room for Meks, and his Datastreamers illuminated five more, all performing the same tasks. He read the Meks' systems and found only one command echoing over and over again: CLEAN.

"Why is this stuff so valuable?" Hoku said. "There's a little tech, but it's too old to be reused. Most of this stuff seems functional, or maybe like art."

Hoku wandered down the path and kept scanning. He told Zorro to do the same. He refused to believe that Karl Strand would keep a room full of junk that served no purpose. Aluna kept up with him, but her eyes were on the Dome Meks and the door, not the mishmash of artifacts.

"At least we know why there wasn't anything in the house," Aluna said. "Judging from the size of this cave, Strand must have scavenged every object from the entire citywreck."

They wandered deeper and deeper into the cave.

The Dome Meks buzzed and clanked softly as they worked, and the incessant *drip-drip-drip* of water from the ceiling had a comforting rhythm.

They should have known it was a trap.

In the back of the cave, a massive shadow shifted in the darkness.

"What is it?" Aluna whispered. "It's huge."

Hoku's Datastreamers scanned the shadow and flashed HYDRA across his eyes, along with references to ancient mythology that he had no time to read. He took another step forward. His tech tried to make sense of the creature's outline, but the wild images it threw in front of his eyes made no sense. Unless . . . unless he and Aluna had wandered into the prison of some ancient Above World monster.

The creature lumbered out of its alcove, its clawed feet scraping the ground, and Hoku gasped. It was big as a whale, but covered in shimmering scales of green and purple. Its wide body looked like a rhinebra's, striped and armored and indestructible. Its four finned legs were bent at angles, like a lizard's.

But from the hydra's massive body sprung the real horror—seven sinuous necks, each thick as a tree trunk, each ending in a vicious, fanged reptile head. Fins flared out from its jaws and ran over the tops of its heads.

Most of the creature's heads twined around one another, hissing and spitting. Forked tongues shot out and retracted. The three heads in the middle swayed back and forth amid the wild writhing of the others. The biggest head sprang out of the creature's centermost neck and turned its terrifying gaze upon them.

"There's something wrong with its heads," Aluna said. "They look like lizards, but they almost look Human, too."

Hoku used his Datastreamers to magnify the head in the middle and shuddered. Aluna was right. The hydra had unmistakably Human eyes. And when it opened its mouth to speak, a Human voice filled the cave.

"Welcome to my home," the creature hissed, five of its seven heads speaking in perfect unison. "I am Karl Strand."

Strand's words echoed in the cave, and for a moment, all Hoku could do was listen and try to process what he'd just heard.

The monster was *Strand*. Strand, who wanted to rule the world. Strand, who had wanted to live forever, and had found a way.

Then Aluna screamed, "Attack!" and the world zoomed forward, as if Hoku had told Zorro to speed up a video. Aluna took off, her arms pulling her body and tail over the smooth rock of the path, straight at Karl Strand. Her Kampii body looked so tiny, like a dolphin swimming at Big Blue.

If Strand was inside the hydra somehow, then he must have used tech to do it. Hoku scanned the creature, looking for a computer connection he could exploit.

"Got it!" he said, and Zorro danced on his shoulder. Hoku's Datastreamers connected to the monster and started to sift through the system, looking for vulnerabilities.

At the other end of the cave, Karl Strand laughed. Five of his heads tilted back and cackled, their forked tongues flicking between the daggerlike fangs.

"How many traps will you stumble into today, boy?" Strand asked.

"Barnacles!" Hoku said, and started to pull out of Strand's network, severing connections as fast as he could. He wasn't fast enough.

Searing pain shot through Hoku's head. *His eyes!* His eyes burned as if they were burrowing into his brain. He screamed and fell to his knees. His fingers found his face, eager to claw away the flesh.

Aluna's voice found him anyway. "Hang on, Hoku. I'll try to subdue him as fast as I can. Don't give up!"

Invisible flames engulfed his head. Hoku screamed

again and dropped to the ground. He rolled, desperate to smother the fire, and smacked into a pile of artifacts. They fell on him, sharp and heavy, and such simple pain was almost a relief from the torture in his skull.

Tiny licks covered the backs of his hands. Hoku slapped Zorro away. He didn't want comfort; he wanted to die.

CHAPTER 39

*C*ALLI LEAPED INTO THE AIR to escape Odd, Mags, and Pocket. She forgot that Nathif couldn't follow her.

"Odd and I will get the snake," Mags snarled. "Pocket, throw something at the girl. Knock her out of the air!"

Calli looked sharply at Pocket, but the boy only seemed confused. Mags pointed to the tracking device in his hands and repeated slowly, "Throw something at her!" Pocket hesitated a moment longer, then nodded vigorously, as if he finally understood.

Out of the corner of her eye, Calli saw Odd stalk toward Nathif, slapping his club into his empty hand. Mags already had a needle out, a clear liquid sloshing inside.

"Ooh, what's in the needle?" Scorch asked. "I hope it involves disfiguring boils. They're my favorite."

"No boils. Old allies earn a quick death," Mags said.

Scorch huffed. "Boring, but suit yourself."

Calli flapped her wings and kept her attention on Pocket. She'd never seen the boy hurt anyone, but then, she didn't know what he kept in most of his "pockets," either.

"Don't do this, Pocket," she called to him. "You're my friend! We're here to save Vachir and Dash!" He pulled back his arm and whipped the device at her head. She dodged and managed to catch the tech in stinging hands.

"Throw something else!" Scorch yelled as if she were watching sport combat and not a group of friends trying to kill one another. "Shoot flames at her!"

"No flamethrower," Pocket said, lifting his hands to show they were empty—of items and of tech enhancements. "I do what I can!"

"Well, at least throw something sharp," Scorch commanded. "But I don't mind a long show, as long as you get the finale right."

Odd had Nathif in a hold and the two struggled back and forth. Nathif was clearly trying to maneuver Odd into the force wall. Calli was surprised that Odd hadn't already beaten Nathif senseless with one blow from his club. And there was Mags, slinging insults but getting no closer to shoving her needle into Nathif's flesh.

Calli stared down at the device in her hand. Dash's dot blipped on its tiny screen. The small piece of tech wouldn't have hurt her even if it had struck true. Why had Mags been so insistent that Pocket hurl it at her?

Unless . . .

"Oh, Mags, I could kiss you," Calli whispered. She flew to the nearest wall and smashed the tech against the rock, careful to catch all the pieces.

The device's innards were rudimentary. Calli started twisting wires out of the casing. The homing scanner didn't have much power, but force shields — like the one trapping them by the door — were remarkably fragile when faced with a certain kind of conflicting current. She'd seen that again and again while helping Hoku with his force shield in the desert.

She felt objects hit her wings and back, but they didn't hurt. A piece of fruit, a small rock, the tiny toys Pocket had whittled for himself. She cried out when Pocket's next missile hit her, pretending that he'd damaged her wing.

"Ha! Stupid bird!" Pocket called.

Calli spared another glance at Nathif. Odd had him pressed up against the wall. Mags shoved her needle into his shoulder and pressed the stopper. Nathif hissed, his eyes wide and wild. Hopefully Calli was right and the syringe was full of nothing more potent than anti-infection syrum.

"Lady's paying for pain," Mags said. "Be a good snake and suffer for her."

Calli threw the modified scanner at the force shield and covered her eyes with her fingers. As the tech arced through the air, she wondered if she'd been wrong about Odd and Mags and Pocket. If so, this fight was about to go from doomed to utterly hopeless.

The device hit the force wall and the wall exploded in sparks. Pocket yelped and patted down a fire in his hair. Scorch, who had almost had her nose against the force wall on the other side, leaped back and shook her head, dazed.

The force wall was down. Calli looked at Odd and Mags and held her breath. Had she been right? Had Mags been trying to send her a signal?

"Bright bird," Mags said with a grin. "Now let's show this bit what loyalty is and means and does."

"For the kludge!" Pocket yelled.

Odd dropped Nathif and patted him on the shoulder. "Good show." Then he turned, growled out a battle cry, and charged Scorch, his club already raised.

"She's got swords in her arms!" Calli yelled, remembering the sick sound of flesh parting when Scorch had extended them during the Thunder Trials. "Be careful!"

She flew down to Pocket and helped him damp the last flame on his shirt. As soon as it was out, she grabbed his arm and pulled him toward the back of the room. "Vachir. Dash," she said, but she didn't need to. Pocket knew what to do.

Scorch smacked Odd in the face. It would have sent a normal person flying across the room, but Odd only smiled. A trickle of blood seeped from the corner of his mouth. He grabbed Scorch in a bear hug, trapping her arms against her sides, and yelled, "Now!"

Calli and Pocket scooted past and made it to Vachir. The horse lifted her head, stomped a chained hoof, and shoved Calli toward Dash's cage with her nose. Calli pressed a gentle hand against Vachir's forelock and nodded. "But you after, brave one."

Pocket was already working on the locks to Dash's cage when Calli knelt beside him. She snaked her arm through the bars and pressed her fingers against his neck, feeling for a pulse.

"He's alive," she said, and was surprised to feel tears spring to her eyes.

The metal bars sprang open a moment later. Pocket helped Calli drag Dash out of the cage and turn him onto his back, then hurried off to work on Vachir's bindings.

Calli swept the hair out of Dash's eyes and pressed

her palm against his dark, bruised cheek. "Wake up, Dash. We need you. Wake up!"

Behind her, Odd grunted in pain and Mags shrieked. Calli saw Mags's tall body slam into a wall and slide to the ground. Her hair billowed over her face, and Calli couldn't tell if she was alive or dead. Nathif was by her side a moment later, lifting her chin and checking her eyes.

Dash groaned. His eyes fluttered briefly, but he fell unconscious again. Calli probed his ribs, looking for damage, and found his shirt stiff with dried blood. "He's hurt. Nathif!" she called. "He's not waking up! Help me!"

She glanced away from Dash and saw Odd fighting Scorch. Odd was losing. If Dash didn't stand up and help, they were all going to die.

Calli squeezed the tears out of her eyes and tried to harden her heart. She pulled back her hand, took another breath, and smacked Dash in the face as hard as she could. His head jerked to the side.

"I'm sorry," she said. "Oh, Dash, I'm so sorry." She hit him again. His eyes sprang open and he gasped.

"Scorch," Calli said. "Scorch!"

Dash grabbed her arm and she helped him to his feet. He seemed unsteady but stable, his eyes darting around the room, taking it all in.

"Weapon," he rasped, his voice barely audible.

Calli pulled out Seeker, extended the spear to its full length, and pressed it into his hand. He nodded once.

"Dash is alive!" Pocket shouted.

Odd looked up, an expression of hope on his bloodied face. Scorch used that moment to drive both her fists at his chest.

"No!" Calli yelled.

She heard the swords slide out of Scorch's arms and into Odd's flesh. His hope turned to wide-eyed surprise. The massive club slipped from from his hand and thudded to the floor. A heartbeat later, his body followed it.

CHAPTER 40

ALUNA CHARGED, her head filled with Hoku's screams, her arms straining with the effort of pulling herself down the path. How was she going to fight this thing? Strand's enormous body was covered in thick scales, his four lizard legs ended in claws half a meter long, and his heads darted and twisted, lightning fast. Even his tail looked barbed and dangerous as it swished and swung behind him.

This wasn't the first time she'd be facing a larger opponent. Almost everyone was bigger than her. Anadar trained her for this, even though he'd been thinking of sharks and Deepfell and Kampii at the time. She remembered his lecture well: "Larger opponents can strike from a distance; that's their advantage.

Your goal is to take that advantage away. You'll want to run away—trust me, we all do—but you have to do the opposite. Get in close. As close as you can. Then the advantage goes to the *better* fighter, not the bigger one."

She stared up at Strand and slowed, wondering how she could possibly get close with all those snapping mouths and wicked claws. The monster's heads twisted back in openmouthed grins, and Karl Strand's Human laughter echoed through the cave.

Aluna could tell he was watching her from seven sets of eyes. Well, from at least five, since two of his heads seemed asleep. Were they? Or were they simply occupied doing something else? This creature may look like a beast, but it was no natural thing. Karl Strand had made it for himself, then transferred his mind into it. The ultimate upgrade.

"So this is what became of Sarah's little Kampii?" Strand said, his five heads speaking together. "How singularly unimpressive."

Aluna ignored him. Let him talk, work himself into a fury. She needed to stay calm, let her battle-mind take over. Another one of Hoku's shrieks cut through her ears and she cringed. *Push,* she told herself. *You can't help Hoku if you let yourself get killed.*

When she got within range, Strand stopped talking long enough to attack. One of his heads struck at her, fast as a snake. Aluna rolled left. The serpent snout smacked into the ground. Another head darted in from the side. Aluna hopped onto her hands and vaulted out of the way.

She pictured the cappo'ra circle in Coiled Deep. The drums echoed in her head, giving her a rhythm and a power she'd never have on her own. She spun. Twisted. Dodged. Tried to get closer even as Strand worked to keep her at a distance.

The heads kept coming, their mouths snapping shut just centimeters from Aluna's face. One long fang caught the point of her tail and ripped through the delicate membrane of her fin as it lay wrapped against her scales.

"So fragile!" Strand said. "I would have designed you far better than *she* did, not built you from bubbles and fairy tales."

Aluna clenched her teeth. The only thing saving her right now was Strand's incessant talking, and the fact that he used all of his functioning heads to do it. She couldn't get any closer on the ground. She needed to try something new.

His central head tilted to the side, a distinctly Human motion. "So many advancements in polymer technology back then. So many building materials to choose from. And yet *she* chose flesh and hope. A failing proposition from the start."

Aluna rolled onto her back, pushed off, and hopped up onto her bleeding tail. Before the next head could strike, she unclipped her talon weapons and whirled them on their chains.

"Such a silly little thing to have caused so much trouble," Strand said, and three of his heads snapped at her at once.

Aluna leaped to the side of one of the heads and unleashed her talons. The thin metal chains wrapped around the sinuous neck and hooked into place.

Strand jerked the head back, then swung it back and forth. Aluna dangled from it, her breath coming in gasps, her body whipping around wildly. Another head snapped at her, trying to pluck her off the first. She clubbed it with her tail, pleased to see its eyes roll back into its skull from the pain.

When a neck swing brought her close enough to another head, she used her momentum to swing onto its neck. She dropped her talons and gripped the scaled trunk with her arms. If only she still had legs!

The head bucked and screeched, trying to turn on itself. Aluna grabbed the blue ridges over its eye sockets and hauled herself up even farther toward its face. *Get in close,* Anadar had said, and she planned to.

"Insolence!" the heads yelled. "Futility!"

Aluna secured her left hand, then unsheathed

her knife with her right. It would never penetrate the creature's thick skull, so she drove the blade into its eye. Pushing, twisting, then pulling out and plunging it in again.

Blood drenched her hand. Aluna's grip on the knife started to slip, but she couldn't bring herself to clamp it in her mouth. Not when it was covered in so much gore. If she gagged now, she might lose the knife and fall.

Her hesitation cost her. The wounded head dropped suddenly, and she lost her hold. A second head snapped her out of the air. Its needle-sharp fangs slid into her tail and she screamed.

But she didn't drop her knife.

Aluna folded at the waist and wrapped her left arm around the serpent's maw. She couldn't reach its brown Human eyes, so she shoved her blade into its nose slit instead.

The creature's jaw opened instantly, releasing her. Aluna dropped five meters and crashed against the stone floor. *Tides' teeth.* She was back where she started.

"You're just like *her.* Selfish!" Strand's chorus hissed. "I know what's best for the world. I'm here to save it! Defying me is akin to spitting on Humanity. I am our best hope for the future."

Aluna groaned and clutched her chest. Something inside her body felt wrong. She needed to keep Strand talking to give herself time to recover.

"Sarah Jennings cared about you," Aluna said. Her voice came out weak. She tried again. "Sarah Jennings never stopped loving you!"

"Lies!" Strand's heads roared. "She never thought about anyone but herself and her precious, pathetic Kampii. I could have given her eternal life, and she refused. Is that respect? Is that love? Is that common sense?"

Only six of his heads still functioned, and the two in the middle still swayed dully on their stalks while the others spewed evil words. Aluna would never be able to destroy all of them before Strand killed her. Taking the first one down had left her bleeding and broken. And Hoku—poor Hoku—only writhed and whimpered somewhere behind her, his voice in her ears a painful echo of her own.

Were her sister and brother outside, facing the same fate? She could picture Fathom's octopus tentacles wrapped around Daphine, squeezing the life out of her while Anadar watched, helpless and wild with grief.

Calli was off somewhere with the Aviars, probably fighting for her life in the middle of the battlefield if she wasn't already dead. How would that smiling girl survive? She was never meant to be a warrior.

"There is a place for everyone in my new world," Strand said, his voices growing louder, "but there will never be a place for the Kampii. I will destroy every last one of Sarah's beloved people, and she will finally be gone forever."

Vachir. Dash. Aluna didn't want to think about Dash especially, but his face floated before her, dark eyes grim, his black hair long as a horse's tail. At least she would not live to see his disappointment.

"You look like her," Strand said, and three of his heads finally stopped talking and attacked.

CHAPTER 41

DASH WATCHED Odd slide to the ground, a shadow of dark red expanding around him. Dash wanted to scream, but his throat was raw and broken. He had done too much of it lately.

Calli had pressed a spear into his hand, and he was relieved to find that his fingers had enough strength to grip it. Its weight reminded him that he was alive, that the horror of the past few days was over. He would do anything to ensure that his fate did not befall his friends as well.

Scorch stood a few meters away, leering down at Odd. *Mocking* him, even as the man died. Dash expected no honor from her, but her unbelievable cruelty awoke a new energy inside him. A fresh anger.

It coursed through his body, replenishing him like a long drink of water after days spent in the desert.

Dash lunged forward and drove the spear through Scorch's back while she laughed at her fallen prey. The sound died in her throat. She twisted to face him, her body still impaled by the spear. A bubble of red appeared at the corner of her mouth. She raised her arm and aimed the tip of her sword blade at his heart.

He could not move out of the way. The act of thrusting the spear, of seeing it pierce Scorch's body, had emptied him of vigor. Scorch spoke, her twisted mouth betraying her sentiment. Her words came to him softly and muffled, as if he were hearing them over a great distance.

Pocket leaped up and grabbed Scorch's arm, attempting to slow her blade. Calli was there, too, and Nathif—Nathif!—was pulling Scorch away from him and yelling at him to move.

He did not. He could not. He could only watch as Vachir bolted into view, reared up on her hind legs, and brought her two front hooves smashing down. Scorch's eyes fluttered and rolled to white. Her neck twisted. She fell to the ground at an odd angle, the butt of Dash's spear still protruding from her back.

Calli's arms were around him. And then Nathif's. And then Pocket's. Dash tried to smile and to hug them back. His arms, as heavy as horses, would not budge. Vachir huffed in his face and he reveled in the warmth of her breath on his cheek.

A path cleared to Odd. Dash stumbled forward and fell to his knees by his side. He wished Odd had not chosen to wear goggles, for he dearly wanted to look into the man's eyes.

Odd was so close to death that Dash imagined his spirit halfway to the Sunshine Lands.

"Brought your swords," Odd said, fumbling at his waist with one meaty hand. And that was all. His body gave up its fight and fell slack while Dash was still summoning the strength to say thank you. He wanted more time. He had so much he wished still to say.

"Me and Pocket, we stay with Odd," Mags said. She sat down cross-legged on the floor, and Dash saw the bruise blooming on her face and the way her left arm hung oddly from her shoulder. "Don't forget us when you're done."

"I will stay with you," Nathif said. "I will see to your injuries."

"Cuts and scrapes will still be here when you're done," Mags said. "Run off, now, and fix this. Fix it all."

"Swords," croaked Dash. Odd wanted him to have them, and right now, he could think of no better way to honor the fallen hero. "Help?"

It took their combined strength to roll Odd off the

swords. Calli and Pocket cleaned them while Nathif and Vachir helped Dash to his feet.

"You are looking particularly handsome today, Dashiyn," Nathif said, smoothing the hair away from Dash's face. "You simply must share your secrets with me."

Dash blinked, the closest thing he could do to laughing, and was rewarded with Nathif's relieved smile.

With Blaze and Shatter once again sheathed at his side, Dash began to feel like himself again. Or, at least, like a shadow of himself. It was a far better feeling than he had had in days. He gripped Vachir's mane to steady himself and felt his strength slowly returning.

"Aluna. Hoku. Safe?" he asked.

Calli raised one eyebrow. "Did you really just ask if Aluna was safe? Maybe you're not recovering as fast as we thought."

Vachir whinnied at the joke, and the sound lightened Dash's heart. Vachir had been through as much as he had during their days of captivity. He would not have survived without her.

"We do not know where they are, brother," Nathif said. "But if you are feeling well enough, we will go find them."

Dash looked at Pocket and Mags, sitting on either side of Odd's body. He winced, but managed to lift his hand and touch two fingers to his heart.

CHAPTER 42

HOKU'S WORLD WAS ENDLESS FIRE and searing pain and no hope of escape. He writhed on the ground, clutching his face and expending all of his will to stop his fingers from clawing out his eyes. Each moment felt impossibly long. He was sure he could never survive another, but then, miraculously, he did.

When the pain ended suddenly, it felt like a trick. Hoku stayed on the ground, wrapped tight against himself, and waited for it to begin again. That sort of cruelty would suit Karl Strand.

Or . . . Strand had been distracted. Hoku could hear Aluna's ragged breath in his ear, her grunts, her yelps, the effort in her every move. Something she'd done had made Strand angry enough to forget about him. He might only have a few moments before Strand remembered.

Despite the respite from pain, Hoku's vision stayed dark and blurry. A shiver crabbed down his spine. He was almost entirely blind.

Fur grazed Hoku's hand. He picked up Zorro and clutched the animal to his chest. "Be my eyes," he said, issuing the commands to his Datastreamers. Their surroundings were projected inside Hoku's eyes, but from Zorro's perspective instead of his own. The effect disoriented him, so he stayed on the ground and assessed the fight.

Aluna had taken out one of Strand's heads and wounded another, but the monster showed no signs of slowing down or surrendering. His heads snapped and snarled, fangs flashing. Aluna didn't have long.

Hoku poked around with his Datastreamers, looking for new holes in Strand's security. He found them immediately. When Strand had forgotten about Hoku, he'd apparently also forgotten to close the connection between them. Hoku had only to follow it back in order to access whatever computer system Strand was using inside his creation.

He used his tech to swim through Strand's network, being careful not to trip any of the alarms. It only took a flash of a tail before he uncovered the secret behind Strand's two dormant heads.

They weren't sleeping at all; they were working! Messages flowed into the heads from Strand's generals. The two serpent brains ran scenarios, calculated victory rates, and sent orders back to the front lines. He had discovered Strand's war room!

Hoku saw a message arrive from Fathom asking for more reinforcements. His stomach clenched. Fathom, that horrible octopus thing, was still alive. He watched Strand process the information and inform Fathom that more troops were on their way.

But when Strand sent the message to activate more Deepfell slave soldiers, Hoku snagged it. He let Strand think the message had been sent, but he deleted it instead. Strand didn't seem to notice. *For Daphine,* Hoku thought.

If he could do that, what else could he do?

He dug around in the data, pulling up names, and found messages from a General Gator stationed at the war front. Hoku wrote a fake message from Gator informing Strand of a surprise attack from the south by a huge force of Aviars and Equians, and asked for orders. Strand's brains crunched the fake numbers and sent back elaborate orders for Gator to split his force in half, hold his position with the smaller force, and await the arrival of another army.

Hoku deleted the orders to that second army, too. No reinforcements for Gator, and now half his troops would be marching off to attack nothing, leaving the real Aviars and Equians to fight a vastly reduced army to the east.

It wasn't enough—stealing a few messages here and there, moving troops, causing chaos. As soon as Strand figured out what had happened, he'd issue new orders and fix everything. Hoku needed to take the serpent heads out for good.

Strand's multiple voices echoed through the cave. "You are pathetic," he said. "If *she* saw you . . . you, whom she sacrificed everything to create, she would regret everything. She would regret leaving me."

Hoku remembered the letters he'd found in Seahorse Alpha. "She" was probably Sarah Jennings, Strand's long-ago partner and the mother of their only child.

Hoku reached into his satchel and pulled out the water safe. He told Zorro to input the combination and open it while his Datastreamers pulled up every scrap of correspondence he could find between Sarah Jennings and Karl Strand.

When Zorro had the water safe open, Hoku used the raccoon's eyes to find the small carved-wood dolphin. Hundreds of years ago, Karl Strand had made the toy for his son, Tomias, and then given it to Sarah Jennings after their son had died.

He put the dolphin on the ground and told Zorro

to scan it. Hoku's vision flickered green as Zorro obeyed. Hoku added the image to the hundreds of electronic text and voice messages his tech had dug up from the Seahorse Alpha records.

Hoku ran his hand down Zorro's back. "Ready, boy?" The answer flashed before his eyes: *Yes, yes, yes.*

Hoku gathered all the files and sent them like one long harpoon, straight into Karl Strand's brains. He told the image of the dolphin to get inside and multiply as fast as it could. He wanted Strand to see it everywhere, no matter which of his brains he was using.

For a long moment, Hoku wondered if his plan had worked. The hydra continued to attack Aluna. She valiantly bashed aside its heads and stabbed them with her knife. Even through Zorro's eyes, Hoku could see the scrapes and bloody puncture wounds covering her body.

He should have disconnected himself from Strand. He should have put up some sort of shield, or tried to hide his mind. But he needed to know if his plan worked. If it didn't, he might not be able to open the connection again to try something else. Strand was the one who had made it so deep in the first place.

But then, all at once, Strand stopped battling Aluna. All six of the remaining heads reared back and roared.

"Tomias!" the hydra screamed in a chorus of tortured voices. "My son!"

"Now!" Hoku shouted, hoping Aluna could still hear him inside her ears. "Go now!"

Strand struck an instant later, but not at Aluna. Burning pain ripped through Hoku's skull, even worse than before. Images of the wooden dolphin appeared in his mind, over and over and over. Strand was beating him with it. Hoku screamed and curled into a ball and silently begged Aluna to hurry.

CHAPTER 43

ALUNA KNEW SHE WAS LOSING. Her arms were kelp, her tail as graceful as a dead fish, her strength had fled. The monster that housed Karl Strand attacked her tirelessly, pausing only to tell her how worthless she was, how weak, how disappointing.

She couldn't help but think of her father, and her heart ached. However much she guarded her heart against him, the words still burrowed deep and tried to rot her from the inside.

Unworthy. Disrespectful. Rude.

A dishonor to the whole family.

A dishonor to all Kampii.

But although the list of her failures might fill one of Hoku's books, she would never let it be written that she gave up. She would fight until her last breath was taken from her. Strand wanted to kill her, and he probably would. Until then, she intended to make his life as difficult as possible. Let her father at least acknowledge that his youngest daughter was stubborn to the end. Let Karl Strand choke on her bones.

Suddenly Strand's heads reared back, all six at once, and roared. Aluna covered her ears and tried to protect herself from the deafening sound. "Tomias! My son!"

Hoku's voice cut through the chaos, his Kampii devices feeding directly to hers.

"Now!" he yelled. "Go now!"

Strand's scream echoed anger and anguish to every dark place in the cave. His heads swung wildly, even the ones that had been still up until now. They thrashed, hitting one another, snapping their maws in midair. Strand's cool intelligence was gone, swallowed up by wild, incoherent rage.

Hoku had given her a chance.

A familiar blur of white and brown wings darted overhead. Aluna's chest tightened and she wanted to whoop with joy. Calli dodged between Strand's heads, her spear flashing. Calli couldn't kill Strand, and she knew it. But she was doing her best to keep him angry.

"Aluna!" a voice called—a voice she hadn't expected to ever hear again. It was followed by the high, shrill neigh of a horse.

Aluna pulled her eyes from Calli and saw Dash and Vachir galloping toward her. They both looked scarred and battered, barely able to hold themselves up. Yet here they were, racing into battle. Racing to help her.

"We have to get in close," Aluna said. "Stop fighting the heads, go for his heart instead." Which is what Hoku had done, she realized, but in a different way. He'd gone after Strand's connection to his son.

Aluna flipped onto her wobbly hands and vaulted onto her tail. Pain flared. For a moment, she didn't know if she could stand, or if her body had simply had enough. Dash slid off Vachir's back while the horse was still moving and tucked his shoulder under Aluna's arm just as she started to fall. She leaned on him and steadied herself, trying to ignore the gentle touch of his hair as it brushed her cheek. He handed her a sword, flipping a switch on the handle so that it burst into flames. Aluna grinned.

Vachir roared her battle cry and raced for Strand's lizard claws. She bit and tore at the scales with her teeth, then reared up and brought her hooves down with shattering force. Two of the hydra's clawed toes snapped. Strand bellowed and shifted his weight to the other leg, suddenly far less agile than he'd been a moment before.

Aluna leaned on Dash and hobbled toward Strand, the fiery sword gripped in her right hand. Vachir and

Calli kept up their attacks. Strand's heads snapped and hissed and darted in every direction without reason. When one got close, Dash batted it out of the way with his sword of ice.

"For Tomias!" Strand screeched. "I will kill you for my son!"

Aluna wasted no time. When they got close enough, she drove her sword into Strand's chest. Strand jerked back and tried to rear up, but his broken feet stopped him. Aluna's blade snagged on his armored hide. She shoved harder, pushing the tip through skin and muscle and bone.

Strand yelled, "Impudence!"

She pulled out her sword and plunged it in again. She ignored technique, ignored training. She used nothing but her remaining strength and her surging will and the knowledge that — by her side, and in the air, and crumpled somewhere in the back of the cave — her friends were counting on her. *Push,* Anadar's voice said to her, and she did.

She was not useless. She was not weak. And if she was a disappointment to her father or Karl Strand or anybody, then that was their problem, not hers.

Finally, she found Strand's heart. A spray of warm droplets covered her hand and she yanked her sword out quick, letting it flow.

Dash dropped his sword and pulled her backward

with both hands. Strand's body fell slowly, like Big Blue the whale drifting to the bottom of the sea to die. She and Dash tumbled to the ground, just out of range of Strand's death throes.

"You did it, Aluna," Dash said. His eyes were black and warm in the cave's shadows, and his voice was just for her. "I never doubted you. Not once."

Somehow, she found the strength to lean up and kiss him.

CHAPTER 44

ALUNA AND VACHIR GALLOPED through the surf toward the cove, and toward the small but growing city of Horizon's Reach. It had taken them weeks to find the perfect location—a place with easy access to water and sky, to mountains and trees, and to great open spaces. Some of the others had wanted to give up, or reclaim HydroTek or the SkyTek dome. Aluna remained adamant. They needed someplace new. Someplace that hadn't belonged to anyone before.

As they got closer, Aluna smelled smoke from the forging fires and heard the heavy clank of hammers echoing in the trees and cliffs. They had so much building to do. So much planning. But in every meaningful way, Horizon's Reach was already home.

She leaned forward and patted Vachir's neck. "You assured me your injuries were healed," she said, "and yet here we are, barely trotting back home."

Vachir whinnied and drove forward, her legs pounding the sand even harder. Aluna laughed and sank low in her saddle. They were both so predictable and stubborn. They should never have been friends, and yet here they were: two parts of the same heart.

The cove nestled between two curved fingers of land, creating a deep, protected bay. With only one small opening to the ocean, Kampii and Deepfell could live safely inside, with or without their breathing devices.

Some Kampii were digging their nests underwater, but a surprising number had chosen surface homes. Aluna wondered if their younglings would take the Ocean Seed and grow their tails, or if a new sort of Kampii would emerge—Kampii who kept their legs and walked Above World. She smiled. What a sight that would be.

"Anadar," Aluna whispered.

Vachir huffed and took her down a small slope toward a quiet patch of pure white sand. Two ends of a broken spear crossed each other behind a heavy stone that Aluna had hauled up from the training dome in the City of Shifting Tides. No other grave marker had seemed right.

Aluna had been giving Anadar updates almost every day, but this time it had been a week since her last visit.

"Daphine has been voted onto the council to represent the Kampii," she said. "No surprise there, of course. And her scope will give her an edge. The Humans—that's what the Upgraders want us to call them—have chosen a man named Kettle. Renowned for his cooking, I think. Hoku was hoping they'd pick Rollin, but Rollin wanted nothing to do with long meetings where you can't throw things at people."

Vachir whinnied lightly, sharing the joke.

"Tayan will represent the Equians," Aluna continued. "You never met her, but you'd like her. Before she was injured, she could have taught you a few things about swords. Master Sefu will speak for the Serpenti, though not many of them are making the long journey through the desert. Flicker is the likely choice for the Silvae, and Prince Eekikee is still deciding whom to appoint. I don't think we'll see much of the Deepfell, honestly, but our alliance is still strong."

A strong breeze raced over the water. Aluna lifted her chin and let it whip her short hair around her face. "Oh, and as for the Aviars . . ."

Calli stood at the construction site for Cloudpoint, what would someday be a graceful spire overlooking

Horizon's Reach, and the home to its Aviars. She held her arms and wings out while a woman with giant green-tipped wings briskly recorded her measurements.

"I don't need new armor," Calli said.

"Yes, you do," her mother countered. President Iolanthe leaned against a partly built stone wall, her one wing folded behind her back, and crossed her arms over her chest. "What do you think, Electra?"

The High Senator snorted. Her left arm hung uselessly at her side, but the injury had done nothing to soften Electra's attitude. "I think anyone representing us on a council ought to look like a warrior, not some rumpled fledgling fallen from its nest."

Calli rolled her eyes. "As soon as you two go back to Skyfeather's Landing, I'm wearing my old clothes again."

The armorer finished her task, bowed to her president, and flew off. Iolanthe took three quick strides and wrapped her arms around Calli. Calli pressed her cheek into her mother's shoulder and felt the whisper of a kiss on her head.

"I'm so proud of you, my daughter," her mother said. "So very proud."

Calli closed her eyes. "I'm proud of me, too."

"No, over there," Tayan said. "I like it better by the door."

Dash sighed, but Pocket picked up his end of the table eagerly. Dash suspected the boy had developed feelings for Tayan, khan of Flame Heart and newly appointed Equian councillor. He imagined there were worse choices for a first crush, but none came readily to mind.

They moved the table—one of the many artifacts they'd recovered from Karl Strand's hoard—and Tayan finally seemed pleased.

"We have other homes to furnish," Dash said. "Perhaps perfecting the table's location can wait. My family will not arrive for many days. Erke and Gan only left to fetch them a week ago."

Councillor Tayan smiled. It was unnerving how often she did that nowadays. "Flame Heart and your family are leaving the desert, the only home they have known for centuries. This is a great, terrifying thing we have asked of them, Dashiyn. A great breach of tradition."

"If they do not wish to come, they—"

"No. Listen," she said, stomping her hoof. "Change can be a daily battle. A warm fire, a tasty skewer of scorpion, a well-placed table—these details may mean the difference between thinking of Horizon's Reach as a place to live, and thinking of it as a home."

"I love the way you talk," Pocket said, then immediately clamped a hand over his mouth, horrified.

Tayan laughed. "Go. Both of you. It is almost sunset."

Dash lifted the heavy fur covering the door and blinked in the fading light. He stared at the tiny drawing of a closed fist that Pocket had etched into the skin of his forearm. Odd's mark. "It is time for new traditions."

Hoku waited on the beach, just out of the surf's reach. His vision was slowly returning, thanks to the drops that Nathif and Mags had made for him, but he still preferred to use Zorro's eyes. He'd gotten used to relying on the little guy during the long weeks after the battle with Strand.

Rollin coming, Zorro told him. *Apple, maybe?*

"Scan her and see for yourself," Hoku said. His vision switched to analysis mode, and Rollin's stocky form sprouted labels. None of which said APPLE. "Sorry, Zorro. Maybe next time."

"Sun's almost down," Rollin said as she lumbered toward him. "They're all late, the gobbly basics."

"They still have six-point-three-one minutes," Hoku replied easily. "Give or take a few seconds."

Rollin grunted and lowered herself to the ground. She was old. Older than she looked. But Horizon's Reach had given her new energy, new purpose. She pored over the city's planning schematics every night.

The ramps and elevators had been her idea, so every person could go every place, whether they had wings or tails or hooves or legs. Given enough time, she'd probably find a way to let the Aviars live underwater if they wanted.

Rollin's ideas and energy were exactly what they needed to make Horizon's Reach the city that they all wanted it to be. The city of their brighter future.

"Did you talk to Squirrel?" Hoku asked.

"Started yesterday," Rollin said. "Already tried to cut her own thumb off. I throw things at her, she throws them back."

Hoku chuckled.

"Brave girl, though. Quick mind. Wants to make things." Rollin sighed. "So do I. Things for bettering, not for breaking. No more weapons. Not ever again."

"In that case, I'll be visiting your workshop more often," Hoku said.

"You visit, you work," Rollin said gruffly, but Hoku could hear the warmth in her voice.

Nathif. Calli. Zorro announced. *Dash. Pocket. Aluna. Vachir.*

Hoku smiled and watched his friends walk, slither, and trot over the sand. They smiled and greeted one another, and his heart swelled to the size of Big Blue.

Aluna slid her tail out of her saddle and hopped to the ground beside him. She was finally wearing her mother's ring—not hidden in the pouch hanging from her neck, but on her finger. Her wild hair danced around her head. Through Zorro's eyes, Hoku saw her stare at him with nothing but love.

"You thought I'd be late," Aluna said.

"The sun would have waited," he answered.

They stood together on the cool sand and watched in silence as the sun drifted peacefully toward the sea.

ACKNOWLEDGMENTS

The *Above World* Team really came through for me on this book. Thanks to Stephanie Burgis for her amazing pep talks and advice, to Chris East for his love of spies and Upgraders, and to Deborah Coates, Sarah Prineas, and Greg van Eekhout for their continued support and friendship. Christine Ashworth, Sally Felt, Yvonne Socks, Anne Nesbet, and Sabine Watts were always ready with virtual cupcakes and confetti. Thanks to the Blue Heaven crew, led by the inestimable C.C. Finlay, and to the incredibly supportive middle-grade and young adult authors in Los Angeles who spend all their evenings at one another's book events.

My editor, Sarah Ketchersid, helped me make this the book of my dreams with her perfect blend of kindness, savvy, and creative inspiration. Our partnership has been one of the best parts of this whole process. I treasure the entire Candlewick team, including: Melanie Cordova, Erika Denn, Tracy Miracle, Hilary Van Dusen, Andrea Tompa, Rachel Smith, Katie Ring, Hannah Mahoney, and the hard-working sales and marketing team.

Thanks to Joe Monti, my agent, for countless things, but especially for wanting Hoku to get an upgrade; to Patricia Ready for running everything with style and humor; and to Barry Goldblatt for bringing the agency together in the first place.

Thanks to Kate Rudd for her riveting narration on the audiobooks and to Alexander Jansson for his gorgeous cover art.

Big thanks, too, to the great local bookstores who've welcomed and supported me: Children's Book World, Curious Cup,

Flintridge Books, Mrs. Dalloway's, Mrs. Nelson's Toys and Books, Mysterious Galaxy, and Once Upon A Time Bookstore, among others.

And last of all, I want to thank a few of the readers who've taken the time to share their enthusiasm (and sometimes even their fan art) with me: Federico, Sophie, Jillian, Ethan, The Maud, Samantha, Shelby, Rihanna, the Munoz family, Claudia, friends both near and far, and whole hordes of book bloggers. Your passion has meant so much to me.

I treasure this journey with all my heart and am grateful that I didn't have to make it alone.